SLEEPING
WITH
Deception

SLEEPING
WITH
Deception

L.A. WHITE

AUTHOR'S NOTE

I want to dedicate this book to the woman who struggles to understand her true value and how to demand what she wants: may you find your voice and may it be loud and commanding.

-LA. White

Contents

Chapter One

"Crap, crap, crap, crap," I chant in time with my footsteps as I run toward our office building on Sixth Avenue, trying not to knock into any more people before I reach the glossy, double doors. My morning is a disaster! The alarm clock I had since middle school decided to stop working at 5:30, leaving me with the impression that I can take my time to look fabulous: strappy wedges to go with my royal blue and tan full-length summer dress with the perky hemline and its matching headband that pulls back my kinky yet soft curls and makes my blue eyes sparkle. More than enough time.

Until I got to my favorite bakery, ordered my usual breakfast with a light cappuccino frappe with an extra pump of cream, looked up at the clock—and dropped my

Danish smothered in caramel sauce down my skirt in shock, the sauce blending in with the tan bits. I had five minutes to get to work, *three blocks away*! That is when I started running, thanking God I changed from the swim to the track team during high school. I just wish I used that brilliance to put my trainers in my bag this morning!

It fills me with pride when I see the reflective plate-glass doors, my job's name neatly painted on the list of companies that occupy the tall building. I push through the double doors and only just make the elevator as the doors slide shut. Dabbing the thin layer of sweat from my forehead in the reflection in the mirrored finish and reapplying my peach-flavored lip gloss to my full lips, I hope no one will notice that I am a few minutes late— especially not my boss, Maggie Sheffield, the deputy director of the start-up company I just started at. I boot up my computer as I slide into my chair, placing my purse under my desk as I scan the vast walls of cubicles that stretch between me and Maggie's office.

I suck in a gasp as the well-dressed figure of my boss drapes herself on the edge of my desk, her black satin pantsuit, olive-green frilled blouse, and matching rhinestone black stiletto pumps emphasizing her five-foot-two svelte frame to perfection. Her silky yet wavy black hair, just barely touching her shoulders, bouncing as she sits. The red lipstick she wears makes her olive skin pop. People often underestimate Maggie because of her size and the perception that she is fashion-crazy, but she is an incredibly smart woman with an incredible mind, and she runs the business with precision. One of the things that helped me decide to take this job is the reports about how cutting-edge she is in the industry. She pushes her silky black hair behind her ear and arches a perfectly trimmed black eyebrow at me. Her greenish eyes are unreadable.

"Medium iced almond caramel macchiato," she rattles, the slight Greek accent making the words sound magical. Words that do not make any sense.

"Excuse me?"

"That's my coffee order for the next time you try to sneak in when you're late."

"I… uh…" She holds up a beautifully manicured finger to stop my mumbling as she answers her tinkling phone. I stare after her, not sure if I should laugh at the wink, she throws at me before walking back to her office, her expensive perfume still wafting in the air. With a deep breath, I turn back to my computer and hope my day doesn't get any worse.

At lunchtime, I take my beautifully prepared lunch to the seating area on the roof and look out over the city I now call home. New York and Chicago have their differences—NYC is always busy, giving your heart a different beat compared to Chicago's easier pace. But they also have their similarities in that they offer new opportunities for growth, friendship, and freedom. It was the ideal opportunity I needed to break away. I was so happy when I saw the ad for *this* job and the opportunity to work for Maggie Sheffield over Christmas. I had to take the gamble. After four months, I still can't believe how fortunate I am to work here.

Since I've moved here, I've been exploring my new home. It's particularly been fun finding new running routes through the city, especially those close to my apartment. And when I power up with some Beyonce in my earbuds as I challenge my body with different terrains, I discover gems of the city. Though it started as a means to work off the nervous energy I had from moving to the Big Apple, it's now the way I prefer to boost my mood without using different forms of medication or resorting to copious amounts of tequila. It has also helped me survive without coffee, for the most part.

Distracted by my thoughts as I scroll through my messages, I miss a dollop of mustard falling from my chicken and rye sandwich onto the bodice of my dress. I close my eyes in exasperation. It's the dress. It's a sauce magnet.

"I could think of better ways of cleaning you up, sweetheart." I glance up at the man sitting at the other table, and I purse my lips, contemplating my response. He works as a draftsman for the architectural firm on the floor above ours, as we've had the privilege of sharing an elevator ride a time or two. He is cute in a boy-band kind of way with dark wavy hair, hazel eyes, and a smile that probably gets him out of trouble with his mom.

I flash him a cheeky smile as I get to my feet and head for the door. "I prefer more than five minutes even if that's all the time you need."

I hear him laugh as I close the door and allow a small grin of satisfaction for my witty response. I make my way to the bathroom to freshen up my look. My brown curly hair has a mind of its own and has now grown big and wild on my head. I lean in closer to check the false lash strips I applied this morning to ensure they are still there. I find that lashes with applied eyeliner make my uniquely blue eyes pop. Not many black women have blue eyes. In fact, I've only known one other black girl to have blue eyes like me, my sister. I stare at my reflection, wondering at the fact that I still feel slightly lost. I'm still new to the city and at Urban Design Studio while all the other staff members had been together when the company had only been a vague concept 18 months ago. I probably haven't given them, or myself, a chance to get to know each other better.

My fingers gently rubbing the twin butterfly charms on my necklace catches my eyes.

All things take time, Kerri, my sister's voice floats through my mind. I briefly close my eyes at the thought that 10 years was a long time to still hear her voice, but it was still as clear as the last time we spoke. No one understands that the connection has never broken for me. I know she's dead, but we were twins. And though Elise Carnegie is my best friend and made up the third of our trio during high school, Ana and I had a special bond *because* we shared an umbilical cord.

Yes. I just have to give it time.

Back at my desk, I open the design I was working on before lunch, embracing small layout changes to enhance the background I was sent from another designer. I am looking forward to the day when I'll manage my own designs, because my portfolio is overflowing with ideas. After a while, I become aware that there is an unusual hush over the office. Normally, the place is buzzing with conversation and laughter while someone plays some soft jazz from their workstation, or a group is winning or losing at foosball. I haven't been here long enough to experience this quiet.

At the end of my workday, I sit back and look over the work I've done, rubbing my eyes from the screen glare before I pack up my things. A flowing shadow in black stops at my desk, and I brace myself as she lounges on the corner. What does Maggie have in store for me now?

"A group of us are going out tomorrow night." I look at her with a frown, not sure what she is saying. "We're meeting up at Illicit, a new club over on Bleeker."

"That sounds like fun." I could feel my smile slipping slightly.

"I'm glad you think so." She flashes me a smile that

displays a dimple on her cheek. "We've been working our asses off the last few weeks, and we all need to blow off steam, you included. You are hereby ordered to come bond with us or spend your life in loneliness for eternity."

I arch an eyebrow at her. "I don't think it will be that bad—"

"See? You can't even recognize when I'm messing with you!" Maggie whines, throwing her hands into the air. "Say you'll come?"

"Fine, I'll be there," I agree, feigning reluctance but already feeling the excitement bubbling in my veins. She claps her hands as she straightens from my desk.

"Nine o'clock. Illicit!"

~ ~ ~

I enter my cozy loft with a sigh of relief, taking off my wedges at the front door before putting my bag down on the end table beside my white sofa. I still feel a sense of pride when I see the pop of white against the redbrick wall that holds a large photo of Elise, Ana, and myself on Elise's fifteenth birthday, so carefree. While I wait for the water to boil for my tea, I water my plants, which enjoy the sunshine streaming in through the floor-to-ceiling windows that line one side of the room. With a last turn of the flowerpot that resembles Papa Smurf, I make my tea and take it to my desk in an alcove at the back of the loft, then open the design I've been working on in my free time.

A message notification distracts me, and I see that it is from the dating app I have on my phone. So far, it's been doing its job helping me meet people since I've been in New York, but it also shows me that there are weirdos here. I enjoy dating, but not the numerous people I have to meet. I would love to have many dates with just one special person, but until I meet *him*, I will keep dating.

My phone rings while I'm still holding it, and my heart drops at Mom's name on the screen. It's not that I don't love my parents—we just don't have the chatting type of relationship. It's more of a mom-will-call-once-a-week type of relationship. "Hi, Mom."

"Hey, honey. How're you doing?" I can hear that she is driving, probably just finishing her shift at the hospital.

"I'm doing good. Missing your special pecan pie, though." *Please don't say I should have stayed home*, I beg silently.

A small pause follows, and I find myself holding my breath. "How's the job going?" she asks instead.

I let out the breath in a sigh of relief. "It's doing good. I'm still enjoying it."

"Good. We're so proud of you." *And...* "You know that if things don't work out, you can come home. We'll be happy to have you home." *There it is...*

"Mom…" I drawl. "I haven't been here long enough to know if it will work. Thank you, but everything is great. Really."

"I know, honey. But if things don't work out—"

"Sure, Mom." I hope she doesn't hear the impatience in my voice.

"Well, you can come and visit soon." She hears it. "We miss you."

"Mom, I just started, and it'll be a while before I can take off. But I'll visit soon, I promise."

"Okay, honey." The line goes still for a heartbeat. "Your dad hasn't been doing too well, Kerri. With you gone, the house has just been quieter. With both of you gone…"

"Mom, I have to go. We'll chat soon, okay? Tell Dad I love him." My heart is beating a mile a minute as I hang up, my palms sweaty from the anxiety I always feel when my mom brings up the past.

Closing my eyes, I sip some of my chamomile tea and dial my best friend.

"Kerri!" She greets me, making me smile. Elise is always so effusive and makes me laugh when no one else can.

"Hey, Lis."

"Not the 'I-just-spoke-to-mom-voice'."

I laugh. "The one and only."

"Was this the 'visited the high school' conversation?"

"No," I scoff. "The 'house is empty without you' conversation."

"Not that one again." I laugh again at her dramatization. "You obviously convinced her that everything was sushi and white wine." A pause. "Is everything okay?"

"You know me too well." I get up and pace my living room, catching glimpses of the setting sun through the windows. "I'm just struggling to settle in, you know. And then with Dad being Dad before I left, I'm wondering—"

"You listen to me, Kerribel Townsend. You are strong and capable and haven't needed your parents' help since our first summer camp. You can do this."

"Elise…"

"Today might not have been the greatest, but tomorrow is an opportunity for a do-over. Grab it with both hands. And soon a year will go by, and you won't even remember tonight. You'll just remember you and me having a great time when I come to visit in a little while. And I want no sulking before I get there."

"Me? Sulk?" I laugh while I wipe away tears.

"Now, repeat after me. I can do this."

"I can do this." I don't say it loud enough, and she exaggerates a sigh.

"Excuse me, I don't think I heard you."

I chuckle. "I can do this!"

"You are Kerribel Townsend, swimming champ of John F. Kennedy High School, Chicago, Illinois. You can do this!"

"I'm Kerribel fucking Townsend, and I can do this!"

Chapter Two

The summer sun is hanging low in the sky when I make my way toward the bar, dodging taxis, and sleek, black cars as I cross the busy streets. I'm trying to look as confident as I can, like I belong in this city, but it's difficult when I have to check my phone's GPS every 30 seconds. I'm glad I chose to walk the mile and a half from my loft to the bar, even though I look like a tourist. The bar is crowded when I arrive. The lighting is strategically set in the corners, which allows you to see around you but also gives the place a dusky, intimate atmosphere. The music isn't blaring but loud enough to dance to on the hardwood floor in the middle of the large space. The bar area takes up an entire wall with a large mirror running behind it, along with glass shelves full of bottles of liquor from medium priced tequila to high-end collector's whiskey.

I'm sitting alone at the bar, anxiously twirling Ana's butterfly charm between my fingers. I'm contemplating my grand escape before everyone arrives when Maggie sits down next to me. She catches the bartender's attention with a mere glance, and he promptly takes her order. I've spent the last five minutes trying to get his attention to order a drink. Maggie was able to do it effortlessly. I'm impressed, but not surprised.

Does this woman even know how to dress down? Her dark gray tube dress hugs her perfectly curved body beautifully, leaving nothing to the imagination, the fringes swaying with her every move. Even the messy ponytail that her hair is in is stylish. Her chandelier earrings tinkle as she angles her head to look at me, a teasing smile on her lips. I give myself a quick glance and suddenly remember I haven't been to a mall in over a year.

The bartender mixes the drinks, adding some flair for our entertainment, and with a gentlemanly bow of his head, he sets the martini glasses on white linen cocktail napkins in front of us.

Without acknowledging the bartender, Maggie slides one towards me sand says, "C'mon, have a drink with me." She lifts her glass and pauses, waiting for me to join her. I take my glass by the stem and lift it in the interest of solidarity. Maggie smiles victoriously and clinks the lip of her glass to mine in a toast.

"To your future with us." I nod appreciatively in response to her sentiment while she takes a gulp from her glass.

I bring the glass to my lips and sip, "I'm nervous," I admit.

"I know," Maggie twists the tips of her fingers around the stem of her glass, "You're allowed to let loose," She leans over and shakes me gently by the shoulder.

"Don't get me wrong, I love your professionalism. But this isn't the office, Kerri. If you need permission, consider it granted. By me." Maggie throws back her martini and flashes another glance toward the bartender while she pops an olive into her mouth, "Don't you just love an olive?"

"They taste even better when you let them soak in the gin," I say, sliding the olive off my toothpick and into the bottom of my glass.

Maggie laughed triumphantly, "Ooh, dirty! I knew I liked you."

I feel accomplished somehow. In truth, I am in awe of Maggie. She is so elegant and carefree. I've seen her at work, and she is stunningly flawless in her approach. She handles every detail exuding confidence. In a way, I feel inferior to her, but only because I admire how put together, she appears to be.

"So… what's your deal?" Maggie asks as she tilts her head slightly to the right.

Not sure what she means I give a puzzled look feeling all the blood rush to my cheeks. "Huh?"

"Your deal!" she repeats. "Are you dating, or do you need a wing girl tonight?" giving a slight grin and lifting her eyebrows in anticipation of my response.

I shoot a quick glance at the wedding band on her hand and cringe at the thought of admitting my current lack of love situation.

"Spill it!" Maggie insists.

Here goes nothing. "Well, I just joined a dating app to meet new guys in the city" I immediately regret my words the moment they leave my lips. I bury my face in my palm.

"Shut up! Hand me your phone. I need to see your profile" I hear Maggie squeal.

I lift my head in complete shock at her request thinking I should have escaped earlier when I had the chance. Also, I'm not quite sure if it's a smart idea to share so much detail with my new boss. Reluctantly, I grab my phone, open the app, and hand it over. Maggie spends about three minutes scrolling and making various facial expressions I cannot decode.

The bartender sits a drink on the counter breaking her

concentration. "Holy shit! You're hot" a bit of Maggie's Greek accent appears thick. She hands my phone back to me and grabs her drink.

"Not sure the men on there are worthy of your time but it's a start" she chuckles and orders me another round from the bartender.

I'm sucking my second cocktail through a stirring straw when I hear a man's voice behind me. A shudder runs through me, and I fall silent. *Damn.* I felt that voice between my thighs. Maggie notices my reaction and gives me a look that says, *What the hell is wrong with you?* My eyes widen in silent communication as I point discreetly behind me. I see her eyes flick up and she offers an exaggerated nod of approval with an enthusiastic thumbs up. I can't help but giggle from the look on her face. I cover my mouth, muffling the sound of my uncontrollable laughter.

"Excuse me," the voice is speaking directly behind my ear. I can feel his breath against the nape of my neck, and I feel myself quiver. I turn around only to be met with the broad chest of a tall man. I lift my chin up and feel like I've been hit by a brick when I see him. This man is divine. He has chocolate skin that literally looks as smooth as whipped butter, and dark brown eyes. I can see the tiny muscles jumping in his sharp yet sexy jawline. My first thought is that I so badly want him to kiss me.

I stare into his eyes, attempting to send the message telepathically. It doesn't work. I tell myself to gain some composure, knowing alcohol is making me delirious.

"…Yes?" I look up at him with a coy smile and bat my eyelashes.

"I just had to see the face of the woman with the most beautiful laugh I've ever heard." The resonance in his voice carries a comforting vibration as it lingers in the air around me. I feel the sensation on my lips and my chest. My face relaxes into a smile, "Oh," I almost start giggling again, but I stop myself and quietly clear my throat, "I'm Kerri."

He stares into my eyes for a few extra seconds before saying with a slight grin "Alex." He continues in a sultry voice, "Looks like you're alone now."

"Not anymore," I hum dreamily before I fully comprehend what he meant and spin around. Maggie left! I search the crowded bar with my eyes before I spot her wiggling her fingers and winking at me. I give her a smirk and playfully roll my eyes. She's a good friend, I think to myself.

I turn back around, "I don't know why she would just leave like that." I say, apologetically.

"Because she's a good friend," he says, reading my mind. I curl my fingers around my ear absentmindedly and feel heat rush to my face.

"We work together. I'm a graphic designer," I tell him with a detectable sense of pride, "I just started working for this design company. It's still in its startup phase, but it's really exploding! I've been so busy lately; I'm used to sitting at my desk all day. This is the first time I've been out since I moved here. Well, other than walking to the bakery." I feel myself start to ramble, so I take a sip of my strawberry mojito to shut myself up.

"Have you been to Harriet's?" He says, reading my mind again, and my eyes light up.

"Oh my god, they have the best macarons! I could die from the sheer volume I could consume." He laughs deeply and I feel my heart flutter in my chest. My fingers take hold of Ana's butterfly charm, a mindless response as I think about wanting to gush about this man to my sister.

"That is a beautiful necklace," he says, as he watches me.

"My sister…" I begin, then decide against it just in time. Alex is seemingly so easy to talk to, I almost ruined our moment. I reposition myself and continue, "We have this thing about butterflies. It's our favorite swim stroke."

"You swim?" He asks, leaning in closer as the music in the bar seems to get louder. I feel the beat pounding against the walls around us. He is so close to me now; I can smell his delicious cologne. My head spins as I breathe in his alluring scent.

"Yes, I mean-I used to. I do a lot more running nowadays." I say carefully.

"I know you'll be running through my mind all night." He says without any trace of irony.

"Oh my god, you did not just say that!" I giggle and throw my hand on the bar, highly aware it fell beside his hand, nearly touching him.

"Yes, I did. And I don't regret it for a second." He laughs. I feel his hand move and I watch as he gently claps his hand over mine. I hold my breath and gaze into his eyes, sinking into this perfect moment between us. I hadn't noticed but he's in a dark blue suit, with a crisp white button-up that's slightly unbuttoned at the neckline. So much so I could see the start of a tattoo on his very defined and muscular chest.

Alex jerks his hand away without warning. I flinch in surprise. His hand disappears inside his suit jacket, and he pulls out his phone. Reality just came crashing down on me and I suddenly feel awkward and out of place. The bar music is now loud and the noises around me come back full throttle. I take a long sip of my drink, patiently waiting.

He stares at the screen for a second, replaces his phone, and says, "I've got to run" and walks away. Turning for a moment he gives me a wink before disappearing into the crowd. It happens so quickly; I don't have time to respond. I choke slightly on my drink in disbelief. I finally swallow and lift my hand in a confused wave.

"Okay," I whisper to myself. I can still feel the warmth

and comfort of his hand on mine and then I realize he didn't even ask for my number. "Shit."

He's too good to be true. I hear Ana's voice and I grasp her charm, taking a deep breath, "But, Ana, he was perfect…"

Chapter Three

"So? How was your night?" Maggie sings as she drapes herself over the half-wall of my cubicle, the flared sleeves of her lilac shirt swaying as she waves her hands to accentuate her words. She is knocking the five-inch heel of her Christian Louboutin softly against the floor as she leans against the perspex wall, eagerly waiting for my answer. I can see the matching belt on her gray pinstripe pencil skirt.

I shake my hair out of my face as I blink up at her owlishly, my eyes blurry from focusing on my screen. "My night?"

"Yeah… When I looked for you, you and that tall drink of chocolate had disappeared." She folds her arms along the top of the wall and rests her chin on her fisted hands. So often, Maggie reminds me of a middle school girl with her constant excitement and optimism.

I scoff lightly. "He ran. I left. There is a difference."

"Aw, Kerri, I'm sorry." Her eyes darken brown in disappointment but then spark back to life. "Tell me you got his number, though?"

I shake my head sadly. "That fish got away, hook and all."

"Well," Maggie drawls as she pushes away from the wall. "At least you're still swimming. So, no moping is allowed."

I laugh softly. "Just be glad you found your *forever guy* and don't have to deal with all the sharks, never mind slippery fish, out there anymore."

"I seriously don't miss the longing and the yearning, and all those frogs." She shudders, making me laugh again. She points a perfectly French-manicured finger at me. "But who knows what fate has in store for you, Kerri Townsend."

"What? *'If he comes back to me, he's mine'* type of thing?" I quip, sarcasm dripping from every word. I'm not the fate-makes-life type of girl, so putting my proverbial eggs in fate's basket is not my idea of fun.

She gives me a sassy shrug as she makes a shooing

motion with her hands, the gold bracelets at her wrists clinking musically. "Back to your cave, Miss Skeptical You never know."

"You're a hopeless romantic," I accuse.

"Romantic, yes. Hopeless, no." She smiles as she walks to her office. I can't help but chuckle at her eternal optimism. She really is a bubble of joy, again reminding me of a little girl playing dress-up. She seems to have the world at her feet, with nothing to stand in her way.

It takes me a while to get my focus back on the design I'm working with, my mind floating to the mystery man I met last night. Sometimes, a shade of brown will remind me of the tone of his dark skin, a certain filter will imitate an emotion flashing in his gray-brown eyes, or the shape of a line will imitate his jawline—even the lemon poppyseed muffin I had with my lunch reminded me of his cologne! It's frustrating, because the design is on a fine deadline, and I can't afford to be distracted… But oh, what a distraction he is! Especially when I think about the way his strong thighs framed his—

"Kerri?" I look up at the bike messenger standing at my desk in relief, needing the interruption to get my mind back in the present. I nod, and he hands me an iPad to sign. He places a box on my desk and smiles. "Enjoy your day."

"Thanks," I mutter as I stare at the large bow securing the box. Not only is the bow large, but the box itself takes up at least half of my desk. It is white with tiny blue dots covering the surface. I am confused about where it could have come from. My heart beats frantically in my chest, and I don't know if it's because of excitement or anxiety. It isn't my birthday, and no one I know would send me something like this—certainly not my parents. And they don't know my work address. Elise, maybe?

"Is it going to bite?" Maggie asks as she stands against my cubicle wall again. I'm so focused on the box, I didn't even hear her stop at my desk until she spoke.

I shake my head with a small laugh. "I don't know."

"Then open it," she urges me, clapping her hands together like an excited little girl. She comes around the wall and settles on the edge of my desk. I glance up at her before cautiously tugging the ribbon and lifting the lid of the box. We both gasp as the air is filled with tiny paper butterflies flitting between us. I allow myself to be lost in the fluttering of the wings, and I'm transported to the picnics my parents took us to in the national park when the grass was long, and the butterflies danced above our heads. Ana and I would spend hours chasing them. I catch one and smile at the iridescent shades of blue and silver in its wings. A long, thin gold string holds the crafted beauty attached to the edge of the box.

"This is gorgeous." Maggie laughs.

"It's magical," I say in agreement as I gasp. I see another

box with a familiar name written across the lid in different fonts inside the first: Harriet's scrawled over the white background in gold ink. My mouth waters at what seduction is waiting for me from my favorite bakery. If the box is filled with the crumbs from yesterday's icing sugar, I will still devour it with relish. I partially lift the lid and giggle at the rainbow of macarons winking at me from between wax paper. Now I am curious about who sent it.

A sheet of blue paper flutters in the corner of the bigger box and I pick it up, hoping…but I resign myself to a cheerful message from my best friend. The handwriting is bold and neat, the black capital letters are written in tidy lines, and the actual words take my breath away.

> Kerri,
>
> I enjoyed meeting you last night. I need to hear that beautiful laugh again soon.
>
> Alex

My stomach flips over at the sight of his phone number beneath his name, and I want to grab my phone and call him instantly, but I'm hesitant after his disappearing act the other night. It has been a while since I've met someone as interesting as Alex. To give him some credit he did remember my name and where I work and made an effort to make sure I can contact him. My knees are feeling like Jell-O and my heart melting at the very thought.

"The man sure knows how to impress a lady," Maggie says, opening the Harriet's box and helping herself to a macaron. She closes her eyes and moans loudly, her head falling back as she chews the treat, savoring the crunchy smoothness. "These things are so damn delicious."

"He sure does," I mutter, tucking the note into my purse. I reach for a cheerful yellow macaron and barely smother the moan at the lemony flavor.

"Are you going to call him?" she insists, reaching into the box for another treat.

I snap the box shut and shoo her away from my desk. "No, I think I'll make him sweat for a while after last night."

"That's my girl!" She laughs as she walks back to her office, waving at me with a purple macaron in her hand.

~~~

I make myself wait until I am comfortably settled on my sofa with a cup of chai tea and the box of macarons before I take the note and punch his number into my phone. After approximately four attempts to send the perfect message later, I scoff and, with a heavy sigh, retype the first message before closing my eyes as I press *send*.

> Me: One box of heaven does not mean you're forgiven.

Even when he responds immediately, my heart is still
~~~

beating quickly, and I hold my breath as I watch the bubble box appear.

Alex: Sorry about last night. Can I make it up on Sunday? There is a place I know of I want to show you. It's on the water where we can kayak. Maybe have a picnic on a floating dock?

I shudder. There is no way I'm going to be stuck on a large body of water in a tiny fiberglass vessel that offers me no protection at all against my biggest nemesis.

Me: How about a hiking trail?

Alex: Your world. I'm just living in it.

Me: Is that right? lol

Alex: Definitely. I will pick you up. Let's say around 11 am?

Me: I can find it if you send me a pin.

Alex: Great. See you on Sunday.

Me: Ok. :)

Those pesky goosebumps run up and down my arms as I put down my phone. I haven't been this excited about a date since high school. Double dating with Ana was the best time of our teen years. It was the best feeling of getting ready together, borrowing hair clips and dresses, and the excited chatter of the boys we were crushing on. The last date I had with Ana was the weekend before she—

Right now, Ana, I want to think about the happy stuff and not dwell on the hurtful shit, I tell her, my thumb furiously rubbing across the gold pendants.

~~~

Yes! I am three seconds faster on this route than the last time I ran it! is the thought that fills my mind as I check my vitals and slow my steps. I allow the exhilaration to flow through my veins as I do a few stretches on the park bench and enjoy the summer sun on my skin, tilting my head back and turning my face toward its reaching rays before drinking deeply from my water bottle. I know that New York can get cold in winter so I am determined to soak up every drop of the early summer sunshine I can get.

I can't stop the smile from spreading as I think about the last couple of days. Things are really looking up for me, just like Elise said they would. I am meeting new people. I have adjusted well to my workload, especially now that I am getting more responsibilities at work. An email I received from HR before I left work yesterday also made my happy hormones bounce uncontrollably when I read that I was made team leader. Add in the fantastic loft I scored just a few blocks from my office, and that I am going on a date that I am looking forward to with a great guy, and I am over the moon with how things are turning out for me.
~~~

I look out over the lake, marveling at the way the water reflects on the trees and how tempting it looks to just break the surface. I close my eyes, and it's as though I can feel the water touch my skin, running smoothly from my pointed fingers, covering my shoulders and over my body, enclosing me in a hug so warm, soft, and welcoming as my heart pounds, making the ripples lap gently from me. It could just be a matter of kicking off my shoes, diving in, and swimming to the—

With a hard shudder, I take two steps back and wrap my arms around my suddenly cold body. I haven't been in the water since I was 15, and I have no intention of entering it again. All the enjoyment I used to have for the water left the day Ana died.

Chapter Four

I watch the sun stream through my floor-to-ceiling bedroom windows and enjoy the way the rays feel across my exposed skin. I look over at my alarm clock as it rings, and with a huge smile, I reach over and turn it off. *This is going to be a great day*, I think as I linger for a few more minutes. Eventually, I make my way through a leisurely shower, Lizzo blasting on my Bluetooth speaker. I'm singing along at the top of my voice as I wash my hair, shave every inch of my body, and luxuriously rub apple-scented lotion all over me, making my skin shine with a soft copper light. I, then, pull on my favorite pair of blue jean shorts that perfectly match the multicolored workout top from Savage X Fenty that gives me the perfect cleavage for a hiking date. I define my curls using my fingers and style over my right eye adding two bobby pins to hold everything together. All that I have left to do is figure out what to pack for this date as I tie the laces of my white and yellow sneakers.

After a quick scan of my fridge, I carefully select a couple of bottles of water, yogurts, and a variety of juicy fruits. As I prepare for our outing, I can't help but feel a flutter of excitement in my chest. I know that today's adventure will be special, and I want everything to be perfect.

With an apple in hand, I eagerly descend the stairs to meet my Uber. Breakfast can wait; I am far too thrilled to savor a solid meal. The anticipation courses through my veins as I arrive at Van Cortlandt Park Alliance. Standing at the entrance, nervous energy courses through my veins as I take in the surroundings. Each breath I take fails to calm the rapid thumping of my heart. Perhaps it's the magic of being amidst the trees, feeling the earth beneath my feet, or maybe it's the intoxicating thought of seeing Alex once again that sets my pulse racing.

"Kerri!" his voice breaks through my thoughts, and my breath catches in my throat as my eyes land on Alex. His presence is magnetic, drawing me in like a moth to a flame. Every inch of him exudes confidence. The morning sunlight caresses his perfectly chiseled face, emphasizing the sharp angles of his jawline and the subtle dimple on his chin. His dark, tousled hair adds a touch of ruggedness to his otherwise polished appearance.

His muscular legs, sculpted from countless hours of physical activity, peek out from beneath his camel-colored shorts. As my gaze travels upward, I can't help but be captivated by his broad shoulders, which strain against the fabric of his white golfer shirt. The material clings to his taut skin, accentuating the contours of his well-defined muscles. A black sport cap slightly shades his eyes, adding an air of mystery. He is undeniably a sight to see. "Hey."

As he approaches, I can't help but notice the way he moves. Every step is purposeful and filled with a quiet strength. I steal a quick glance up and down one more time before I realize that I am stumbling over a simple word. Clearing my throat, I manage to whisper a breathless, "Hi..."

"You look amazing" he compliments leaning forward. The scent of his cologne envelops me, leaving me intoxicated and craving more. It's a subtle yet alluring fragrance with a blend of woody undertones and a hint of citrus that lingers in the air, heightening my senses. I hold my breath as he comes closer. I hold out my cheek, not wanting to seem too eager— only to feel a pang of disappointment when he leans past me to lift his backpack to his shoulder. Regardless, I summon a small smile and reply, "You too."

Together, we venture onto the trail that winds through the park. The park isn't very large, with a few hiking trails that we can follow, all of them curling around a small lake.

The view is truly breathtaking, and I find myself dawdling as I take it all in, enjoying the spots of sunshine through the leaves of the trees. I love summer, and the city is showing off its true colors this early in the season. It's amazing to think that a city as busy and dazzling as New York can have pockets of such peace and quiet. Even the sound of traffic is gone while we walk in the depths of the woods. I come to a standstill at a small rocky outcrop overlooking the water that is as clear as a mirror, exactly reflecting the azure blue sky and trees on its edge.

"Breathtaking."

I blink at Alex's voice close to my ear and turn to find him staring at me. Watching him look at me so intensely has me suddenly feeling the heat radiating from my skin. *Is he talking about me?* I can't breathe, hear the birds singing in the trees, or focus on anything other than Alex's grayish brown eyes. He blinks and gives a tiny squint now focusing even harder on me. With a gasp, I realize that they aren't only brown, but have the tiniest flecks of gray, and that they are sending heated messages I am surely misinterpreting.

I take a step back and draw in a much-needed oxygen-filled breath, licking my suddenly dry lips and then glancing sharply at Alex. He lifts his cap and wipes the sweat from his forehead, and I watch as he tips his head back to drink some water. Now, I can't stop staring. I am fascinated by the way his Adam's apple moves up and down as he swallows. *How the fuck can a man swallowing water be so sexy?*

"So, Alex." I clear my throat, "I… um… really enjoyed our conversation the other night. I thought we… *zinged*…"

"*Zinged*, huh? Is that what you're calling it?" His voice deepens as he teases me, his teeth flashing white against his dark beard when he grins.

I feel myself blush but blame it on the sun shining warmly on my face. "But…I wasn't sure if you felt the same since you left so suddenly."

He looks out toward the lake, and I wonder at the look of pain that crosses his face. He is quiet for so long that I doubt he's going to answer. Instantly, I regret bringing it up. After a few more awkward seconds pass he says softly, "Kerri, you have no idea how much I enjoyed the other night."

I smile at him, but inside, my stomach… and other parts… tingle making me into a bundle of nerves. I think a part of me needed that confirmation.

"I enjoy being with you too," I respond softly.

He looks at me, and I can see the emotions chasing each other in his eyes. "I want to enjoy the limited time we have together as much as possible."

I narrow my eyes at him as I consider his statement. *What the hell does that mean?* I quickly decide on a flirty response, killing any curiosity it brought me. "Well, I guess you'll have to keep surprising me to keep the *zing* going."

He licks his lips, and I feel my sex tighten in response. He leans in close to my face intoxicating me with his delicious scent causing my shallow breaths to return. "Consider it done."

I tilt my head as I look at him, narrowing my eyes as I decide if him saying that is enough for me to take the plunge, delete my dating app and devote my heart only to him. But I veer away from that thought as quickly as it comes. *This is only the first date.* I could hear Elise's voice telling me. Plus, I'm still a bit curious about his disappearing act. "You're not an assassin or an international spy, are you? Or worse—" I widen my eyes at him. "Are you a serial killer?"

He laughs again, the sound rumbling from his chest, the humor still sparkling in his eyes when he looks at me. "I was kicked out from the spy academy when I lost top-secret documents, and blood makes me nauseous…so nope…not a killer either."

"If you say so" I mumble underneath my breath as I turn around and start up our hiking adventure again.

He reaches past me to push some branches out of the way for me to pass, and his scent weaves its spell around me. I can feel the warmth of his body behind me even though we aren't touching. Not sure if he's perfect for me in the long-term, but he most certainly feels perfect for me now.

Together, we hike to the picnic area at the end of the trail. There are a few picnic tables scattered on the grass, but though the park is busy, most of the families present are sitting on blankets under the trees at the edge of the lawn. This allows us to find an empty table easily, and Alex unpacks his backpack. Glasses, plates, a bottle of wine, and then boxes of pastries from Harriet's, and I gasp at his consideration.

"I wasn't sure which you would prefer, so I bought a selection of all they had to offer."

I smile at his gesture. It is the best peace offering he could extend. I immediately take a caramel Danish and bite into it with a soft moan, closing my eyes to savor the delicacy. "So, if you're not a spy, then what do you do for a living?"

I look up to find him staring at me, his eyes that fascinating deep brown with a gray shimmer, and I forget that I had asked him a question. As it is, I am not sure if he heard me. But then he clears his throat and makes a selection out of the box before turning back to answer me with a smile. "I'm an intellectual property lawyer."

I raise my eyebrows and chuckle. "Yeah…that still tells me nothing. Give me the social media version of what you do not your resume version."

He laughs, and the deep sound sets my soul alight. "I

don't really have social media, not since college. After someone hacked my account and posted a lot of crap on it, I've been careful about my online interaction since then. And besides, I've heard too many scary stories of judges and questionable behavior on their Instagram pages."

"Yeah, I know what you mean. I only have my social media to follow trends for work and just a few special celebrities." I shrug, then give him a teasing smile. "Judges, huh?"

"Yes! I would love to be a judge someday. To sit on the bench and help people in more ways than I can as a lawyer is one of my life's goals. But for now, I'll settle for being a partner at my firm."

I take a bite of a strawberry croissant smothered in chocolate sauce and take a moment to savor the flavors exploding in my mouth. "I like a man with ambition."

"I think my father wishes that my ambition was to take over the restaurant, but fortunately, my brother has more skills in the kitchen than I ever showed." He bites into a croissant with a cream and jam filling and chocolate sauce drizzled over the top. "He was a dishwasher at the place in the '70s, worked his way up, saved his ass off, and then bought the place. So, Anthony is now running Dad's business, and I am their legal consultant."

"Okay… So, it's Dad and Anthony. Anyone else in the family?"

He laughs. "My mom is a nurse, Helen. My dad is Robert, then there's Anthony and Andrew, as well as our sister Ashley."

"Your mom's a nurse? My parents are both doctors. I'm sure your dad made sure you guys at least had warm meals."

"Let me guess. You and your sister survived on burnt toast, peanut butter, and bananas," he teases. But I can only stare at him. He remembers that I mentioned a sister.

It takes me a moment to recover before I retort, "Actually, Mom made our dinners in the mornings before she left for work, and Ana and I had to just finish them off. Admittedly, Ana was better at it than I was."

"Is she still in Chicago?"

I pause unsure how to respond. I don't want to talk about her and risk changing the vibe. "No, she hasn't been there in many years." I take the first pastry that I can reach out of the box. "These are so good! I love Harriet's!"

Our conversation is easy after I change the subject, and we enjoy a couple of hours of teasing and meaningful conversation. As the sun begins to fall in the sky, we decide to pack up our idyllic picnic, and walk side by side, our shoulders delicately grazing as we veer towards the gate. When we make our way to the front I wait patiently as he hails a cab for me. We turn towards each other as he holds the door open for me and with pulsating excitement,

I reach up towards him, feeling my lips tremble with longing. I feel my lips tingle in anticipation.

"Bye, Kerri. I don't know the last time I had so much fun," he whispers, and my breath hitches as he brushes a kiss on my cheek before turning and walking away. I watch him as he disappears among the crowd. As the cab drives through the bustling New York streets, I remind myself that it's entirely too soon to think he's *the one.*

Chapter Five

"You've got to be kidding me!" Elise explodes during our phone call later that afternoon. I am sitting on my couch after I changed into my favorite yoga pants and tank top, with a glass of iced tea in hand and my laptop on my knees as we talk. I can almost see her hazel eyes spark with fire through the phone. "He said that?" I must admit, it was an odd statement... *the limited time we have together.*

"Yep. That's what he said."

"Geez. That sounds like he has commitment issues, KB." Elisa spats. I can't help but think she may be right. Elise sighs. "I just don't want you to get hurt. I want you to be careful with him. You're worth more than someone not being able to give you their all—not when you're always giving more than you should."

My heart melts at her serious tone, and I know she cares about me. Elise became my protector after Ana died, especially at school after the rumors spread, even going so far as to knock Kelly Lesley on her ass when the girl tripped me at track practice one day. But sometimes she took her role just a little bit too far. "What about just having fun, Elise?"

"There's that. But remember, Kerri, anything is fun until something breaks. And I'll break his *cazinga* if he breaks your heart!" she warns, and I laugh. My fingers tangle in my butterfly charm necklace as we speak, my thoughts on Alex and what Ana would have thought about him. It's like she is reading my mind. "Ana would have liked him because she loved you and would have loved who you loved. But don't live your life according to what we think Ana would want for you. Live it for you, Kerri."

I sigh. It's hard for me to explain to Elise that after Ana died, a large part of me died with her—that I feel almost guilty when something good happens in my life, because she should be here to share it with me. "Thanks, Elise."

"So? What does this Alex look like?" I laugh as I send her photos of the hike, the beautiful scenery, and the lake with the eagle flying overhead. Half-listening to her commentary, I flick through my photos and realize that I don't have a single shot of Alex. I'm sure that I took some pictures with Alex and the fantastic view in the background.

"Damn"

"What?" she asks, concern in her voice.

"I don't have a single photo of him!"

"Ahh!" she groans. "What if he's a psycho killer? I need to put a face to the man, the myth, the legend! Or at least have something to show the cops…"

I laugh so hard that I sputter iced tea across my laptop screen. "Well, we've already established he's not an assassin or killer on our date. I guess you'll have to just trust my word, Elise."

"Girl, you'd go crazy over Steve Urkel, and not even his alter ego version but the suspenders-wearing version! So, I am not sure why you are surprised that I am asking."

"My supposed best friend," I scoff. We hang up just as I receive a message alert on my phone.

Alex: I really enjoyed our time together today.

Me: Me too. Can't say my sore legs agree lol.

Alex: Can we repeat the experience this weekend?

Me: Minus the hiking?

He sends me laughing emojis along with his message.

Alex: We can try.

Me: Great!

We share a few more texts to finalize the time and date, and I set my laptop aside as I think about the day and what he has planned for next week. With the joy still bubbling in my chest after my fantastic date today, and the plans for the next exciting one, I get ready for bed. I'm about to switch off the light, but a text comes through on my phone. The sender is not listed in my contacts, and I delete it. It was obviously sent to the wrong person.

Unknown: Go back to the hole you crawled out of, bitch.

~~~

I find Maggie lounging on my desk when I arrive at work on Monday morning, her ivory shirt highlighting her golden skin tone, the burnt orange silk pants flowing over her long legs, giving them the appearance of being endless. I raise my eyebrow at her "cat-ate-the-canary" smile, but it only brightens as she glances at my desk. I stare at the package while I put away my purse and activate my computer.

"You are driving me crazy!" Maggie whines, and then giggles as I bat her hands away from the ribbon. I lift the
~~~

tall box out of her reach and am surprised at how heavy it is.

"Fine." I pull the end of the yellow ribbon and smile when I see that it matches the poppies on my summer dress. A gasp escapes me as I lift the crystal cut vase out of the box, and immediately the lemony fragrance of the Phalaenopsis orchid fills my cubicle.

"Oh, they are so gorgeous," Maggie practically purrs as she leans forward to smell them. "I'm not sure which one is better, his first or his second impression…"

"Don't you have work to do?" I shoo her away from my desk, and her laughter tinkles over the cubicles as she sways to her office.

I am about to leave for lunch on Wednesday when I hear someone calling my name. A delivery man comes over to my desk and hands me an envelope. Again, the weight of it surprises me. I reach in and pull out a large glass frame with my picture in it. It is one he took at the picnic when I was enjoying the sun on my face at the picnic table.

A note drops out of the back of the frame when I extend the stand.

Now you know how beautiful you are to me.

"Aw, that is so sweet," one of my colleagues coos as she peeps over my cubicle wall. I can't help but agree with her, placing a hand on my stomach to calm the butterflies taking a flighty path to wreak havoc on my intimate places.

I am a bit disappointed when Friday ends and there is no gift to make my heart melt. Even Maggie arches an eyebrow when she leans onto my cubicle wall. "Did I misread the pattern or miss the day? Today is Friday, isn't it?"

I smile sadly as I hook my purse over my shoulder. "Maybe he was just busy today. Besides, it's sweet of him to send the gifts, but totally unnecessary."

"*Unnecessary?*" Maggie lays her hand on her chest as she gasps in shock. "Honey, it might not be necessary for you, but it sure as hell doesn't hurt when it comes to tipping the scales for some horizontal salsa."

"Maggie! Seriously?" I laugh as I walk away from my desk.

The journey home is long, and all I want to do is take a long bath to soak away the busy day. I groan when I get to the elevator in my building and read that it is out of service, and I take a deep breath as I climb the five flights of stairs to my apartment… in heels. *When will I learn to put my trainers in my purse?*

When I eventually get to my floor, my legs shaking from the unplanned exercise, I pause as I emerge from the stairwell. I squint my eyes at the strange bag at my door, and I feel my mood lighten as I see the balloon animals tied to the handle. This time, I groan for a whole other reason as I read the name of my favorite Moroccan takeaway on the bag, and the aromas wafting from it make my stomach rumble. And it is still warm!

On a napkin at the top of the bag is a note from Alex.

> I wish I could be there in person to enjoy this with you, but I hope you can feel my hands giving you the best neck rub you can imagine.

What do you do with a man who is so thoughtful? I close my eyes, and I can almost feel the heat of his fingers against my skin, gently massaging the kinks from my tired muscles, and bringing my body to full alertness when his hands venture to my waist and back up to my—

My eyes fly open at the sound of a door banging further down the hallway, and I realize that Alex had me in a dreamy haze even before I opened the door to my loft!

~~~

On Saturday morning, I wake up to find rain falling softly against my window. I snuggle deeper under my comforter and watch the water slide down the glass pane for the next thirty minutes before deciding to get up. Today, I am set to see Alex again. I guess my thrill has the best of me because I wake up before my alarm once again. I stretch luxuriously and smile at the weak ray of sunshine coming from a tiny break in the clouds. Tiny rainbows fall across my white comforter with its multitude of different colored
~~~

butterflies. With a final glance at my clock, I deactivate the alarm and slowly leave my bed.

I smooth my hands down the sides of my wide-legged jumpsuit with the pink and orange hibiscus, fluff my hair, and place a large white hibiscus behind my right ear. Some mascara and a soft pink lip gloss finish my look, and I smile at myself in the mirror. I always thought Ana was the beauty between us, and she would always laugh when I said so. But today, I look like a million bucks.

I am still smiling when I put my bowl of oatmeal in the microwave and check my phone while it cooks. The sinking sensation of my heart pulls the smile from my lips the moment I read Alex's first text message.

> Alex: Good morning, my beautiful butterfly! I hardly slept thinking of you all night. I hate to do this, but I can't go today.

Feeling the red, hot blood drain from my 5'7" frame leaving me with a pale expression, I click in the message box and begin typing.

> Me: What do you mean?

> Alex: I have a bit of food poisoning, and I'm not feeling too great.

> Me: Damn. I'm sorry. I hope it's not too bad.

> Alex: No. I knew the place my client suggested

was dodgy, but their shrimp scampi looked too good to pass up.

Me: Oh, I see... Need me to bring you anything?

Alex: Besides you? No, I'll be fine. I've got to go.

Me: It's not a problem. I'll bring you soup or something.

Alex: I'll be okay. Speak to you soon.

In disbelief and disappointment, I push the call button, but the call goes straight to voicemail. Frowning, I put my phone on the counter and finish my breakfast. I try to call again as I drink my tea, but it keeps going to voicemail. *He's probably sleeping,* I rationalize with a shrug, but I can feel my logic cracking as his words ring in my ear *I want to enjoy the limited time we have together as much as possible.*

Chapter Six

After my disappointment with Alex on Saturday morning, Maggie calls me and invites me to go shopping with her. She doesn't mention that she needs to restock her father's wine cabinet, so this trip is as much a wine-tasting as a shopping expedition. From there, we meet up with some friends of hers, which results in us visiting new bars and sampling their menu specialties. Falling into bed at 3 in the morning is a novelty for me, so getting a call from Maggie at 10 to say that she is downstairs and giving me 15 minutes to make myself presentable is an exciting conundrum. We meet up with the same group of friends for Sunday brunch, which flows into lunch and then dinner on one of their yachts. I enjoy myself so much with them, but my tolerance to alcohol will need years to adjust to their levels.

Monday morning has me walking to my desk on shaky legs, and I sink into my chair, sure that my hangover will probably only pass later in the week. My hand is shaking as I reach forward to switch my computer on, and I can still taste the fruity white wine at the back of my throat. If only my stomach stops revolting at every movement, I'll be okay. Is this really what a Monday morning feels like after a weekend of taking freedom by the horns?

My hands hold my head up as the kaleidoscope image of my start-up screen makes me dizzy, and I make an extremely silent vow to change that as soon as my fingers can move without causing me a headache.

"Aw, this is so adorable," Maggie sings as she makes herself comfortable on the edge of my desk. I glare up at her outfit of the day, her brown wide-legged pants and daffodil yellow sleeveless silk blouse giving her such a fresh look. How the hell did she look so good on a Monday morning after a weekend of "wine-tasting"? She reaches for something on my desk before frowning at me. "Are you okay?"

"I will be when you stop singing, and why do you always use my desk as a chair?"

She laughs, and I close my face with my hands. She tries to smother her giggles. "Too loud?" I nod, and she coos softly, "I'm so sorry, KB. I'll make you some coffee."

She hops off my desk, and I moan as I shake my head. "Tea. Chai, preferably."

"On it!" Peering through my fingers at her retreating figure, I try to focus on the item that had caught her attention. Next to my screen is a tiny bear with a contrite look on his face holding a box of macarons from Harriet's. The balloons floating above his head spell the words, *I'm sorry.*

Squinting through bleary eyes, I send Alex a text to ask how he was feeling. He responds immediately, apologizing again, but I brush it off and ask him if he is okay. I don't get a chance to read his response as Maggie puts the tea on my desk and tells me to take it easy with a naughty glint in her green eyes.

For the rest of the week, there is a gift on my desk when I reach it in the mornings, every gift with a different breakfast delicacy. On Tuesday, it is banana caramel crepes with a 4-by-4-inch scale model version of Harlem. On Wednesday, it is a set of minuscule people for the model with a frosted cinnamon Pop-Tart. Thursday, I am greeted by the rest of the miniature set, including trees and cars, and the most delectable raspberry cream cheese pinwheels. At the rate this man is feeding me, I won't be able to fit through my front door, but it is nice to be spoiled. Even Elise is warming up to him for the way he is making me feel. And everyone in the office is taking a great interest in what he will send next. So, on Friday morning, it isn't a surprise to me when I can't reach my desk because everyone was surrounding it, speculating about what this gift will be.

Maggie is lounging on my chair, tapping a small blue envelope in her hand with an arched eyebrow. At least it's still sealed. I sigh with relief as I push through the crowd. "Can I have my chair back, please?"

She looks up at me with a wicked smile. "On condition that you give me a full report of this invitation."

"You've read it?" The horror of my boss reading my mail gives me chills down my spine.

"Really, Kerri! I'm not that immature!" She scolds me, with a look of shock on her face. I raise my eyebrow at her. "Okay, I didn't this time."

She hands me the envelope, and everyone stops breathing—or at least that's how it feels as I take the small square and pull up the tab. A heavy ivory card with a pretty, curly font in blue ink is inside, and I frown as I read.

> *Meet me at the Crown Plaza Hotel at 8 a.m. for breakfast. And bring that sexy smile of yours…*
>
> *Alex.*

My lips are hurting as I try to contain the smile that wants to burst from them as I replace the note. On my desk is a tiny helicopter with a miniature teddy bear as its pilot, and one of the girls whispers, "He is so romantic. If you don't want him…"

I laugh as she leaves the thought unfinished, and I shake my head. "Can you guys please let me get to work?"

"Again, only if you tell us *everything*." Maggie wags her finger at me with a stern expression as she vacates my chair.

"Well." I smile in return, putting my purse under my desk and sitting down before she changes her mind. "Maybe not *everything*."

"Kerri!" she groans, and I give her a wide smile as I switch on my computer.

~~~

I make my way through Times Square and walk through the doors of the impressive hotel 10 minutes before 8 a.m. and am surprised to see him already here. His tall figure dressed in blue jeans and a white shirt so casual yet distinguished. *Staring at him never gets old.* I think to myself as I tug at the bottom of my shirt adjusting its wrinkle. My heart beats so hard in my chest that I'm sure he can hear it from where he is standing. I take a deep breath in and exhale praying that helps slow it down. And then he reaches out, and the world blurs around me except for that hand he holds out to me. In a slow-motion haze, I see my hand moving forward, and the electricity stings at my nerve endings as his fingers close over mine. And everything comes to life in a heartbeat. I can hear the footsteps of the
~~~

people around us, the clinking of cutlery on fine China, the soft buzzing of the front desk telephone, the hushed whispers of the staff, the swish of the doors as they open and close behind me, and Alex's deep, strong voice when he smiles at me and speaks.

"Hi, Kerri."

"Hi," I breathe in return. He leads me to the elegant dining room, and I find myself lulled into the magic that is Alex Carter.

Breakfast is an out-of-this-world experience and not just the food. Listening to him speak about the last two weeks since we last saw each other, I realize how much I've missed him. He is such an easy person to talk to. Though we've texted each other over the last few days, especially me thanking him for the gifts and him sending me a *good morning* or *evening*, it's not the same as hearing his voice, seeing his face and the expressions that bring it to life, or smelling his cologne. And then he steals my breath with a smile that reaches the deepest parts of my body.

"Ready for step two?"

I tilt my head to look at him, not wanting to admit how that glint in his eye is affecting me. "I think so."

"Good." Again, he holds out his hand, and we make our way to the elevator. I look at him in surprise when he pushes the button for the roof. His excitement is infectious, and I feel the buzz of it flowing through my veins. The ascent is long, and being confined in this small space with Alex is exhilarating. I can feel the warmth of his body radiating into me, through me, filling me, enfolding me to the point that I can hardly take it. And just when I think I am about to pass out, the doors open, and I suck in a deep breath.

Alex escorts me toward a red and white Bell 407 helicopter on the helipad, the life-sized version of the toy he had sent me. The sight of a large helicopter has me wondering what Alex has in store for me next, especially when the pilot comes forward and introduces himself to us, informing us that the preflight inspection is done and that he is ready for take-off.

I turn and look up at Alex, my eyes wide in sheer shock. *Is this really happening?* He looks at me with his strong jawline and presses his lips together giving me an intense stare. "You ready, baby girl?"

He grabs my hand not giving me a chance to respond and leads us to the helicopter, helping me on board and buckles me in securely. I stare at his hands pulling on the straps confirming they are secure. Each tug has his muscles jumping in his arms. I watch as he straps himself in the same giving the pilot a thumbs up that we are good to go. And then we are up in the air, the cityscape beneath us with the shadow of the helicopter flitting across the buildings. The pilot, Brad, hovers over specific landmarks, and seeing the Statue of Liberty up close blows my mind. Then there is the Chrysler Building, and I gasp at the sheer height of it, and then Alex points out the Rockefeller Center with its summer café, which in winter would be frozen over for the infamous ice rink. Brad and Alex laugh when I coo "Adorable!" at the tiny tables and colorful umbrellas surrounding the pond.

Alex points out different boroughs of New York as we fly over them, and it is amazing to see the people relaxing in Central Park, the Brooklyn Bridge, Times Square, and the Empire State Building. The helicopter hits an air pocket as we round the stately building, and Alex's hold tightens on my hand.

"Are you okay?" I ask into the mic of the bulky headphones.

He gives me a shaky smile. "This is a first for me."

My heart melts. *I can't believe he is doing all of this for me.* I feel a rush of emotions take over me and intertwine our fingers and clasp his hand more tightly. He leans forward, so close to my face. I can't help but think *this is it.* I turn my face to him, only he stares into my eyes and then my lips not moving any closer. Him kissing me is all I've been able to think of lately. Well, that and in Maggie's words doing the horizontal salsa. I can almost feel his soft lips collide with mine causing my insides to ignite a fire. I swallow big with anticipation. Just as I see him move in closer, we hit another air pocket causing more rocky turbulence, breaking the moment we shared. "Fuck." I mumble under my breath.

"I feel like an alien with these things on," he gives a nervous laughter.

"Best looking alien I've seen," giving in to the redirection.

"At least the force is with you!" He glances out of the window as the helicopter banks and his face lights up. "If you look over there, that's Harlem. Do you see that street with the elm tree on the corner? I grew up on that street."

Really?" I gasp as I look over the area he shows me, honored that he feels comfortable showing me where he grew up. And then the week's gifts make sense—he was sending me bits of himself in the tiny replica of the neighborhood he grew up in. "Will you take me there sometime?"

"Sure." His smile brightens his eyes, and I feel the butterflies in my stomach flutter.

"Do you still have family living there?"

"Yeah, my grandmom and parents still live there."

I watch him as he stares out the window talking about his family and showing me places he grew up as a child. He's opening up to me and sharing a part of his world and I can't think of any other place I'd rather be right now.

"Couldn't you just hide up here all day." I say taking in the sight.

His gaze turns towards me. "As long as you'll hide up here with me."

Chapter Seven

Brad flies us back to the hotel, and our helicopter ride comes to an end with a slight bump as it comes to rest on the helipad. Alex grasps my hand tightly at the drop and doesn't let go, something that I am grateful for because my knees are still wobbly as we disembark, and I hold onto Alex for support. He takes my hand and kisses my knuckles, making tiny sparks explode along my nerve endings, prickling my scalp and making my body tingle. I can feel myself responding in ways that have been asleep for a while, my blood thrumming through my veins in the same thumping rhythm of the mighty rotors of the helicopter. My cheeks heat up at the thought that maybe wearing the white lace lingerie set might have been the right choice.

"That was incredible!" I breathe. I pull him to a stop and turn to look at the view from the beautiful hotel's roof. All around us, the rooftops of famous buildings reach for the sky, the early afternoon sun glinting on their surfaces and bathing New York in a sleepy glow. The soft breeze is tugging at my burnt orange culotte and gray frilled tank top, giving the day a fresh scent and cooling the heat that I can feel radiating from the buildings around us. From here, the sound of the traffic is distant, giving the idea that we are on our own cloud.

Alex pulls me closer to his side as he admires the view with me. "*This* is incredible!"

We're standing close to each other in the elevator, our hands still linked as we take the incredibly slow descent to the reception. The ride seems to take forever. The feelings of our earlier ride in the elevator threaten to overwhelm me again, only this time they are intensified, and I take deep breaths to steady my heartbeat. Each breath is filled with the wonderful, sexy, fresh lemony scent of his cologne, and I smile at the idea that I will be smelling of him for a long time. I glance up to find Alex watching my breasts rise and fall in my near-panic, and instantly my nipples harden as the air leaves my lungs with a soft *whoosh* when he looks into my eyes. We're both still staring at each other when the doors slide open into the lobby.

"It was an experience for me as well," he murmurs,

closing his eyes and taking a deep breath. With a gentle tug on my hand, he pulls me closer, and with slow steps, we walk toward the front desk. His hand tightens around mine when he stops in the middle of the large and bright hotel atrium. "How about some lunch? I'm starving."

"That's a thing for you, isn't it?" I tease, trying to divert my reaction to him with humor.

"I do my best thinking when I'm eating. I blame my parents. I've been bussing tables since I was fourteen, and we would have 'staff meetings' around a meal after the restaurant closed. So, brainstorming took place around the possible new menu options," he says, looking into the dining room. "There doesn't seem to be a free table."

"Can we sit outside? It's such a fantastic day," I ask, peering through the large windows to the sunshine brightening the street outside.

"Great idea," he agrees, and we make our way out of the air-conditioned hotel. The heat of the day swoops down on us. We stroll down the block to find a café with an empty table outside, but it seems that everyone in New York has the same idea of enjoying the summer sun. "Let's see if there is anything in the park. It could be cooler under the trees as well."

Nodding, I follow him down a path covered with trees, and there we are met with a dozen pop-up food trucks selling everything from seafood burritos to pistachio ice cream. The aromas wafting in the air have my stomach grumbling and my mouth watering. We are spoiled for choice, and I can't make a decision when Alex asks me what I want. He leads me to a truck with picnic tables set out. After ordering a sampling platter and beers, we sit under a colorful umbrella and explore the food. Everything looks and smells so delicious, from the deep-fried prawns, pulled pork sliders, beef strips, and apple salad to the mouthwatering rainbow trout and orange glaze.

"I cannot imagine my mom sitting in the park and enjoying a lovely meal like this. If it's not in a restaurant, then it's not a proper meal." I can't contain the giggle at the image of my mom sitting at a picnic table in her designer suit eating the beef strip and apple salad with a plastic knife and fork, the paper napkin blowing off her lap.

"My dad would love having your mom in his restaurant, then." Alex laughs as we eat. "I can see Anthony having a truck like this somewhere in the city, but it's too casual for Dad."

"Your family sounds interesting." I would really like to meet his family, but I know it's too soon for that.

"I suppose they are, but I can tell you for sure they are not half as interesting as you." His eyes darken, and I suddenly find a shortage of oxygen in the air as he draws me closer, hooking his finger under my chin and lifting my face to his. My lips are suddenly so dry, and I put the tip of my tongue out to lick them wet, only for Alex to groan softly before he lightly brushes my mouth with his… And my world dissolves until the only thing that remains is the sensation of his warm lips against my own.

His hand curls around the nape of my neck, and he pulls me closer. I shiver as his tongue glides across my bottom lip, and I gasp, allowing him the entrance he is asking for, deepening the kiss as his tongue sweeps in and makes me shiver again. My heart is beating so fast as I cup his strong jaw, and my hands are shaking when I pull him closer, his beard tickling my palm and making my body tighten. *I'm in trouble!* This is the last coherent thought I have before giving in to the taste and feel of Alex's kiss.

I loop my arm around his neck as he slides his hands to my waist, pulling me flush against his chest. My nipples instantly harden at the feel of his hard body against mine. Every breath causes friction between us, which has me sighing into his mouth. He moans in response, and the sound vibrates down my spine and settles in a puddle between my legs.

We break apart, breathless, unable to look away from each other. And I am giddy with the knowledge that his world is affected as much as mine. Without saying a word, we throw our empty plates into the trash and wander back through the park, our hands still intertwined, our steps unhurried despite the tension sparking between us. It is one of the best dates I have been on in a long while.

Though contact between us is only through our clasped hands, the heat still smolders on the surface, and I feel that I will implode if he snaps his fingers. It continues to sizzle as we stand next to each other in the elevator to my floor, the walk from the park a blur after the way he kissed me.

Both of us are breathing shallowly as we exit the elevator car, and time slows down. Each step takes forever to land. My body feels heavy with need: My breasts are swollen, my nipples are sensitive, and my thighs are quivering. Each brush of his arm against mine has my body pulsing in response.

We eventually reach my door, and we turn to each other, our arms winding around the other of their own free will. Our mouths melt together like we are each other's survival. He pushes me against my door, and I feel my body flush as his erection presses against my stomach. Our kiss turns frenzied, his hands sliding over my butt and lifting me higher against his body, and I cling to him as my hips rock forward.

Without breaking contact with him, I blindly reach for my keys and unlock my door. At the sound of the lock clicking open, he slowly withdraws from me, his breathing uneven. I manage to pry my eyes open to look up at him, and I suddenly have a feeling this is not going to end as I expected.

"Alex?" My voice is husky, unrecognizable with desire and confusion.

He leans his forearm against the doorframe, and I feel his breath warm against the skin of my neck, stirring the thin silver threads of my earring. "I'm sorry, Kerri. I can't."

Cold air touches me as he widens the space between us, the tension still humming between us as I wait for him to decide between staying with me or walking away. He leans closer, and I part my lips when his breath brushes over them, but then he pushes away from me abruptly, and I watch in disbelief as he walks away without an explanation.

Filled with anger I enter my apartment with short, jerky movements, almost slamming the door behind me. I put some water on to boil for tea and then run a bath—the two things I know will calm me down. My body is still pulsing with unfulfilled need, but I try to ignore it as I carry the mug into the bathroom, still feeling edgy. I fill the bath liberally with my favorite gardenia-scented bubble bath and start undressing.

I gasp at the friction of my bra rubbing against my sensitive nipples, the pull so deep it hurts. Even the brush of the water against my skin has tiny explosions popping off in my heated core as I slide into the bath. Closing my eyes, I lay back, and I can still feel Alex's hand on my arm. Without realizing it, my hands trace the same paths, and I take it even further when I massage my eager breasts, my nipples hardening even more as they lift out of the water and the cool air touches them.

I can barely open my eyes when I moan deeply, my

exploring hands coming to rest between my legs. My back arches and my legs fall apart as my fingers open my lips and find my throbbing clit. I moan again as I circle that sensitive area, enjoying the tension it creates. My breasts quiver as my breathing becomes faster, and I slide my fingers into my yearning pussy, gasping at the fires that the friction ignites. My heated walls tighten around my fingers as I feel the tension build. I remember the feeling of Alex's warm lips on my own and his eager hardness pressing against my pussy as I rub my swollen knot of nerves with my palm. My fingers thrust deep and fast, bringing me to an explosive orgasm, my shuddering body sending waves of bubbles over the edge of the bath.

Chapter Eight

Alex: I feel bad about how I left things the other day. I hope you can give me a chance to make it up to you.

With a sigh, I place my phone beside my keyboard and think about ignoring his text, but my concentration is shot at the sight of his name. It's the second time he's left me hanging, and this has me second-guessing myself. It also makes me wonder who Alex really is, because I cannot shake the feeling that he is hiding something.

It doesn't help that my mind is still reeling from the other text I received the morning after our date.

Unknown: Are you deaf, bitch? Crawl back

into your hole, or I will dig a hole for you!

It was from the same unknown number as the first text, and the anger in it is still sending shivers down my spine. With a shudder, I deliberately push that text out of my mind and concentrate on what I need to do about Alex.

I lean back in my chair, the images on my computer forgotten as I think about the time I had spent with Alex and the way we respond to each other. And the way he makes me feel! *What do I do, Ana?* Biting my lips, I disentangle my fingers from my butterfly charm necklace and pick up my phone. Holding my breath, I send him a text.

> Me: It will have to be epic.

> Alex: Central Park with fireworks over the harbor?

I won't lie; I am intrigued. The thought of spending a romantic night watching the skyline light up with fireworks while he holds me sounds amazing, but I also don't want to make it too easy for him.

> Me: So, we're going to study the grass in the park and watch fireworks between two tall buildings?

He responds with laughing emojis.

> Alex: There is a wide variety of grass in the park.

Me: You're supposed to entice me to watch the fireworks…

Alex: Trust me?

I take a deep breath and consider his question. *Do I trust him? Should I trust him?*

Since Ana died, I've been playing it safe, doing what is expected of me. I went to medical school because that is what my parents wanted for me, and I was too afraid to venture into the field I wanted to. When I fainted one too many times in anatomy, one of my lecturers suggested I change my major. It took me a full semester to tell my parents. Even moving to New York is a huge risk for me. But my instincts tell me that Alex would be the biggest risk I can take and that he will change my life in the biggest way. With my heart beating a mile a minute, I take the leap.

Me: Okay.

~~~

The Fourth of July is my least favorite holiday ever. I usually spend it hidden in my room with the curtains drawn tight. It was the last weekend I spent with my sister—the weekend of our last fateful swim meet. So, it is not a surprise when I receive a voicemail from Alex that simply says, *"Kerri, I'm sorry, but something's come up. I will make it up to you, I promise."*

I groan aloud as I pull the covers back over my head. I
~~~

had gone out with Maggie and a couple of her friends last night, and my phone battery had died before I got home. As a result, I didn't get his calls, only the voicemail when I turned on my phone this morning.

My phone buzzes on the bedside table. I glare at it from beneath my cozy cave, but it doesn't stop, so I reach out and answer it, my voice muffled by the duvet.

"Do you have plans for today?" Maggie asks, her voice bubbling with excitement.

"Not anymore," I mutter, glaring at the sunshine streaming through my window.

"Great! I'm picking you up in an hour."

"Why?"

"To get you out of bed, obviously." She pauses for a moment. "It's just a barbecue with some friends. It'll be fun."

"Says the person before boarding the *Titanic*," I whine.

"Will it help if I say *pretty please?*"

"Okay," I groan as I push the covers off.

"Yes!" she crows as we disconnect.

~~~

Maggie hooks her arm through mine as we walk into the
~~~

yard filled with people. The smell of charring meat fills the air and makes me realize how hungry I am. A drink is pressed into our hands by a waiter as he passes us, and I take a sip of the rich white wine, wanting to feel the buzz it will give me on an empty stomach.

"Mags!" someone squeals, and Maggie bounces in that direction in excitement, her arm still hooked through mine. A stunning woman appears before us, her sandy brown hair hanging in curly waves to her voluptuous hips. Her olive skin is highlighted by the fuchsia pink halter top and denim shorts showing off her mile-long legs to perfection. I admire her skill of walking on four-inch stilettos at a barbecue without getting caught in the grass. Her soft pink shade of lipstick compliments her rosy cheeks. She even makes Maggie look girlish in her lavender skort and white sleeveless shirt.

"Demi! Come meet Kerri!" The two of them embrace, and I am automatically pulled into the circle because Maggie still has a strong hold on my arm. "Kerri, this is the most talented artist you will meet on this side of the Hudson River."

"Only on this side of the Hudson?" Demi teases as she extends her hand out to shake mine. Her upper arm covered in a tattoo sleeve full of tribal symbols, hibiscus flowers and roman numerals giving her total look an Amazonian goddess vibe. "I see your warden is here already."

A strange look flashes on Maggie's face and I'm not sure how to interpret it. "I needed to pick Kerri up. Where's your other half?"

Demi grimaces and looks around the yard. "Hopefully getting us more drinks."

Two tall men walk toward us, and Maggie empties her glass in one gulp before putting a smile on her face. She holds out her hand, and the taller of the men takes it and pulls her to his side. "Um, Kerri, this is Preston."

Preston smiles and shakes my hand, a silent expectation in his blue eyes. He is incredibly handsome, with dark brown hair and bright blue eyes, and a body you can see he spends a lot of time in the gym for. He is at least a foot taller than Maggie's five-foot-two, but they seem to complement each other well. "It's great to finally meet you, Kerri."

Something about the way he looks at me makes me uneasy, and I am relieved when Demi introduces me to her boyfriend, Julius, diverting the attention away from the sudden tension that filters into the group.

Music starts across the yard, and Maggie takes my hand. "Come on, let's—"

"Food sounds like a good idea, Maggie," Preston says, patting her hand at his waist. Her smile freezes, and she nods.

"Yeah, sounds great," she agrees, and we make our way to the tables heavy with the summer feast. I'm watching as she makes his plate. It seems that some of her vivacity is gone. This is a different side to Maggie, and I'm not sure what to make of it.

"The food looks delicious."

She nods in agreement, both of us dishing lightly before heading back to the table. Conversation flows easily as the men carry the bulk of it, Demi and Maggie occasionally adding their own contributions.

"Oh, Demi, you must see the graphics that Kerri is busy with! She took your artwork and turned them into masterpieces for the Jenkins account—"

"There's Clifford and Jean Lincoln. Let's go and say hi," Preston interrupts, not giving Maggie a chance to refuse before pulling her to her feet and leading her to the couple he pointed out.

A silence settles over the table after they leave, and I sip some wine before turning to Demi. "How did you and Maggie meet, Demi?"

She doesn't answer me immediately, and I notice that she is looking at something in Julius's lap. I quietly clear the knot of discomfort in my throat, wondering how I can give them some privacy without being obvious when Julius looks up, a tinge of red on his cheeks as he glances at Demi.

Something that looks like pain flits in her light brown eyes, but her lashes lower as she takes a sip of her wine, and her expression becomes an impassive mask. Julius clears his throat as he looks at her before tossing his phone on the table and getting to his feet.

"I'm off to get a drink." He kisses Demi before walking to the bar. Both of us watch his broad back retreat, his jeans hugging his tight behind—those hours in the gym have clearly paid off.

"I'm sorry, Kerri. Did you say something?" Demi smiles at me, shaking the bangs out of her eyes.

I repeat my question, and we chat about Maggie's ambition and what it feels like to work with her, both of us having that experience in common. The DJ starts playing more lively music, and Julius catches my eye as he pulls an older lady onto the dance floor and starts dancing with her. His movements are exaggerated and comical, making his partner laugh as well. "Julius seems quite a character— sweet."

"Lover to all, faithful to none," Demi murmurs before sipping her wine again. I gape at her, not sure what to say in response. She glances at me and gives me a wry smile. Before I can respond, Julius jogs from the dance floor and pulls Demi to join him, a fond smile alighting on her face. I watch them dance, then spot Maggie and Preston deeper in the crowd. Their conversation looks intense, and I'm sure that she is wiping away a tear. She looks so miserable—a mirror of my own despondent mood.

I'm not sure why I agreed to come to this party except that I needed to be around people, and I thought being in a new city would help make new memories to replace this heavy weekend. I was wrong. Watching the sunset on a day that didn't start well is a relief to me because it means the day is nearly over. I really want to call a cab but I'm not sure what the address is. I'm afraid if I don't, I'll have to sit for another hour watching Maggie pretend to smile.

My phone vibrates, and it's a message from Alex, but I ignore it. I can't help but think, would my day have gone better if he had followed through on our plans? I wouldn't be ending this day alone again if he had just kept his promise?

These are questions I cannot answer, and I get to my feet in frustration and look for a bathroom. Instead of returning to the yard, I walk out the front door and take a deep breath of the sultry summer air. Standing on the porch, I send Maggie a text and make my way to the end of the street, where I find directions to the train station.

With relief, I close the door to my apartment, make myself some tea, and watch the fireworks shoot across the sky from the large windows. As they pop off, I remember watching them with Ana from the roof of our house, each Roman Candle, Strobe, and Parachute belonging to a particular princess who found her happily-ever-after.

Chapter Nine

There is a bowl of Chow Down*'s* hot and spicy chicken Chow Mein set out on my coffee table, a glass of Merlot breathing beside it, a movie with Michael B. Jordan ready to start, and my favorite leggings and loose sweatshirt giving me as much comfort as my heart needs. Fireworks are still popping off around the city, the different colors flaring through my drapes, and I can hear parties on different floors of my building. I settle down and turn up the volume to make the most of my night the best way I know how, not wanting to think about Maggie and Preston, or even Alex at the moment.

After the movie, I took a long bath, talking to Elise the entire time. The chat helped, as it always does. She is always able to get me in a better frame of mind, and the idea of her coming to visit in a few weeks definitely helps. I'm already planning our itinerary with excitement bubbling through me at the prospect of seeing my best friend after such a long separation… introducing her to Maggie… and maybe even taking her to the bar where Alex and I—

Knock.

I glare at the door. My eyes narrow and my lips purse as I wonder who would be so rude as to interrupt my comfort. Maybe they will go away if I just stay quiet and pretend I'm not here. I softly slurp the broth of my meal and lift my glass from the table. Another knock sounds, more insistent than the first. With a sigh, I put down my glass and answer the door.

I blink up at Alex, who stands there with his hand raised, preparing to knock again, wearing a look of determination. His shoulders lift as he sighs heavily, and I am entranced by the movement, unable to pull my eyes away from the way his chest expands and how his t-shirt folds around his lean waist. His jeans-encased legs are long, and I swallow the sudden dryness in my throat. He is looking particularly good tonight.

"Why aren't you answering your phone?" His tone has my eyes snapping up to his with a frown to match his own. A muscle jumps in his jaw as he grinds his teeth impatiently.

"I turned it off." I shrug, and his eyes narrow in anger. "I didn't know I was supposed to answer *every* call I get."

"Why?" I watch as his poor teeth grind some more causing his jaw muscles to jump again.

"Because I didn't want to be disturbed, especially by you." I turn back into the apartment, not wanting to care if he follows me or goes away. I am unable to stop the bubbling up of hope that he'll stay. I cannot believe how much it hurts hearing the door snap shut, the sound echoing the loud crack of my heart. A soft thud has me spinning around with my eyes wide as I see Alex leaning against the door, his arms crossed over that broad chest. "What are you—"

"I thought we agreed, Kerri. "His voice is soft as he walks towards me, his steps slow and calculated.

"We agreed to enjoy every moment together, but that's hard when—" My words are cut off by his warm hands cupping my jaw and his hot lips claiming my mouth. I try to push against his chest, but his tongue sliding along my lip, which he sucks softly, has me moaning, and I find myself wrapping my arms around his waist. He tilts my head up to place a trail of hot kisses down my neck and to my shoulder, which is exposed by the drooping neckline of my sweatshirt.

I gasp when his teeth graze my collarbone, and my eyes fall closed as I shudder. His hand skims beneath my sweatshirt and sets my skin on fire. My body responds immediately; my pussy is swollen and weeping, needing him as I've never needed someone before. He murmurs my name as he pulls me closer to his growing erection, his mouth returning to mine with a silent demand. And I gladly open up for him.

"Kerri," he gasps when we break the kiss, both of us breathing heavily. He rests his forehead on my shoulder, his hot breath blowing across my hardened nipples and stoking the fire even higher. His hands flex on my hips, and I sense him withdrawing from me. I shake my head, taking hold of his face to pull him back towards me, not wanting to lose the connection we've just created.

"Oh, fuck, Kerri," he whispers before he takes my mouth again. With a groan, he lifts me onto the counter, and I wrap my legs around him, his erection cupped between my legs as though we are made for each other. His hand settles on my ass, and I arch my hips, the friction making us both moan as I rock against him.

"Alex, please," I plead, sucking his tongue into my mouth, catching it with my teeth, and then running the tip of my tongue over it. My hands cup his head as I hold him close to deepen the kiss.

"Kerri," he growls, plowing a hand into my hair. His other hand finds my naked breast under my shirt. My legs tighten around his hips when his fingers massage the swollen nipple, and I cry out as my inner heat squeezes painfully. He pulls up the hem of my shirt and replaces his fingers with his mouth, sucking the hardened tip. His tongue flicks over it, sending aftershocks through my body and making my pussy clench painfully. I cry out, and his erection jerks against me. His fingers push past the waistband of my leggings, and I widen my legs to give him access to my wetness.

"Yes," I gasp, hardly breathing as he slides a finger into me, my body greedily pulling him deeper. My back arches over the counter when he withdraws, and I moan when his thumb finds my sensitive bud between my hot folds and circles it. I hiss when he inserts a second finger, and I grasp his wrist as I rock on his fingers, their length finding the magic spot deep inside. My heart beats in rhythm with my body's throbbing.

"You are so beautiful," he murmurs against my shoulder, his mouth moving back to my own.

"Please, Alex…" My breaths are nothing but heavy panting as I feel my orgasm building. "I need you… Ohhh… Please, Alex, I need you inside me…"

He stops his movements, and I arch my hips higher to keep the momentum going, but he slowly withdraws his hand from me. I moan in protest, but he takes a deep breath as he steps away from me, his hands shaking when he pushes them over his head. Despite the heat of wanting fulfillment deep inside me, I feel the coolness of his withdrawal like a bucket of ice water on a hot July day.

"Shit, Kerri," he breathes, his hand cupping my cheek as I blink up at him. "I'm sorry, I got carried away. I'm so sorry."

My hold tightens on his wrist. "No, Alex, don't do this again."

"I'm sorry."

I bite my lip as I watch him leave…again. The quiet click of the door snaps through my body like a whip.

I sit frozen, unable to move as I try to understand what just happened. *What the entire fuck! Did I say something wrong? Was I too forward? Was it too soon? I know he wanted it just as much as me.* I blush as I think about the way I begged him to fill me while the pain from the blow of rejection settles in my stomach.

My throbbing body and sporadic shivers of desire remind me that I had voiced my need, and he had walked away. *Maybe he doesn't want me in that way.* But then I remember his insistent erection flush against my body. There was no way he didn't want to finish this as much as I did!

I close my eyes, and all I see is the regret on his face as he turns to walk away, his lips swollen from my kisses and his eyes hot with lust. Then the anger strikes, and my body hums with a different kind of energy as I push myself off the counter. The pull of my pants against my sensitive folds sends another shiver through me, sparking another round of intense anger. I curl up in the corner of the couch and reach for my phone, turning it on as I lay it on my lap. Five text messages and even more phone calls beep through, most of them from Alex.

After skimming through the last of his texts, I quickly type out a message and turn off my phone, not wanting to be disturbed again.

>Me: You have done this one too many times, Alex. And I'm tired of it. Please leave me the fuck alone.

Chapter Ten

Two weeks later, and my life settles into a routine. I run for an hour in the mornings, go to work, have occasional drinks with Maggie and friends when we finish, and enjoy the evenings by myself. This is besides the nights I wake up sweating and breathing hard, my body throbbing and only allowing me to sleep after I bring myself to orgasm, the thoughts, taste, and feel of Alex filling my dreams. So, as of this week, I have decided to go on dates again.

I haven't heard from Alex in all this time, and I'm starting to really miss him. I tell myself that I am relieved that he left me alone, but that doesn't stop me from checking my phone throughout the day for a message. I reactivate my old dating apps as well as sign up for more, hoping to meet someone who will make me forget about Alex.

"There are so many fish in this very tiny pond, Kerri," Maggie reminds me as she slides on the edge of my desk. She wags her finger at me. "I know we miss the gifts, but there's no sulking allowed. There are many young and lively men who will gladly pay for a glass of wine with you."

"Well." I shake my phone at her. "You'll be glad to know that I've reactivated my accounts, and I have a match. We are going on a date tonight."

"Yeah!" Maggie whoops as she gets to her feet. "I want details."

"Maybe!" I sing as she walks away. As I turn back to my screen, I tell myself that I am looking forward to it.

~~~

As I step back from the mirror, I can't help but feel a rush of excitement and nerves coursing through my body. The cobalt-blue, off-the-shoulder silk dress hugs my curves in all the right places, accentuating my femininity and making me feel undeniably sexy. The dress effortlessly glides down to rest enticingly at mid-thigh, leaving just enough to the imagination. I take a moment to appreciate the way it clings to my figure, reminding me of the confident and alluring woman that I am, especially when I finish my look with a sky-high pair of strappy silver sandals. I smack my lips after I apply the cherry-flavored lip gloss, then fluff my curls
~~~

hanging over my left eye, adjust the silver headband that holds the rest back, and declare myself ready.

I make sure that I have my phone, credit card, and some cash in my silver clutch purse, then grab my keys as I rush out the door, my mind focused on the excitement of the night ahead, I suddenly come to a halt. Standing there, leaning against the wall with his hands casually tucked into the pockets of his perfectly tailored gray pants, is Alex as if he was deciding between knocking or walking away when I opened the door. His eyes flash with appreciation when they run up the length of my bare legs to the soft swell of my breasts heaving with the thud of my heavily beating heart. As his eyes reach my face, I can feel my cheeks become flush and I briefly get lost in the depth of his grayish-brown eyes. *Keep it together, Kerri!*

And then I remember the way he left me, hot and ready, the last time we were together, and every night in my dreams. I slam my door shut behind me, not allowing him entry into my home… and possibly my life. His shoulders jerk slightly at the click echoing softly in the hall as he acknowledges what it signifies.

"What are you doing here, Alex?" I try to infuse as much ice in my tone as my overheated body will allow.

"We need to talk, Kerri." He comes closer, and I take a step back, knowing that if he gets too close, I might unlock my door and not let him leave again.

"I'll check my calendar for an opening," I retort. "I don't have time now."

I take a step away from him, but he takes hold of my wrist and turns me to him, my body flush against his. A shiver runs down my spine as he pushes me against the wall, his wonderful scent filling my senses. I try to push against his chest, but he easily catches my hands and pins them above my head, automatically arching my back and pushing my eager breasts tighter against his white shirt. The friction of the silk fabric rubs my nipples raw.

He leans forward, and my stomach clenches as he places a kiss softly on the curve of my neck, barely touching my skin. The heat of his tongue traces a path along my shoulder until he reaches the strap of my dress and follows it down to the curve of my breast. And then he thrusts his tongue between my breasts, exactly above the spot where my heart is thundering, and places a hot, wet, open-mouthed kiss right there. My knees buckle and I can feel the wetness in my panties. My pussy tightens when he playfully tugs at my earlobe, and I swallow the gasp. He flicks my hardened nipple with his thumb, and I frown at him as I fight to suppress the reaction he is eliciting from my body.

His gravelly whisper sends more shivers down my spine. "I bet he can't make you feel like I just did."

I close my eyes, partly in exasperation, but also to block out the sight of his full bottom lip so temptingly close that if I turn my head, I can touch it with the tip of my tongue. Locking my knees to keep them from collapsing like overcooked spaghetti, I push him away from me. I slide my hands down my sides to straighten my dress and fix my hair, before eventually having the courage to look him in the eye. "You can go now."

Hoping my stilettos don't disappoint me, I use this opportunity to walk away from him, his soft laughter following me as the elevator doors ping closed.

~~~

I blink to stop my eyes from glazing over as my date talks about the stylish lines of the Empire State Building. I smile and nod, sipping at my warm white wine that has gone acidic. As it trickles down my throat, it reminds me of Alex's tongue against my skin, and I shiver, my nipples puckering against the shimmering silk. I can smell his citrusy scent on my skin when I lift my glass. *How the hell did I end up here?*

Oh, yes… I am here because Alex is a tease. I am here because of the damned dating apps. I am here because my luck has me matching with the architect who works in the same building as The Urban Design Studio, the same one who flirted with me when I dropped mustard on me. I am here because Alex made me so hot that I was hoping this poor man—*What the hell is his name?*—could ease the yearning. And it is obviously not going to happen. *Damn*!
~~~

The meal of sea bass fried in lemon butter on a bed of delicately blanched vegetables is as tasteless as ice, and my date's conversation is as interesting as watching water freeze. I swallow a yawn and try to take another sip of wine when I spot a movement over the shoulder of—*whatever-his-name-is*—and gasp in indignant shock. I narrow my eyes as I recognize the white shirt that Alex had been wearing earlier. You're kidding! He did not just follow-

"Kerri, are you okay?" Mark—Michael—*Martin?*—asks.

"I'm okay." I smile reassuringly. "That's fascinating, but can you excuse me for a second? I just need to run to the ladies' room."

"Sure," he agrees quickly.

I place my napkin on the table as I get to my feet, and saunter past the table where I thought I saw Alex hiding behind a menu. I release a heavy sigh as I confirm his presence, the cheeky smile he gives me over the top of the menu on the table spiking my irritation. I am so tempted to tip the pitcher of iced water into his lap as I walk past, but I bite my lip to contain myself. Once I am in the bathroom, I take out my phone and send him a text with a multitude of angry emojis.

Me: What the fuck are you doing here???

His response comes through immediately.

Alex: Having dinner.

Me: Why here???

Alex: I hear this place has great reviews.

Leaning over the counter, I look up at the mirror, and I'm surprised to find my cheeks flushed and my eyes sparkling. I can see the pulse beating in my neck. I let out a soft breath, blowing the bangs off my forehead, but I know that the heat deep inside will only be extinguished in one way, and only by one man. Having him "present" at my date irritates me, but it also makes my inner walls clench, soaking my panties once again in anticipation.

Alex: Your date is watching the door anxiously. I think he realizes that you could do better.

Me: I sure as hell can!

Alex: I hope you weren't planning on dessert because he is checking his cash.

Me: Stop! He is a sweet guy!

Alex: Being sweet won't let him make you wet.

My sex throbs inside my panties at his text, and this only irritates me more. And the realization that I can't hide in the bathroom any longer has me seeing pink. I dab some cool water on my wrists and, with determination, make my way back to—Martin—Mark—*Paul!* That was the man's name, Paul!

"Sorry, I had to answer a call."

Paul smiles forgivingly. "Do you want to order dessert?"

"I'm so sorry, Paul, but the call I got was from a girlfriend of mine needing my help. I really need to go."

He smiles a little sadly. "But we will see each other again?"

"Sure," I lie, tamping down the temptation to run. My phone vibrates as I walk to the door.

Alex: Illicit in 15.

Me: Not a chance.

Chapter Eleven

And yet, here I am, 10 minutes later at the very spot Alex and I first met, sipping some drink I can't pronounce and waiting for a man I can't resist. I shiver as a finger lightly brushes across the back of my shoulders just above the neckline, and I look up into the mirror behind the bar, my eyes clashing with those of Alex—and my body forgets to do what it is supposed to do except respond to him in the most primal way.

"What the actual fuck, Alex? Stalking me on my date?" I go into attack mode, trying to ignore my body's need to be close to him.

I could see him trying not to smile. "I told you…the reviews."

"Screw you, Alex," I retort, not as hotly as I would have liked. I scold myself as I sip my cocktail.

"You would love to," he says softly, his lips almost brushing against my shoulder, and I shiver. My tongue inadvertently flicks out to wet my lips, and his eyes darken in response as they meet mine in the mirror again. I lean back to get some breathing space. "Let's face it, Kerri. We can't stay away from each other. Tell me you weren't as miserable as I was the last couple of weeks."

He is saying something, but I am distracted by the various shades of brown in his irises. But then I shake my head, breaking the spell he has cast on me. I wrap my arms around my waist, my shoulders almost sagging. "What does it matter, Alex?"

He is quiet for a heartbeat too long, and I realize he is staring at my cleavage that I had pushed up when I crossed my arms. He strokes his large fingers up and down my arms before wrapping them around my elbows. Bending his head, he looks at me. "What do you mean? Of course, it matters!"

"Why?" I shake his hands from me and turn to reach for my drink. He sits down on the stool next to me, his leg sending sparks along my nerve endings as it brushes against my own when he places it between my knees.

"Because I want to be with you," he says softly. "You give color to my world, Kerri, that I have not found anywhere else.”

“I doubt that.”

“Why?”

“There is obviously someone else, Alex. Why else would you keep running out on me? Or cancel dates? Or not take me to meet your family?” I challenge him. My eyes narrow as something that looks like guilt shimmers across his face for a moment, but it disappears so quickly I tell myself it is my imagination.

“I’m sorry I’ve canceled so many times, Kerri, but you are the only girl for me.” He takes my hand, linking our fingers together, his eyes begging me to believe him. “The last few months have just been hectic for me. My workload tripled since I was elected as one of the partner candidates at my firm. And then I’ve been helping Anthony at the restaurant as well, preparing for Dad’s retirement. And to add to that, I can’t keep my mind from you, and think about all the ways I want to make you… *extremely*… happy.”

Shaking my head, I hide my moan in my alcoholic concoction when his finger runs a silky path from my knee to the hem of my skirt and back, moving over to the more sensitive skin on the inside of my thigh. I bite on my teeth, denying my body the need to express what his words and errant fingers are doing to it. I don’t want to make a decision about Alex based on what my body wants. I need to understand how he makes me feel, emotionally. And so far, he is filling my heart with happiness, but he is also leaving me with equal amounts of frustration.

He makes me feel special and cared for, considering the gifts he sends me, little things that make me smile, and I missed that over the last two weeks. I miss the way he can make me smile. I glance over at him and admire his strong profile, his soft beard tempting me to stroke it, his full lower lip calling for my teeth to bite and pull... and suck.

My breath catches, and I gulp my drink, blurting out the first thinking that pops into my mind... or, more accurately, the second. "I don't even know if you live on your own or if you still stay in your parents' basement somewhere in Harlem!"

"My parents' basement—" He stares at me for a second before starting to laugh, and my stomach clenches at the rumbling sound. "I don't live with my parents, Kerri. I have a place of my own that my mom wants to lay her hands on to decorate, but that I continuously avoid."

"Sure," I drawl, sipping my drink. "Your parents' pool house then."

Again, he laughs. "My parents don't have a pool, and Anthony lives in the apartment above the garage. I, on the other hand, live in a cozy condo just on the other side of town."

"I don't believe you," the pretty drink I've been sipping

on challenges him.

He smiles and strokes my cheek with his thumb. "Will you believe me if I show it to you?"

I cock my head. "It could belong to your dad."

"Trust me, it doesn't."

"I'll want proof."

"I'll give you all the proof you want."

"Now how is a girl supposed to refuse that offer?" I put my glass down on the bar, pick up my purse, and walk toward the door. He joins me just as I reach the sidewalk, taking my hand and leading me in the direction of his supposed *cozy condo*.

~ ~ ~

Alex looks at me in shock as the elevator doors close. "How can you still doubt I live here when the doorman just greeted me by name?"

"He could be paid."

"Kerri! He *is* paid," Alex scoffs. "To be the *doorman*."

"Oh…" I bite my thumbnail as I consider his logic, watching the numbers flash by to the 11th floor.

He shakes his head and puts his hand on the small of

my back as he guides me to his door. The heat radiates from that spot to the rest of my body, and I know that this would be the best point to change my mind. But I don't want to change my mind.

The moment I step into the penthouse apartment, a sense of luxury washes over me. The entire floor space is adorned with exquisite hardwood floors, their smoothness caressing my feet as I slip out of my high heels. As I enter the short entrance hall, I am greeted by a grand foyer that leads to three magnificent bedrooms. To the right, a large family-sized bathroom beckons with its opulent fixtures and sparkling cleanliness. To the left, the main bedroom awaits with its regal presence, adorned with a lavish king-sized bed that promises restful nights. Making my way further into the penthouse, I find myself in an airy den, surrounded by bookshelves that reach from floor to ceiling. The room exudes sophistication with its elegant design and a large desk placed perfectly in the center. I quickly notice Alex's law books scatter on the desk. The den seamlessly opens to an expansive room that boasts floor-to-ceiling windows. These windows are adorned with long, white, filmy curtains that delicately filter the city lights, illuminating the space with a mesmerizing glow. Adjacent to the living room, a grand dining room that commands my attention immediately. Its centerpiece is an antique redwood dining set that can comfortably seat 12 people. The thought of Alex's parents and siblings sitting at the table brings a subtle smile to my face. Separating the dining room from the kitchen is a large island, adorned with soft gray marble countertops and pristine white cabinetry. The kitchen floor matches the countertops with its sleek gray tile, while a six-burner gas stove and oven beckon with their culinary possibilities. He had said his place is *cute*…this place is incredible! I can't imagine what it cost to live here, more than I could ever afford.

"What do you like the most about this place?" I ask him, trying to squelch my awe.

He tilts his head as he looks at me. "This."

He leads me to the living room and opens the doors that lead to the balcony. Before me are the twinkling lights of lower Manhattan and the majestic nighttime outline of Carnegie Hall, so graceful and full of intrigue, drama, and life, the lights across its roof giving it the eternal character that everyone loves. It is breathtaking. I can see myself sitting on the beautiful cane furniture with a cup of chai tea and my laptop while the sun rises over the rooftops.

Alex comes up behind me and wraps me in his strong arms, and I lean back against his chest, my hands crossed over his. Immediately, I can understand why this spot would be his favorite. It is so peaceful as you look out over the city, and you can be forgiven for thinking that you are alone in the world. "*This* is breathtaking."

"It is. I come out here to clear my mind when things get

to be too much. I just wish they could do something about the traffic."

Laughing, I turn in his arms to face him, draping my arms over his shoulders and pressing my breasts against his chest. "That is the music of New York!"

"It can be damned distracting when I want to do this." He bends his head as his hands slide around my waist and, with a gentle finger under my chin, he tilts my head up and kisses me. I hold on to his neck as my knees get weak, the movement causing the silk to brush over my hard nipples and igniting a fire between my legs.

Chapter Twelve

Being in his arms is heavenly, and I lean into him as I savor his kiss. He tightens his hands on my hips, and I break away from him breathlessly when I feel the soft summer breeze brushing against my thighs. He pulls me into the apartment, his hand firmly around mine. My skin burns at his touch. Holding me close to his body, he locks the door, and I can't resist placing a kiss on his neck, and he groans deeply.

"Kerri…" He kisses the corner of my mouth, teasing me until I cup his face and take control of the kiss.

"There's nowhere to run this time," I murmur against

his mouth, pulling his shirt from his pants.

"Who says I want to run?" he retorted, his voice vibrating against my throat. His teeth scrape against my pulse, and my legs weaken even more. "Not here. But first, would you like some coffee?"

I stare at his mischievous smile as he walks into the kitchen, and I follow him, unable to close my mouth in disbelief. I find myself following him through the vast, open-plan living room and into the dining room, where I sink into a chair at the large redwood table, my body thrumming with desire and my heart heavy with disappointment. The man is *humming* as he makes coffee!

He sits down next to me, placing two cups of steaming Irish coffee on the table, and I frown at it, my lips pursed in frustration. "Alex, I don't want *coffee*," I emphasize.

He smiles and begins stroking my arm. His fingers gliding across my skin send shivers down my spine. I watch as he gapes down at the silk shimmering over my breasts and his reaction as my nipples harden like rocks.

"Kerri," he groans and pulls me into his lap flexing his muscles. The very ones I've grown to love so much making my thighs straddle his and my heat flush against the ridge of his hard cock. I lean my arms on his shoulders for balance. I watch as he dips his finger into the coffee cup close to him, and then gasp when he circles my lips allowing the hot coffee to drip down my bottom lip. A slight groan rumbles from him and in one quick swoop his hands slide down my back pulling me tighter against him. He cups my face and draws me to his lips sucking every drip of coffee that has fallen down my face. His kiss is hungry. A kiss that I cannot refuse. His hands clench my ass tighter as I rock on him. He dips another finger into the cup and slides it down my throat, a drop running down my collarbone and onto my breast to bead at the neckline of my dress. I moan as his mouth follows the coffee trail, leaving heated spots of fire down my throat. And then he latches onto my nipple through my dress, sucking hard, and I cry out, my whole body tight with something… His fingers loosen their hold and fists into my dress, and I can feel him in the small of my back. I bit my lip as his fingers find their way under the edge of my cobalt blue lace panties.

My eyes fly open when he lifts me onto the table, pulling my panties down my legs, and I watch, mesmerized as they fall to the floor. I feel my juices flow onto the highly polished surface. I bite my lip as he lifts my legs over his shoulders, and I can feel them lift with the deep breath he takes. "Fuck, you smell amazing."

"Mhmm…" Is all I can manage to gasp as he dips his fingers into the coffee again and slides a trail along the inside of my thigh. I suppress a moan as he repeats it again on the other leg, my muscles quivering with anticipation. A hiss escapes me when he licks the coffee from my one leg, so close to pussy I can feel his breath on my curls, but

I groan in frustration when he withdraws, and then follows the coffee path on the other leg, again stopping short of where I want him to pay attention. He laughs when I cup his head to pull him closer, but he pulls back and dips his fingers into the coffee, and a soft wail escapes me as he smears the beverage over my pussy.

With a sly smile, he dips his head to my swollen pussy lips and places a warm kiss on the seam. I moan so fucking loud I'm sure the neighbors can hear me. I feel his tongue moving from the front to the back and then dipping inside my wetness drawing as much of it into his mouth as he can. *Fuck. Fuck. Fuck!* I cup his head, wordlessly encouraging him to forage deeper, my body molten as lava as the only sounds I can manage are moans and sighs. He slides his hands beneath my thighs and lifts me higher and I lean back on my hands, opening my legs to give him the access he asks for. My hips arch up, eager for the release he has been promising for the last few weeks.

He rubs coffee over my clit and, accepting the invitation, thrusts two fingers into my pussy as he sucks the coffee hard from my throbbing core. And when he repeats the action, my long-denied body responds immediately, his name echoing into the vaulted ceilings as I scream my release, my conscious mind splintering into a million pieces.

After several seconds of pure euphoria, I eventually come back down to earth. He is watching me through lust-heavy eyes, and I sigh as my body trembles. He gets to his feet, and my legs wind around his hips not wanting to let go. I close my eyes as my senses fill with Alex—his taste, his smell, his heat, the feel of him settling above me, his weight pressing me against the table, and his still-covered erection rocking against my greedy pussy, telling me how much he wants me.

I unbutton his shirt and scrape my teeth against the strong column of his neck, pushing the material down his arms and exposing his beautiful dark skin. He impatiently shrugs it off and pulls my straps off my shoulders, our movements becoming more frenzied as our desire rises again. The table shifts and creaks beneath us, and Alex drops his forehead into my neck, laughing softly.

"My grandma will never forgive me if I break her table."

"Wait…what? Your grandma lives here?" I gasp, pushing him up.

"This is my house, Kerri… It's just my grandmom's table."

"Oh…ooooh," I moan as he pulls my dress down further, revealing the strapless lace bra that contains my full breasts, which he is feasting on, nibbling his way to my hard nipples. He places a knee beneath my thigh, opening me even further, and my hands glide down his waist to the waistband of his pants. I am about to reach into those pants when the table shimmies and groans, making us both freeze in our movements.

"Fuck this," Alex mumbles, putting his hands around my ass and lifting me off the table. "I have an incredibly comfortable bed."

I cling onto him as he carries me out of the dining room, his mouth still making contact with the swell of my breast above the lace. Then he groans when I reach behind me to unhook the hindrance, wanting to feel the heat of his mouth without the lace barrier. I gasp when my shoulders hit the wall, and he hitches my legs higher up his waist before cupping my breasts, his hands massaging them. His fingers twist my rock-hard nipples until my body tightens internally, my stomach fluttering with anticipation of the nearing orgasm. He thrusts his hips forward, his jutting hardness pushing against my exposed clit, and I explode, again.

"I can't take any more of this, Alex, please," I murmur against his neck.

"Do you want me to stop?" His eyes are burning with want and humor as he grinds against me.

"Fuck no," I retort, sucking his earlobe, making him cry out as I feel him thicken and jerk against me.

"Kerri," he whispers in my ear as he walks to the master suite, and my breath catches at the sight of the California King dominating the bedroom. The gray and black covers give it a distinctly male feel, and the room smells of his cologne. That is the only impression I can get before he drops me on the bed, a rush of excitement fluttering between my legs. I watch him strip off the rest of his clothes exposing his sexy tattoos giving just a hint of bad boy vibes. *Alex is sexy as hell.*

I can't help but stare at his physique. I knew Alex was in shape but…*damn*…he is ripped! My breath goes shallow as I watch his chest bounce and jerk when he flexes his arms, his arms bulge with tiny veins as he bundles his shirt tossing it to the side, and my eyes follow it down the sculpted valleys of his impressive six-pack… to stare transfixed by his very… *impressive*… erection hanging at my gaze. He's manicured. The smallest jerk sends my juices into overflow soaking the sheets beneath me. I can't wait much longer to have him inside of me.

In a blink, he is settled between my thighs, and our gazes meet as he positions himself at my entrance. My heartbeat is thumping slowly and languorously throughout my body, echoing the throb deep inside of me. And with an excruciatingly slow thrust, he fills me. We both cry out at perfection, trying to remain still to enjoy the moment for as long as possible, but he growls when I clench around him, my body needing fulfillment.

"Fuck, Kerri, you're torturing me," he murmurs against my breast.

I cup his face and pull him up to lay a sweet kiss on his lips. "We can make love later. Right now, I want you to fuck me…hard."

He groans and rises onto his hands above me, and I reach up and cup his chest, dragging my teeth across his rock-hard nipples. A guttural growl escapes him as he withdraws and then slams back into me, his length filling me, stretching me further than I ever could have imagined. With every thrust, my walls clench around him, and I feel his shaft massage my pussy in ways my body can't handle but wants more than anything. And just when I think I have accepted all of him, he shifts his knees beneath my thighs, spreading me more and finding a spot even deeper inside of me. He holds my hips as he increases his pace, moving so hard and so fast that the bed is shaking. All I can do is hang onto his shoulders, gasping with each deep thrust, the sensations driving me to the edge.

"Alex!" I keen loudly, unable to contain everything that he is making me feel. Every cell, pore, and hormone is activated, charged, and electrified by the friction caused by the delicious slide of his rampant erection.

He lifts me, and I wrap my arms tightly around his neck, crying out as he impales me even deeper. I feel the scream breaking from me as I orgasm, clenching so tightly around him, it hurts. He clasps his hands hard onto my hips, holding me firmly in place as he pumps upwards, riding my waves, increasing their intensity. And just when I think I can't peak anymore, he tilts my shoulders back, arching me tighter against him, the base of his cock teasing my clit, and I truly explode, drawing his powerful release into my milking pussy.

Together we collapse onto the sheets, gasping for breath, our sweat-slicked skin reigniting the sparks that had barely tempered between us as our chests slide against each other with our thumping heartbeats.

"Shit, Kerri, that was…" he says with a gasp against my neck, his breath turning those sparks into tiny flames along my sensitized skin.

"Hot." I whisper in agreement, my lips grazing against the pulse point in his neck. He shivers, and I feel him getting hard where he is still resting inside of me. My voice hitches as I moan, "Absolutely fucking hot…"

~~~

As I stretch in the early morning sun streaming through the filmy curtains, my body feels well-loved, thoroughly cherished, and deeply filled with Alex plunging softly and slowly inside of me from behind. I moan as his hand covers my breast, and then gasp when he tightens his fingers on my nipple, his lips grazing heat across my spine. With one hand filled, he slides his other over my leg and pulls it back over his hips, my breath leaving my lungs on a long mewl as he deepens the angle.

My fingers scramble on the headboard for a grip when he slides one of his legs between my own, once again changing the angle. With another swift move, he shifts until my legs hug his hips, withdrawing from me slowly— and then with one hard, full thrust, I shatter around him,
~~~

once again screaming his name as he releases his warm seed into me.

"Good morning, my butterfly," he breathes into my neck as he collapses on top of me.

Chapter Thirteen

I clench my thighs together as I think about the weekend and spending it in Alex's bed. My body is deliciously sore, every twinge reminding me of the many ways he made love to me. I suppress a moan and pick up my digital pen to complete the sketch I need to have finished before lunch. He had once again surprised me this morning with a thoughtful gift from Harriet's and a beautiful bouquet of roses on my desk. Maggie peers down at it pointedly and then arches her eyebrows with a salacious smile before sashaying to her office.

Alex: Are you thinking about me? Because I can't stop thinking about you.

Shit! And just like that, I need a fresh pair of panties

thanks to all the excitement happening between my legs.

Me: No, I'm working. Don't you have work?

Alex: Who can work when I have these distracting me all day.

Alex sends a picture of the panties I must have left at his place. I am one hundred percent sure my chair is wet!

Me: I thought there was a slight breeze on my way home.

He sends me laughing emojis.

Alex: Care to show me what color you're wearing today?

Me: Might be kind of difficult...

Alex: And why is that?

Me: Because I'm not wearing any.

I lie.

Alex: Well then no I'm not working...I'm on my way to you...

Me: Alex! No. I am at work!

I put my phone in my desk drawer and add the last few strokes to the hawk taking flight on my screen, and I become so focused on the details that I am surprised when my stomach rumbles. Checking the time on my computer, I am shocked to see that I only have a half hour of my lunch break left. I quickly grab my lunch bag and make my way to the roof. It is more crowded today than normal because the weather has been unusually hot and humid at the street level, so I make my way to a quiet corner, waving at some of the people I've met during the times I spend on the roof.

With a sigh of relief, I find a semi-private nook overlooking East Broadway and make myself comfortable on the waist-high wall. A gentle breeze plays with the hem of my flirty knee-length skirt as I kick my legs in a slow rhythm while I eat. From my vantage point, I can see the Hudson River and am so enthralled with the view that I am barely aware of someone saying my name until I see Paul standing at the corner of the building, showing someone my hiding spot. Before I can respond, my heart stops at the sight of Alex walking toward me. *Omg, he really came.* I need to shift my legs as I feel my body respond just at the sight of him. His gray suit embraces his broad shoulders and trim waist, while the pants hug his powerful thighs. The navy-blue shirt and tie gives him an air of authority that few can ignore, but the smile he gives me is soft and makes me return it without hesitation.

Our eyes lock, and I can't look away from those swirling gray-brown depths as he stops in front of me, close enough that I need to open my legs. The cotton of his pants brushing against the inside of my thighs sets me on fire, and I moan softly.

"What are you doing here?" I manage to ask over my thundering heart, not really caring for his answer, just the fact that he is here.

"I told you I was coming. Besides, I was in the neighborhood, and thought I'd come and get some dessert with you," he murmurs against my lips, and my eyes close as I accept his soft kiss. My arms wrap around his neck to pull him closer, and he slides his hands down my back until they cup my ass, pulling me closer to the edge of the wall and widening my legs to accommodate him better.

"Alex," I moan softly when he breaks the kiss, and my heavy lashes flutter as I look up at him. He kisses me again, this one hungry and demanding, and I answer in the same way, unable to help myself from feasting on his taste. The trail of goosebumps on my legs is the only sign I have of him sliding his hand under my skirt and exposing me to the soft breeze blowing over the rooftop.

"I can smell you, Kerri, warm and oh..." He groans deeply as he bites my lip, his fingers sliding beneath the lace of my panties and into my slick folds. "... so very wet, my beautiful butterfly."

I gasp, trying to keep my breathing even, suppressing my moans as his fingers find that spot deep inside of me. "Alex...we can't..."

"Shh... keep your arms around me," he instructs softly.

I look down when I hear his zipper open and lick my lips at the brief sight of his hard cock before it disappears into my greedy pussy. His hands cup my ass again, and he rocks my hips, setting a quick pace that has my walls tightening around him instantly. *Fuck.* He leans close enough to make contact with my hard nipples, and the friction through my silk camisole has my fingers digging into the nape of his neck as my pleasure builds. He lifts my hips faster, and I swallow the scream when his thumb circles my pounding clit. "That's it, butterfly, come for me."

He seals our mouths tightly as we moan our pleasure at our climax, my muscles milking every drop of his seed deep inside me, his hands clamped so tightly on my hips I know there'll be bruises. I laugh softly, burying my face in his chest as he adjusts our clothing, his mouth trailing light kisses up and down my neck. "Dessert, huh?"

He gives a wry chuckle before kissing my nose. "No panties, huh?"

Well, he got me there. I smile as I look down double checking that my clothes are no longer crooked.

"I'm sorry I can't enjoy the actual dessert with you." He says as he taps a box that I'd been too distracted to notice earlier. Through the clear window, I see the most delicate chocolate eclairs drizzled with mint sauce. "You need to get back to work."

I check my watch and jump off the wall, clutching his

hands as my knees threaten to buckle after our… *interaction.* "Shit, Alex, I really have to go!"

I hurry off the now-empty rooftop, make a quick visit to the bathroom, and flop into my chair with a few seconds to spare. And all I can think of is his sexy laughter following me off the roof, the feeling of his eyes gazing at me through the glass doors. It heats me from deep within, tempting me to turn back and spend the rest of the day with him overlooking the Hudson River.

~~~

Three weeks later, I dial Elise's number after hanging up with Mom, stretching my legs along the sofa as I think about the conversation we just had. For the first time in a long time, I can honestly tell Mom that I am doing better than okay. I even told her about Alex. I'm still chuckling at her polite, *"That's lovely, Kerribel"* when Elise answers the call.

"I'm not sure I know this number. Is this my best friend, maybe?" I laugh at her silliness.

"Of course, it is!"

"So, no date tonight?"

"Later. He's taking me to dinner."

"You sound happy, KB."

"I am," I reassure her, but I can hear the reserve in her
~~~

voice. "He took me on a sunset dinner cruise around the harbor last night. It was amazing, Elise! And so romantic!"

I can still feel the gentle rays of the setting sun on my shoulders as we toured the harbor and enjoyed a delightful dinner of prawn and pistachio salad with bits of watermelon and feta cheese, sea bass and glazed orange on a bed of sweet potato mash, and a huge slice of pecan and blueberry pie with whipped mint cream. Watching the moon rise over the shoulder of the Statue of Liberty is a magical experience that I won't forget for a long time, especially when Alex is wrapping his arms around me as we stand at the railing. After his hand sneaks into the waistband of my high-split skirt, my ivory sleeveless georgette shirt hiding his actions from any witnesses, I don't remember much else except that he made me see rainbows not long after we reached his condo.

"I sure hope I get to meet this perfect man soon," she teases me. "I still need to see a photo of him."

"Oh, Elise." I frown as I realize that I don't have pictures of Alex and me together, or even of just him. "The times we are together, I don't worry about my phone, because I don't want to miss anything with him."

"Does he at least make you happy?" Her voice drops suggestively on the last word, and I giggle as I feel myself blush, remembering how we ended the cruise last night.

"Like no one else before him."

"He better—his *cazinga* is still on the line if he doesn't."

We chat for another half an hour before I need to get ready for my date, excitement making me take extra time with my appearance. As I apply my lipstick, I realize that Alex has not missed one date so far—always on time, always attentive, and always making it more than memorable. And the sweet treats he sends to my office are always a welcome distraction.

Alex had sent me a message to say that I had to dress for dancing, so I am wearing a bright red dress that flares at the bottom feeling inspired that I'd look like the infamous Baby from Dirty Dancing when Alex spins me around. I finish the look with a pair of silver strappy sandals. With my curls bouncing from a fresh wash and strings of silver earrings, I am ready to dance.

He takes me to a club on the Lower East Side, and we enjoy the Latin vibe, the music making my heartbeat to its vivacious rhythm and my feet tap. Our first dance is a sultry salsa and has us both breathing heavily at the end of the song, staring into each other's eyes as the band starts a new song that is slower and sexier. The slow tease between us is making me hot and wet, and when Alex discovers the slits and how to take advantage of them to gain access to my skin, we both flare up. His eyes become heavy-lidded as he pulls me closer, whispering all kinds of suggestions into my ear that flood my panties. But instead of leaving, we continue to dance until almost midnight, when he eventually succeeds in finding a way to get his fingers against my pussy under my lace panties, his breath hissing out of him when he finds me dripping.

I gasp when his fingers brush against my clit, and I clench, missing the feeling of him inside of me.

"One more dance?" he whispers against my neck.

"Not unless you want me to become a puddle of nothing on this dance floor," I retort, my nipples painfully hard where his chest is rubbing against them.

"Your place or mine?"

I groan at his cheesy question even as my body clenches again. "The closest," I barely murmur.

"The car it is," he rasps as he pulls my earlobe with his teeth. I bite my lip as a mini-orgasm spasms through my body, and I cling to him and try not to moan my pleasure too loudly.

Chapter Fourteen

"Hey, baby." My stomach flutters as his deep voice flows through my system.

"Hey, yourself," I smile, enjoying the first time him calling me baby and the rare opportunity to have an actual conversation with him rather than the text messages we usually share. "It's nice to hear your voice for a change, instead of deciphering your emojis."

He laughs nervously. "It's nice to hear your voice, too."

"But you're not calling to hear me breathe, are you?" I ask, trying to keep my tone light even as I fight the red flag wanting to fly high. I'm already battling to forget the message I received this morning from that unfamiliar number, a message that confirms my suspicions that the others were not so random, the words burned in my brain.

Unknown: I keep warning you, and you keep ignoring me. I know what happened to your sister. You will suffer the same fate, twinsie.

I blink away the memory.

"I like hearing you breathe, especially that moment just before you—"

"Alex!" I protest, already feeling myself respond to his suggestive insinuation, and I grind my teeth to pay attention to what he is going to say.

"Okay!" He laughs. "But you're right. I am calling to apologize, my butterfly."

"For what?" My stomach clenches for a whole other reason at his words. He has been teasing me with his plans for us for the Labor Day weekend, and to have him cancel… again… is worse than disappointing.

"We have a case that's picked up a complication, and I need to work through the long weekend. I was really looking forward to spending time with you, but I promise I will make it up to you." All the teasing has left his voice, and I shiver at the near-distant sound that is separating us.

The disappointment is a sharp jab in my heart, but I have come to realize that he wouldn't miss the chance to spend time together if he could. I infuse a smile into my voice, not wanting him to feel guilty about canceling. "Damn. I was looking forward to making you labor."

"Shit, Kerri!" He groans. I hear a voice in the background, and he muffles the phone when he answers. "Listen, I need to go. Speak to you later."

"Okay." I nod, but the call is already disconnected. My hands drop to my lap, and I fist them so hard the nails are biting into my palms.

"I don't want to take advantage of your disappointment, Kerri, but I am *very* glad your plans fell through," Maggie smirks as she slides onto the corner of my desk, her Louis Vuitton pumps swinging gaily. I didn't even realize that she had been watching me while I was on the phone with Alex. A feeling of embarrassment washes over me but changes to confusion… and apprehension. This is Maggie, after all.

"Oh? Why would that make you so happy, Mags?" I am intrigued even though I don't want to be.

"Because, I get to spend time with my new best friend, and," she says, dragging out the word as she wiggles two fingers in the air, "we can have a girls' weekend."

I purse my lips to stop myself from smiling so that I can tease her. "What if I had a backup date?"

"Oh, please girl!" She waves her hand in the air dismissively. "This is far more entertaining."

"Mmm?" I hum, pretending to turn back to my screen.

"Okay, so this is the deal," she capitulates. "Some old college buddies of Preston are having some event or whatever this weekend, but he isn't able to make it. So, we need to represent."

"*We?* As in…?"

"Demi. Me. And you, of course."

"Of course," I murmur.

"Come on, Kerri!" She pleads with me, jumping from my desk, grabbing my hands, and squeezing them as she bounces. "Labor Day weekend… Long weekend… In the *Hamptons…* It will be fun."

"Says the person testing the first hot air balloon," I sass, knowing I am going to agree anyway.

~~~

Maggie gives me an hour to pack my bag before she picks me up for the two-and-a-half-hour drive to Westbury, where she has booked us an Airbnb. Demi is already seated in the passenger seat. Her high cheekbones and oval face are accentuated by her messy bun hairstyle, and her lilac tank top showing off her tattoos and denim cut-offs show off her body to its best advantage. Maggie pulls her Ray-bans from her head to cover her green-brown eyes and puts the volume up on Doja Cat's "Paint the Town Red," and we sing the lyrics at the top of our voices as we drive out of the city.

We all stare up at the double-story cottage after Maggie
~~~

parks the car, the gabled roof making it look as though it is sleeping. Someone had taken the time to paint the clapboard in blue and white stripes, trim the large white front door and windows in navy, and plant climbing roses at every porch post so that it blooms with a variety of colors. The place is cheerful and so welcoming, and I can't wait to explore the inside.

"Come on, Kerr bear!" Demi calls, and I realize that they have taken their bags from the car and are waiting for me to stop gawking. With a self-conscious giggle at my new nickname given by Demi, I jog to the trunk and hitch my weekend bag over my shoulder, following Demi into the house while Maggie locks her car.

"Let's get the dust from the road off us and find out if that thing works," Maggie says as we stand on the deck that overlooks the shore of the lake, the white sand stretching far on either side of our location. Demi goes over to the jacuzzi and fiddles with the buttons, then squeals in delight when the tub starts filling with water and the jets bubble on.

"Last one in pays for the first round of drinks tonight!" Demi challenges and races into the house. Maggie and I gape after her, and then follow her into the house to change into our swimsuits. Maggie mixes a large pitcher of margaritas, and we settle in the jacuzzi to watch the sunset. The water massaging my tired body is heavenly, and I find myself drifting off, Demi and Maggie's conversation barely registering. We relax in the jacuzzi for another hour, me dozing in and out of a light coma, when I'm suddenly woken by Maggie taking a fork to the margarita glass pitcher. *Clink. Clink. Clink.*

"Girls, I'm starving. Let's find somewhere to eat, and then go to a party to enjoy our girls weekend," Maggie says, stepping onto the deck. "Put on your dancing shoes— we're going to greet the sun tomorrow morning."

~~~

Why do I agree to Maggie's madness? I ask myself the next morning. My vision blurs as I try to eat a bowl of cereal, the crunching sound reverberating in my pounding head. With a heavy sigh, I push the bowl aside and sip deeply from my chai tea, wishing I could stomach coffee. The late morning sun is already warming the deck in gentle waves.

We returned to the house just as the sun was turning the sky pink as it rose over the lake. We had bar-hopped until we stumbled upon party and joined the celebrations. This led to a bonfire on the shores of the lake with loud music, ciders, beers, and tequila that kept us in a happy mood until the sun peeked over the horizon. Tired, hungry, and giggling, we stumbled home barefoot and happy. Maggie had fallen asleep on the sofa with a slice of toast on her lap, and I had gently removed it from her hands as Demi covered her with a blanket before we went to bed.

"Why is it so bright?" Demi groans as she joins me at the table on the deck, pushing her sunglasses onto her nose
~~~

before she sips her coffee. "I am never trusting Maggie again when she says *last drink*."

"I will remind you to remind me to remind you never to trust her." We laugh and groan simultaneously, and then whimper as Maggie floats out the door, a bowl of cereal and a cup of coffee in her hands.

"Good morning, my ladies," she sings as she enjoys her breakfast. Demi glares at her over her glasses, and I massage my temples at her happy tone. "I see the spa treatments I booked are in order, and we will be pampered and get our hair washed today."

I grimace at her jibe and decide to ignore it as I close my eyes and allow the late morning sun to caress my skin. It reminds me of waking up with Alex gently touching my face before he slowly and softly makes love to me. I feel my heart soften at the thought of him, and I realize that I might be in love with him—not completely, just a little bit.

"Mags." I peer at Demi as she sweeps her cup at our friend. "When is this event happening? And where are our official invites?"

"It's tomorrow afternoon, and we are invited through Preston, I told you."

"You sure? I'm not interested in party crashing or even worse getting denied at the door."

Maggie rolls her eyes at Demi's persistence. "Yes, I'm

sure! Plus, my parents know the people somehow—I think through their country club—so that's double protected."

Demi and I glance at each other, neither of us sure if we can trust her nonchalance. We are barely recovering from Friday night's hangover when Maggie drags us out for a day of massages, pampering, manicures, pedicures, and salon treatments. Feeling languid with soft muscles and mimosa-fuzzed minds, we are convinced to relax and allow Maggie to dictate our time without much fuss. We spent the rest of the evening doing low impact activities recovering our livers from the previous night.

Maggie had gotten so excited when we arrived at Westbury Manor. Immediately, we are given a glass of champagne as we enter the hall filled with people either sitting at the elegantly decorated tables set up around the dream of a ballroom, standing in groups around the room and on the patio, or dancing on the large hardwood floor. On one side of the enormous room is a wall lined with arched windows framed with flowy white drapes that are drawn back to allow the afternoon sun to stream onto the honey-colored floor. The ivory tablecloths with their soft pink runners are centered with white and pink roses and baby breath in cut crystal vases. Black dinnerware and sterling silver cutlery finishes the table settings. The long tables set out against the wall covered in floor-to-ceiling mirrors are covered in trays of luxury hors d'oeuvres.

The doors leading to the garden are wide open, inviting

in the gentle afternoon sunshine. The air carries a sense of magic as more and more people indulge in the beauty of the moment. Suddenly, a statuesque woman gracefully emerges onto the terrace, her A-line satin skirt flowing like a delicate dream around her slender legs. The soft hue of dusty pink perfectly complements the radiant glow of her sun-kissed, golden-brown skin to perfection. The black lace applique bodice is covered in sparkling crystals, and her honey-blond hair is twisted into a complicated chignon. She reaches out her well-manicured hand to welcome the couple who are standing closest to us, the diamond-encrusted bracelet matching the necklace around her neck. Though her smile is subtle, her full lips delicately curl at the corners, hinting at a hidden allure. As she delicately air-kisses the woman, her freckles become more pronounced and visible for me to see.

Her expensive perfume reaches us just before she does, her hazel brown eyes barely acknowledging us before they glance over the crowds as though she is looking for someone, and her welcome is distracted as she barely meets our eyes...my eyes. "Please have fun." I shift the weight from one leg to the other and pull down my slightly too tight cocktail dress.

"Oh, we will," Maggie says as she takes us by the arm and leads us to the shiny dance floor. "Come on, let's find us some gentlemen who would take a lady for a spin on that beautiful dance floor."

We are having so much fun as the afternoon continues,

periodically dancing and drinking or enjoying the fantastic canapes that are on offer. Demi follows me to the terrace when the ballroom becomes even more crowded, each of us taking a glass of champagne. Maggie joins shortly after, and we all discuss what our plans will be on our final day. Demi Googles the attractions in the area, and each of us picks an activity before we leave the vicinity. An elderly couple joins us, and Maggie introduces them as friends of her parents. We chat with them for a while until the man hears their favorite song and charms his wife to dance with him. I turn to admire the sunset just before the band leader quietly calls everyone to gather around and refill their champagne glasses to toast the happy couple.

Chapter Fifteen

I glance through the open door to the small bandstand where the woman I saw earlier—Nicole—is pacing in her dusty pink and black dress as she makes her speech, a few people titter at the appropriate times, and then chorus their well-wishes. I'm barely listening to the well-rehearsed speech when she begins telling a story of how her and her husband first met, adding in slightly pretentious jokes for reaction. The crowd coos loudly, and I peer at the gap in the filmy curtains again and see Nicole hugged by her husband. The only thing within my line of vision is his arm covered in a black suit sleeve at her waist appears to lean in and kisses her, but too much of his face is obscured. They seem to fit well together, both tall and athletically built, and by the elegance of the party, both are very wealthy.

"I want to thank everyone for being here and celebrating this day with us." I spin around at that deep, velvety tone, all my senses on full alert. That voice is unmistakable, the same voice I enjoyed earlier this morning. It was one of the rare calls that he had made as the sun was rising, and the conversation might not have been long, but it had been heated, sending fire through my veins, much the same way it was doing now. My heart thuds, hard and loud, before it constricts, my mind going blank except for *that* voice. I don't know what he is saying, all that I am aware of is that my world is moving in and out of focus the longer he is speaking, and that I cannot breathe.

As he continues to speak, I can't shake the ice creeping into my veins as I hear my lover commending his beautiful wife for the impact she's had on his life. His voice is so sincere and genuine. My stomach tightens with anxiety, and my heart is beating so slowly and so hard that I can't hear the murmur of the crowd over its thumping. There's not enough space in my lungs, and when I start feeling dizzy with the lack of oxygen, I realize that I've been holding my breath. I remind myself to breathe. But the next breath is too shallow, and I try to drag in another, but it hurts too much. I find myself gasping for air. My vision is blurring, and I blink to clear it, but darkness is creeping into the edges, and I realize that I am afraid it won't go away.

I take a sip of champagne to wet my constricted throat, but the drink is dry, and the bubbles scratch my tongue and throat as I swallow. I almost gag on the expensive beverage. Though everything in me is sure it is *my* Alex, my heart is having trouble accepting it, and I move to the door for a better view, almost tripping over my high-heeled sandals. But there are too many people who are taller than me in the way, and I move to get a better view without even realizing that I am doing so. I feel Demi standing beside me, and I blink at her to see that we are in the middle of the big room, a distance from the stage but directly in front of it. I look up.

And then the world stops, because there he is, so handsome in his black suit, dusty pink shirt, and silver tie that perfectly match his wife's dress, his arm securely around her waist. My vision swirls as my breath hitches, the edges fading away. I blink, trying to stay conscious, but my fingers have turned numb, and the exquisite champagne flute falls from my nerveless fingers, resembling my heart as it shatters to a million pieces on the smooth white marble tiling of the ballroom.

Everyone goes quiet as they turn to look at me, but all I can do is focus on Alex's shocked eyes as he turns to look at me across the crowded ballroom. I feel my head moving from side to side in denial, but I can't seem to stop it. Someone says something, and people around us laugh. I know it is at my expense, but I can't seem to care enough to be offended.

"Kerri?" Maggie takes hold of my arm, pulling me into the present, and it is as if someone is holding a blowtorch to my nerve endings. "Kerri, are you okay?"

I barely register her concerned face, and when I feel Demi put her arm around my shoulders, I realize that my face must be reflecting my shock—and worse, my heartbreak. I look at my two friends, and I need to get away. "I—I—"

I choke back nausea and make my way through the crowd, blindly finding my way to the door. Everyone seems to part as I approach to give me a clear path. I'm not sure how I get to the bathroom, but I do, and immediately kick off my sandals. I am rewarded with a definite thud as they collide with the eggshell white wall in tandem with my breaking heart. I wrap my arms around my body, trying to maintain what little warmth is left in my veins, but I am overcome with shivers because the ice is bone-deep.

I open the hot water tap, and the bathroom fogs up with steam. It reminds me of the last night I spent at Alex's condo… a condo that has no indication that a wife is a major part of his life. I look at my reflection in the mirror and stare at the stranger gaping back at me. My eyes are too wide and too bright, my cheeks are shallow and pale, and my lips are chewed raw with emotion. A tear falls, and I roughly brush it away, not allowing myself the luxury of crying. But then another falls, and the anger descends.

A refrain starts in my mind in a slow steady staccato, picking up pace as my heart starts beating so fast my ribs hurt. *I am the other woman… I am the other woman?… I am the other woman!* …

"All the missed dates!" I toss my clutch purse at the mirror, but it silently ricochets to the floor and doesn't give my anger credence. "All the texting!" The soap has a louder thud, but not loud enough. "This is for all the lying!" My tears are running uncontrolled down my cheeks as I toss a bottle of hand lotion at the mirror, the thud more convincing. "This is for being so naive!" The spritzer of perfume misses the mark completely, bouncing off the wall and increasing my frustration. I pick up the ceramic incense burner, testing its weight in my hand. "And this is for believing the lying son of a bi—!"

I lift the piece of pottery and prepare to hurl it at the mirror with the entire force of my anger but cry out in frustration when a hand grabs hold of my wrist before I can release the projectile. "Kerri!"

I fight against the hold that Maggie has on me, but she is strong for her petiteness and can wrestle the burner from me. In the meantime, Demi turns off the tap and is holding me around my waist, both of them falling to their knees when mine buckles under the weight of my heartbreak. I sink to the floor, my body hurting with the sobs being pulled through it with a painful force.

"Come on," Maggie says softly when my sobs subside. "Let's get out of here. Expensive champagne has no place at a party like this. Let's go make our own."

This manages to draw a watery laugh from me and Demi as we get to our feet, link our arms, and leave the party behind. My mind is filled with flashes of Alex from the first time we met, the way he smiles, the feel of his warm skin under my fingers, the security of his broad shoulders, the tenderness of his caressing hands, the way he growls when I touch him in a certain way, the fever with which he kisses me, the heat of his arousal against me, the way he feels in me, filling me, stretching me, the way his eyes turn from brown to silver when he reaches fulfillment… The way he makes me feel like I am the only woman he could love… Except that I am not. I am not even the main woman.

My anger rises again… I am the *side chick*, the butt of the jokes, the stupid, naive idiot who is only filling in spare time...

Chapter Sixteen

Our return to the Airbnb is a blur to me. I vaguely remember Maggie and Demi walking on either side of me, and I remember feeling supported and protected by them. While Maggie is putting glasses on the coffee table and I am putting the sofa's cushions on the floor for more comfortable seating on the living room floor, Demi lays out the trays with snacks and a few bottles of wine. When we are all comfortably sprawled on the cushions, Demi takes my phone and dials Elise's number, her pretty face immediately appearing on the screen when she answers.

"Hey, Kerri! How's the weather in the Hamptons?" she teases.

"Um, Elise. I'm Maggie, and this is Demi." Maggie introduces them, and Demi waves before placing the device on the table so that all three of us can be seen.

"Oh, Kerribel, what happened?" she gasps, her eyes filling with tears.

"The son of a bitch is *married!*" Maggie answers, her green eyes spitting angry flames.

"Who's married?" For a moment Elise is confused, and then her eyes widen with realization… and anger. "He's *what?!*"

"He pretended to be so sweet and generous, sending her all those gifts while he is living it up with his wife," Demi fills in during the pause.

"I promise you, Kerri, when I get there, you better keep him far from me because I am going to separate him from his married balls and mail them to the other side of the globe." She shakes her head, and I can see the compassion in her eyes. "I'm so sorry, Kerri. I had such high hopes for him."

"Me too," I say softly. My throat is still raw from my earlier screaming. Demi and Maggie wrap me in their arms, and Elise puts her fingertips against the screen. I do the same, all of us are connected in our anger and my heartbreak.

"I wish I could be there," she whispers.

"I know you've got my back. You always do." I smile at

her.

"You girls take care of KB—she's the closest I have to a sister," she instructs Demi and Maggie as she wipes away tears.

"Of course, we will," Maggie agrees readily, hugging me again before hanging up the call. We fall back against the sofa, and I close my eyes as I remember all the tiny gifts Alex has sent me. The last one was a blue and silver butterfly that is now fluttering above my houseplant in the Papa Smurf pot. Everywhere are reminders of Alex—in my home, on my desk, in my pores, in my heart…

As though sensing my thoughts, Maggie pours us each a glass of wine, although, this feels more like a tequila moment. "I'll tell you one thing, and that is that all relationships have their bumps; some are just harder than others to negotiate. You just need to decide how willing you are to deal with them."

"Come on, Mags," I smile in disbelief. "You're so well put-together, and you and Preston—"

"Also have our issues." She shrugs, the movement so sad that I put my arm around her shoulder. She wipes a tear from her cheek and then empties her glass. "But we're drowning *your* sorrows, KB, so let more wine flow."

"You're a damn good actor, Maggie," Demi says softly, and Maggie shakes her head as she laughs, reaching for the wine bottle.

"When you're thirteen and enter beauty pageants, you learn to apply your makeup so that it hides all the flaws." We both turn to her. I reach for the snack tray and place it on my lap before settling back with my glass. She wipes another tear from her cheek before taking a sip of her wine. "Sometimes, I wish I hadn't gotten married. I really hate to admit it but I just keep thinking about the road untraveled."

"Or stay with someone for so long that you've forgotten who you were before you met him," Demi says with a salute, her glass high.

"What?" Maggie and I chorus, our eyes wide as we stare at her.

She gave a sad smile. "Julius is a good man, but I keep waiting for him to change his ways so that we can take the next step. And then I ask myself if I *would* take the next step, even if he does change. I do love him, but…"

"*Lover to all,*" I murmur.

"*Faithful to none,*" she finishes, wiping away a tear as she clinks her glass against my own. She covers my hand with her own. "We all want that perfect relationship, Kerri. Sometimes, it's best to find the best you and hope someone loves it enough to give you the best of them. We need to make the best of an uncertain situation, but we also need to know when the best course of action is to walk away."

"Well," I drawl, taking my glass and emptying it, then giggling as I empty the wine bottle into it. "If perfect is so overrated, then fuck perfect."

"Fuck perfect!" Demi and Maggie chorus, and we clink our glasses, laugh, and sniff back tears as we huddle together. Demi scrambles around the living room for her phone, and when she finds it, music fills the house, loud and fast. Maggie and I jump to our feet and start dancing, singing at the top of our voices.

Nineties break-up songs are still playing at midnight when we find ourselves in the jacuzzi, a feast of pizza and wine littering the deck among our discarded clothing. I lean my head against the edge of the tub and look up at the stars and realize that they are covered in a heavy haze of clouds and only peek through occasionally. That is my life with Alex, spots of clarity with everything else hidden behind a thick fog.

What was it Maggie said? *Every relationship has bumps… you must decide how willing you are to deal with them…* How does that help me and this disaster with Alex? I can't believe this is my life.

A heaviness settles over my heart as I think about my life without Alex. He came around at the perfect time. I was so uneasy about my decision to move to New York and hearing my mom constantly remind me I had a place at home didn't help my confidence that moving would be a success. With him around a part of me feels like I don't need to hide who I really am— nor hide my personality— and he makes me feel like the most beautiful women in the world, free of the fear of what others think about me. He has made me realize that though Ana was the sunlight of our lives, I have the right to shine in my way without feeling guilty. I have the right to be happy.

Have I known him long enough for him to be my *happily ever after*? Why am I so willing to hang my whole basket of happiness in this man's hands? What if there is someone else out there for me, and I miss him because I'm blinded by Alex? Why am I giving him so much damn power over my life?

"Kerri?" I start at Maggie's touch on my arm. "KB? Are you okay?"

With my decision made, I can meet her eyes with confidence. "I am now."

I get out of the tub and wrap my arms around myself at the sudden chill, the lace of my wet bra scratching my skin. I grab a towel as I walk into the house, lifting pillows and clothing as I search for my phone, my movements spurred on by the anger that has settled like a vice in my heart.

"Hey! Where are you going?" I hear water splash as Maggie and Demi follow me into the living room, their wet feet slapping on the floor. "More importantly, what are you doing?"

I look at Maggie's confused face, and I hand her my phone so that she can read the text I just sent him.

Me: Congratulations on your 10th anniversary! Here's to another decade of never seeing me again.

"Oh shit!" Demi gasps as she reads the text over Maggie's shoulder. "Did you have to put so many emojis in, though?"

"Classy!" Maggie whistles. "I especially like the little champagne glasses… not to mention the number of angry faces."

"I must say, I would never have thought of flipping him the finger like *that*!" Demi agrees, and then bursts out laughing as she accepts a glass of wine that Maggie is handing to each of us. "Kerribel Townsend, I would not have thought you capable!"

"Well, what did you think?" I ask her, fluffing my hair. "I am Kerri *fucking* Townsend, after all!"

"That you are!" Maggie salutes, and we all laugh.

~~~

I lean against the wall of the elevator, massaging my pounding head and looking forward to a long hot bath and watching some series on *Netflix* until I fall asleep. We had not slept at all; instead, we had stayed up all night, emptying more bottles of wine while we dissected our relationships. I don't think I've ever cried or laughed as hard as I did last
~~~

night.

I grimace when the elevator dings my floor number, the sound echoing through my head like a stuck pinball machine. Hitching my weekend duffle higher on my shoulder, I take slow steps to my door, careful not to let my heels fall too loudly on the tiled floor. I think to myself that I should have taken them off my shoes in the elevator. I keep my head down to avoid the bright lights hanging along the hallway. Tiny dwarves are invading my body and have taken up residence at the base of my skull, killing me with tiny, resounding hammer blows.

"Oh, shit, Alex!" I gasp as I collide with his tall body standing at my door, and I immediately take a step back because I know, if he touches me, all my resolve will disappear like mist in the sun. "What the hell are you doing here?"

He seems shocked at my anger, but then reaches out a hand, and I take another step back, falling against the wall beside my door. "I was hoping we could talk, Kerri."

"Don't!" I hold up my hands, hoping he will stay away from me. "Your time for talking was when we met at the bar or the hike, or even the fucking helicopter ride."

Shaking my head to stop him from speaking, I push my key into the lock and quickly open the door. "Kerri, please?"

"No." I say it loudly, for both of us to hear it, and for my heart to heed it. "Go away, Alex."

"Kerri, I don't want to lose you—" I close the door and drop all my bags at my feet before turning and resting my head against the brightly painted wood. I bite my lip as the tears fall. I can hear him still breathing on the other side of the door for a long while. Finally, I hear his footsteps fade as he walks away.

With a sniff, I pull myself together, pick up my bags, and try to find a sense of normalcy. This lasts through my bath and partway through an episode of my favorite series until the female lead is driving away from her love interest. I find my tears falling as hard as hers, and then the sobs come, and my world falls apart on my comfortable sofa. The last thing I remember before falling asleep is fidgeting with my butterfly charms.

How could I have been so wrong, Ana?

Chapter Seventeen

Unknown: You can try to hide, but I still see you. I know what you've done, and I plan to let the world know too.

I groan at the confusing text message that accompanies the pounding headache I wake up to on Tuesday morning. I reread the message several times, each time creeping me out more and more. I call Maggie to ask if it's okay if I work from home. She agrees, and when she goes quiet, I silently curse myself for not texting her instead.

"Kerri, are you sure you're okay?"

"Honestly, no. I feel like I just need to hide for a couple of days, Maggie, and get my head screwed on straight before I face the world again."

"Then take them, Kerri. You've worked hard and

deserve a couple of days off."

"Thanks, Maggie."

"But if I don't hear from you tomorrow at noon, I'm invading your space."

I laugh, then suck in a sharp breath as my head splits even more. "Okay. I'll check in at noon to prevent an invasion."

"Good. We'll see you at 6:30. And we'll bring food and beverages."

"Maggie, wait—!" I stare at my phone as she disconnects. I moan her name as I drop back onto my pillows and look out of the window. With another moan, I pull the covers over my head and stay in bed for as long as I can.

Wednesday sees me staring at a bright September morning. Though the days are still warm, they become cooler as the weather changes, and I decide it is the perfect weather for a run. So, I drag myself out of bed, take a shower, pull on my running tights, grab a bottle of water out of my fridge, and freeze at my front door.

What if Alex is standing on the other side of the door, waiting for me to open it? My finger is pounding, and I realize that I have twisted it so hard in my chain that it is close to snapping.

"Oh, get a hold of yourself, girl! What if he is? You

know how to walk past a mannequin on sale day. You are Kerri *fucking* Townsend." I put in my earbuds, pump *Bruno Mars* on my phone, and pull open my door. Instead of the elevator, I take the stairs down and keep a steady pace for the next hour, using the momentum to concentrate on my breathing, my footsteps, and my heart rate. At the end of my run, I am stretching my muscles and, as I wait for the elevator, an alert vibrates on my phone.

With trepidation, I squint at the screen, equally relieved and disappointed that it's not from Alex, but then frown at the source. I've matched with someone on one of my dating apps that I forgot to delete. "I'll take that as a sign to move on with my life."

The rest of my day is spent finishing the graphic I was working on at the office while watching daytime talk shows, eating breakfast for lunch, taking a late shower, and just keeping my mind occupied so that I don't think about... *him*. And yet, his is the first name I think about when someone knocks at my door.

I sit in my chair, frowning, trying to control the wild thunder of my heart and wiping my sweaty hands down the legs of my yoga pants. I wonder what I would say to him if it is him standing in the hallway. Blowing out a loud breath, I'm psyching myself up to answer the door when the knocking takes on urgency.

"Kerri!" Maggie's voice carries her concern through the wood. "Kerri, I swear, if you did something stupid, I'm going to kill you!"

She is really worried! I rush to the door, and she immediately wraps me in a sweet-scented hug before pushing me away and giving me a once-over. "Hi, Maggie."

"You didn't do anything stupid?"

"Nope." I smile, hugging Demi, who is looking around the loft. "What are you guys doing here?"

"Hello! Invasion?" Maggie says, showing me the numerous bags of take-out and several bottles of wine in Demi's arms.

"Oh man, was that tonight?" I wrinkle my brow, and they laugh.

"Come on, let's see what's on offer tonight!" Demi rubs her hands together as she flips through the TV channels. We spend the rest of the evening critiquing the fashion in different shows and eventually settling on an Anthony Mackie movie.

~~~

Alex: Hey butterfly. I just wanted to say that I'm sorry, again, for how things turned out. I miss you. I miss talking to you. I regret not speaking to you about my situation. I know I would have been able to give you a clearer picture.
~~~

I turn over my phone with a sigh and pay attention to the man sitting opposite me at the table of Mont Le Cleur's, making me so thankful that this is our first—and last—date. He is one of several guys I have met over the last three weeks, and though some of them have been *interesting*, he is the worst of the bunch. He asks me what I would like to order and then changes it, insulting my tastes. I shift in my chair, wishing I'd chosen a more conservative dress than the black shirt dress with the silver belt as he blatantly stares at my cleavage, as well as the ass of the server as she collects our plates.

"Can you hurry up, baby, and bring our dessert?" I gape at the man, shocked by his rudeness. He had asked me what I do for a living, but before I finished my description, he told me all about his position as VP of sales at some high-tech company, and then proceeded to complain about his job, his office, and his staff. This allowed me the opportunity to read the text from Alex.

Even though I am still angry with him, seeing Alex's name on my screen has my body on alert, and I cross my legs. I look at the man sitting across the table from me and wonder if I am a jackass magnet. The man is handsome with his square face covered in a dark goatee, drawing attention to his full mouth and high cheekbones. His narrow eyes are so dark they shine almost back, and I find that his manners are just as dark. Looking at his wide shoulders covered by a black jacket over his white dress shirt, I can't help but compare him to Alex.

This man is no Alex Carter. I always felt like a lady with Alex: respected, admired, and cherished from the very first time. He'd made me feel like an equal, and he had listened to what I had to say. I smile at the server as she places a dessert consisting of a raspberry on a teaspoon of mousse and some cookie crumbs around the large plate, and then shake my head.

"I'm sorry." They both look at me in confusion.

"For what now, baby?" He lays a hand across the table, but I deliberately remove mine from his reach.

"I'm talking to Rachel." I turn to the server and give her an apologetic smile. "I'm sorry you had to deal with him all night."

"What're you saying?" He straightens in his chair.

"Thank you for a… for this evening, but this is not going to work." I get to my feet and hurry out of the restaurant, hoping to get a cab before he can come out. And thankfully, I see him running out of the doors just as the cab is pulling away, and I breathe a sigh of relief. I stare out of the window, watching the famous buildings of New York flash by, a feeling of loneliness filling me from deep within. Tonight, I will admit to missing Alex.

For the last three weeks, he has been calling and texting me at least twice a day, even though I've not responded to any of them. He doesn't say anything in his texts except that it's complicated, and he needs to speak to me in person.

I pay my fare and walk towards my building. My frown is reflected in the mirrored doors of the elevator as I think about the one question, I would like him to answer: *How could he allow me to fall for him, make love to me, knowing he's married.*

~~~

On Friday morning, I freeze mid-step as I approach my desk, frowning at the package sitting beside my keyboard with a silver envelope beneath it. I just know it's from Alex. It's the first gift he's sent me in two weeks. With cautious steps, I close the gap to my chair, place my purse on the floor, and stare at the ivory box with the silver-blue satin ribbon.

"I can have it sent back if you're not ready," Maggie says softly, leaning over the wall of my cubicle, her eyes dark with concern.

I look up at her and shake my head. "I'm not sure what I want to do with it yet."

"Maybe just read the note? It might help you decide about the gift."

"How do you remain so optimistic?" I ask her.

She gives me such a joyful smile. "By always knowing that there is a rainbow after every storm."
~~~

I watch her as she walks to the desk of a colleague who recently had a baby, smiling and cooing over the photos he is showing her. She has a point, though. I can't hide from Alex forever. With my eyes still focused on the package, I switch on my computer and pick up the envelope. Leaning back in my chair, I close my eyes and pull the note free.

> I found this a while ago. It reminded me of your beauty. I appreciated the times we had together even if I no longer share in your life.
>
> Alex

With shaky hands, I pick up the box and slowly pull off the ribbon, unsure of what I'll find inside. The lid and the ribbon fall from my nerveless fingers as I stare at the platinum ring nestled in the black velvet setting. The design is dainty and intricate and takes my breath away. The monarch butterfly has its wings made of onyx, amber, and diamonds spread as it prepares to take flight. It reminds me of who I am when I am with him.

After Ana died, I had withdrawn from everyone except Elise, and it didn't help that my parents disappeared into their work, leaving me to find my own relief from the overpowering grief. If it hadn't been for Elise, I don't know what would have happened to me. I have played it safe since then, especially with the men I dated, because I was too afraid to get too close to them. I was too afraid of being hurt. Until Alex… He gave me the courage to leave the safety of my cocoon, but he also enticed me to open my heart… and taking the risk had left me exposed and heartbroken. But he had also given me a taste of freedom.

Yes. I think I'm ready to talk now.

Chapter Eighteen

Me: I will give you one chance to explain yourself. I will accept nothing but the absolute truth.

I quickly send the message before I change my mind, having typed, and deleted several messages before sending this one, and then find myself holding my breath while I wait for him to respond. My heart still skips a beat when he replies.

Alex: I'm outside. Meet me in the park by the food trucks?

I hesitate before replying, not sure what the conversation will be and how it will affect my memories, seeing that so many of them have been tainted with bitterness. I find myself protective of the few sweet ones left. Maybe it could be the right place to speak about this.

Me: Meet you there at 5.

I'm not sure if I'm making a mistake in hearing him out, but I need to make sense of what is going on for my own peace of mind. I need this so that I can move on and not get stuck on him. Alex has changed my life, but at the moment, I'm not sure if it is for the better or if he just opened my eyes to the hurtful aspects of being in love.

At five minutes to 5 pm, I'm leaning over the railing of the bridge that leads to the area where we found the food trucks. I look down at the stream running beneath me, my fingers tangled in my butterfly charms, looking for some guidance from my sister. Elise is the one who was warning me about Alex—about the questions I have about him, and the way I accepted the fact that I can't make plans with him, either short-term or long-term, or how he never included me in other areas of his life, especially when it came to meeting his family. She will never say "*I told you so,*" but I still feel so stupid for not listening to her—for ignoring her warnings with the determination to live my life for right now. Maybe talking to him will give me the answers I need and the closure I need to move on.

"Hi."

The sound of his voice sends a chill down my spine, and I take a moment to gather all my scattered thoughts before facing him… seeing him for the first time in nearly a month. I fold my arms across my waist and tuck my hands tightly under them to stop myself from reaching for him when I turn around.

"Alex," I whisper. He is still as sexy as always, though he has lost some weight. His cheeks are a bit sunken; his shoulders are a bit sharper under his gray light-knit sweater, and his pants look a bit baggier. His eyes are so dark they appear black instead of the warm brown that I love so much.

"Can we get some coffee? Tea for you?" He points to a truck that has an impressive menu.

We walk in silence for a while as we sip our beverages, the shade of the trees cooling the warmth of the day. Though the silence is strained, it's not as awkward as I had thought it could be. Even the distance between us is comfortable—not close enough to touch, but near enough that I can still feel his heat. I sip my tea, then bite my lip nervously, waiting for him to speak.

"Nicole and I met in law school. She was elegant and flamboyant, and every young man's dream. And I couldn't believe she wanted to be with me. Straight after graduation, I got a job with Newman and Anderson, and it was a dream come true. Things with Nicole and me hit a hiccup just before we graduated, but then she comes to me and says she's pregnant." He stops speaking and stares into the distance. His voice is soft when he starts speaking again. "We got married, and a month later, she lost the baby."

I stare at him in silence unsure what to say. A part of me feels so sad for him but it doesn't excuse his betrayal.

He shrugs and tosses his cup in the nearest trash can. "The thing is, Kerri, there was a time we were happy, and I thought that we had left all the college shit behind. Her insecurities and need to be perfect seemed to be under control, but before I realized it, things spiraled again. We'd have arguments about nothing. She'd dismiss me, accuse me of the worst things, and then not say a word to me for days—yet when we're in public, she expects us to maintain a certain image. I got so used to playing that role of the perfect husband and partner, Kerri, that I forgot there's more to being happy. I didn't think I'd find that again, that my life was going to have something—or someone—in it that makes me happy."

"Then what was the party about, Alex?" I am confused by what he is telling me and what I saw at the party. "If you're so unhappy, why don't you just leave? Why keep pretending that everything is okay? Why do you keep living a lie?"

"It's not that simple, Kerri." He stops and turns to me, his eyes begging me to understand. With a slow shake of his head, Alex puts his hands in his pockets, and we start walking again. "A few years ago, I tried to leave Nicole. It was messy. She somehow hacked my social media accounts and posted some bullshit that nearly got me fired. She knows that the one thing I cherish is my career, and she is willing to destroy everything I've worked to achieve. She's shown me that she would not hesitate. Even more recently…things just got complicated."

"So, you're telling me that you're afraid of her?" He shakes his head emphatically. "If you're not, then what? Your career? Really? Is it really worth more than your happiness? It might not be easy to start over, but it is possible, Alex."

"No, Kerri, not in this city. Her family is influential and powerful enough to destroy my reputation. I will never be able to practice law in the state of New York. Kerri, please understand, my career was all I had to keep me surviving some of the shit she put me through. If I didn't have it, I don't think I'd be standing here right now. Plus, it's not just about my career. There's just so much more to it."

We're standing on another bridge, and I lean over the railing to watch the water bubbling under the bridge. "It just sounds like a bunch of excuses to me."

"They're not excuses, Kerri." He sighs. "Look, I guess I partly feel sorry for her. She's… fragile… and I don't want to be the reason she goes over the edge. There's a lot I can't really get into. We're living separate lives, especially after the last miscarriage."

"How many has she had, Alex?"

A shadow passes over his face, and his shoulders sag. I'm tempted to reach out and hold him. His voice is heavy when he answers softly, "Five. The last one was about two years ago."

I stare down at the water. "I'm sorry, Alex."

"After I tried to leave her the first time, we went for counseling, did all the exercises, went to all the challenges, and we tried so damn hard. It went well for a year, and then… someone said one thing to her at a party, and all hell broke loose again. I just got tired of fighting, Kerri. I got tired of fighting for a marriage I wasn't sure I really wanted anymore. Tired of doing things that would make her happy, that kept the peace, that wouldn't set her off. Until I moved permanently to my condo, and she lives in the house. We meet up for dinner once a week and for every other occasion that requires us to look like a couple."

"Ok and where do I fit in to all of this?" I spit back.

"You are my true world, Kerri. You give my hope that my future can be so much better…with you." Alex comes to stand beside me and lays his hand over mine where it rests on the railing, and I can't help the tingle that races down my spine. "I was ready to live my life for my career with a wife I tolerate. I didn't expect you. I tried to walk away. I tried to resist you, but it was so fucking hard. I didn't expect to fall in love with you so damn quickly."

I feel the air leaving my lungs at the simple way he made the statement—so clear, so sure. My throat burns, and I can feel the tears on my lashes. I blink furiously to stop them from falling. "Okay. So, you live apart and are basically a public couple? So, where does that leave us, Alex?"

"Kerri." I pull away as he tries to reach for me and wrap my arms around my waist. "I don't know yet. All I know is that I want to be with you. And I promise you, Kerri, I am working on a way to be free of my situation without it affecting you or other factors. I am asking you to trust me. Please?"

I shake my head, not wanting to fall for his pretty words. I start walking down the path again, and he falls into step beside me. "I don't want to sound like a diva, Alex, but I deserve more than a promise. What happens when things work better for you and Nicole? Are you going to pull me along out of guilt as well?"

He sighs heavily and pulls me to a stop. "I can't give you more than a promise, Kerri. And I will admit that I am selfish enough to not let you go."

I swallow hard at the lump in my throat and close my eyes as I try to quiet my runaway thoughts. I reach into my purse and hand him the ivory box. "I can't take this, Alex. Not until I know where I stand."

He shakes his head and drops it back into my purse. "Then accept it as a gift from someone whose life you've changed."

~~~
~~~

Back at my apartment, I sit on the couch with a cup of tea that is ice-cold, staring at the ring. It isn't just the beauty of it that has me studying it, but what it represents. Spending the afternoon with Alex made me realize how much I miss him; just being close to him and listening to his voice reminds me of how empty my time had become without him.

He is asking me to be patient, to trust a promise that will leave my life in limbo, to almost put my life on hold for him. The question I know he cannot answer is for how long? A month? A year? A *decade*? It's not fair of him to make me wait. To bind me to him for an indefinite amount of time. I could meet someone else. He must be insane to think I would wait for him while he takes his time to make up his mind. I want a family one day. I can't truly have that as someone's side piece. As I run through all these various scenarios in my head of what life looks like with Alex in it with his *situation*, I slowly get angry again. So many questions and no answers, except that he *says* he wants to be with me. I'm not sure I want this kind of life; to risk it all on a *maybe*.

Chapter Nineteen

"Hey, KB!" Elise always sounds so happy to hear from me, and I can't help but smile at her enthusiasm.

After I left Alex at the park and stared at the ring until I nearly spilled the cold tea over my lap, I realized that I needed another voice other than his and the million thoughts running through my mind. I needed to get some perspective. And Elise will always be honest with me, no matter how much it might hurt me. "I miss you, Elise."

"Aw, Kerribel. I'm sorry I couldn't make our visit." Elise had been supposed to visit with me last weekend, but she was asked to work because of some crises, and we postponed it for another month.

"Work keeps you busy—I understand." I sip some of my tea, grimace, and put the cup down on the coffee table, trying to find the courage to tell her the latest in my love saga.

"Spit it out, KB. I know when something's bothering you. Is it Alex?"

"Well, it's certainly not the jackass I went out with the other night." I walk over to the kettle and put water on for more tea, then return to the sofa and sink into the corner while I wait for the water to boil, pulling my knees up and resting my chin on them. "I met with him today."

"Which jackass are we talking about here?" she asks me, but I can hear by her tone that she knows to whom I am referring, and she is not happy.

"We had a slow walk through the park while we drank some coffee, and he told me all about his wife."

"Let me guess, he told you all about how insecure she is, that they're not communicating, and how lonely and neglected he is. Geez, Kerri, he sang the proper song, and you're thinking about dancing to his tune." I hear her take a few deep breaths, and I know she is trying to control her anger. "I'm sorry, Kerri."

"I know you're just trying to protect me, Elise. That is what a good friend—a sister—would do." I wipe away a tear. "But you're right. That is exactly what he said. Almost to the note."

"Shit, Kerri." She is quiet for a while, and then I hear

her sniff. "Please, Kerri, don't do this again. Don't be drawn in by his promises. Let him go, please?"

"I know that I need to do that, Elise, but…" I take a deep breath and shrug, knowing she can't see it. "Try telling my heart that Alex is bad for my health."

"Well, at least you have a heavy dose of Elise to apply the Band-Aid."

How can I not laugh at that? "I love you, my funky Band-Aid."

"Not as much as I love you."

There is a knock on my door as I hang up, and I frown. I wasn't expecting anyone. I pull the oversized cardigan tighter over my cotton camisole and adjust the sleep shorts I had put on for a date with my remote control before I answer the door. "Oh, shit."

He looks so good in tight blue jeans and a black long-sleeved T-shirt, and a leather jacket hanging from his hand. In his other hand, he's holding a divine-smelling bag of food from my favorite Moroccan takeaway. I'm not sure which package makes me open the door wider for him to enter, the subtle hint of his cologne making me moan out loud. He raised an eyebrow at me, and I blush.

I peer at him through the gap in the door, shocked at his sudden appearance at my apartment. "What are you doing here, Alex? I thought we agreed that you would give me space—that you would consider your situation. So, I take it you've made up your mind?"

"I couldn't think about anything else but you. You looked a little thin earlier, so I brought you food to make sure you're eating enough?" He holds up the bag on two fingers, the aromas closer to my nose weakening my resolve.

I suck in a sharp breath, straightening my spine and trying like hell to ignore that bag. "It doesn't matter, Alex. You still owe me an answer and yet, here you stand, trying to break my resolve with… with…" I point to the food.

He breathes out a loud sigh. "I contemplated sitting outside your door and enjoying this meal, on my own, but close to you. Maybe even enjoy that TV show you are listening to…"

"In the hallway?" I ask with a quirked eyebrow.

"With the hopes that the smell will draw you out of your cave…" That smile should be illegal. His face looks like a sad puppy dog making it impossible to resist his argument.

"That bag smells fantastic… And I am sort of hungry…"

"Just *sort of?*" he teases.

I narrow my eyes at him and open the door further. "But just because you're saving me the effort of ordering food myself."

"Sure," he drawls as he places the bag on the counter. I don't comment as I take out plates and grab a bottle of wine out of the fridge. His glances make me feel hot as I try not to enjoy the feeling of having Alex in my kitchen. He starts dishing food, but he doesn't say anything as he takes it to the coffee table. I settle into a corner of the sofa while he makes himself comfortable on the floor, his back resting against the cushions and his legs crossed under the table.

I clutch my fork tightly to stop myself from reaching for his strong jaw so that I don't trace the high cheekbones, broad, sharp nose, and full lips that hide an enchanting smile. When he smiles, a dimple appears, denting his smooth beard and making my knees weak. From this angle, I can see the thick, dark lashes that frame his unusual gray-brown eyes. And then suddenly I am staring into them. With a deep gulp, I take a large mouthful of food as I jerk my eyes away from his.

The food is excellent, as always, and I force myself to focus on taking each forkful and chewing it, making the excuse that I need it to survive, to stay focused, to—*Who am I kidding?* I am intently focused on using my utensils so that I don't have my wicked way with him!

"Can I take that?"

I blink up at him, not sure when he had gotten to his

feet. "Your plate. Can I take it for you?"

"Oh…Yes, thanks." I nod. He takes the dishes to the kitchen and rinses them before stacking them in the dishwasher. All I can do is watch the way his body moves so smoothly, the tiny muscles bunching under his sweater, and the way his jeans hug his butt as he bends at the dishwasher. I chew my lips, not wanting to admit that my body is on fire just from watching the man tidy my kitchen.

"You need to stop looking at me like that, Kerri." I sit up, my back straight in shock at his comment. I sit cross-legged as I quirk an eyebrow at his back.

"Like what?" His comment catches me off guard. His back is facing me so I'm curious how he can even see me.

"Like you can't wait to get your hands on me."

I scoff. "How would you know? You're not even—"

"I came to spend time with you because I just wanted to be close to you." He leans over the counter as he looks at me. "I didn't think you'd open the door. And not looking so damn sexy in those tiny fucking shorts."

"Alex…" His name slips from my lips with a moan. He shakes his head as he moves back to the sofa, his steps slow, measured, and almost feral.

"I know I complicated things, and it is unfair of me to come here uninvited, but I cannot stay away from you,

Kerri." He sits next to me, then leans over and places his hands on both sides of my shoulders, surrounding me with his body, his scent, and his warmth, though he doesn't quite touch me anywhere. He is staring down at me, his eyes asking me for something I'm not sure I'm ready to give him yet. But my body is more than willing to give him everything else. He must read something in my eyes because he chews his lip, the action making it swollen and even more tempting. "Kerri…"

I uncross my legs and hook them around his waist as my arms wind around his neck. Reaching up, I slide my tongue across his lip before sucking it deeply into my mouth. He groans and twists his tongue with my own, and my heart rate increases even as everything else slows down. I slip my cardigan off my shoulders, and he breaks the kiss to take slow, long nibbles across my collarbone before pushing down the strap of my camisole. I gasp as he pulls down the neckline and sucks my nipple, making me arch my back, the ridge of his hardness fitting so wonderfully into my soaking cleft.

"I missed you, butterfly," he says against my skin, his voice deep with need. I pull his sweater over his head and run my hands over his warm skin, his muscles shivering beneath my exploring fingertips. Kissing his neck, I unzip his jeans and push them down, freeing his throbbing shaft. I moan as he jerks when I circle my fingers around him. His hips pump forward as I slide my hand from the tip to his base where I tighten my hold before sliding it back to the tip.

With the essence dripping from him, I wet my thumb and massage it into his enlarged head, and Alex cries out. He curses as he glances down between us and watches me pleasure him before grabbing my wrist and placing it above my head. He leans down and kisses me roughly, bruising my lips as I open up to him. Cold air covers me, making my nipples even tighter and harder when he pushes upright and looks down at me. I feel my eyes widen, and my pussy becomes even wetter as his cock twitches and grows harder.

Alex slides his hands under the waistband of my shorts and roughly pulls them down my legs, both of us crying out when he plunges two fingers into me, my juices running down my slit. He hooks my legs over his shoulders and lifts my butt, and I scream as he fills me with a hard, swift thrust. He again leans his hands on the arm of the couch, and I arch my back and hang my head over the cushion, both of us moaning loudly at the depth of the angle, his tip massaging the special spot deep within me. I hiss as he pushes deeper inside of me.

"Do not move" he says spurring out a breath with each word. I don't know how much more I can take if he goes any deeper. "I want you to take every inch of it."

I open my eyes enough to peer at him through my lashes. His dark skin is covered in a sheen of sweat, his muscles quivering as he moves. And then my breath escapes as his gaze locks on mine, and beneath the desire burning in them, I see what he is not saying—the care, the passion, and the love.

"Ooh…" I croon as my tunnel tightens around him, and with a few deep thrusts, my world blacks out as I shatter. With a deep, guttural cry, he explodes inside of me, his hips pumping deep, almost painfully so.

He looks down at me before tenderly kissing me. "I think I love you, Kerribel Townsend."

He gathers me tightly in his arms, and I feel his breathing even out as he falls asleep. "I think I love you too, Alexander Carter."

Chapter Twenty

My stylus hovers over my digital sketch pad as I think about the last few days and having Alex back in my life. It's wonderful, for the most part. I'm treated to boxes from Harriet's on my desk when I come into work, dinners at his condo or my loft, lunchtime walks in the park, trying food from new food trucks, and Saturday mornings either going on hikes or visiting New York's favorite attractions. These are magical, and I look forward to them with excitement.

I can't help but grimace when I think about the frown that forms on his face when he gets a text from… *her*. Or the way he now tells me that it's a social thing he has to attend instead of making flimsy excuses about work or helping his family. It's as though a wall has been broken between us, and it has taken our relationship to new heights, but it has also highlighted the huge cracks between us. Sometimes I wish I never knew about her and their situation. It reminds me that a future with Alex is a near impossibility. It might never happen.

Because of my workload, I've been coming in to work earlier than usual, and this allows me to remove the gifts from my desk before my colleagues see them, especially Maggie. I am not ready to explain what is happening between us yet, not when I can't even make sense of it myself. I feel guilty about sneaking around with Alex, but I just don't think they will understand. I've found her looking at me occasionally, and I just smile when she teases me about having a secret man in my life because of the hazy look in my eyes. She doesn't ask, and I don't volunteer any details. Even Elise thinks that I am randomly dating again.

I haven't been spending as much time with them because I am too afraid, I'd let something slip. Every time Maggie asks me if I am joining her and Demi for an evening out, I find a way to wiggle out of the invitation, only attending evenings when the rest of our colleagues are going to be there. Knowing that my friends are thinking that I am not involved with Alex puts a damper on the times I have with him, especially when I feel so crappy about not sharing this with them or getting excited about the tiny gifts, he sends me. I know they have my best interests at heart, and if I am smart, I would follow their advice.

Yet, I am so bound to him that walking away from him and being with someone new is unthinkable. Some of my days are spent missing him and being angry with him in equal parts. And this makes me even angrier with myself, because I *know* I am worth more than being *the other woman*.

I frown at the words appearing on my screen:

> I love the invisible image. Our clients will love it as much as I do.

I blink at the message, then scowl at my stylus, which is now dangling from the beautiful olive-green manicured fingers of my friend and boss, who is lounging on the corner of my desk. The gold pinstripe in the ivory suit pants flashes in the corner of my eye as she swings her leg casually. By the level of comfort, the length of the message, and the smirk on her face, I realize that she has been there for some time. I close my eyes and sigh loudly.

"I'm sorry, Maggie. I'm just…" I shrug helplessly.

She gives me a smile in return. "You free for lunch?"

"For you, any time." I lean down to fiddle with my purse so I can hide the guilty flush on my cheeks, trying to make the statement as sincere as I can.

"Great! Let's go," she says, jumping to her feet and taking my hand.

"Now? Maggie!" I giggle in surprise. "It's only 11:00!"

"I'm the boss, so I say lunch is now."

We leave the building and find a food truck a couple of blocks away from the office, where we each order a pulled turkey taco and sodas and stroll into the park to find a bench to sit on. We eat in silence for a while, and then I take a sip of my soda and turn to her. We ask at the same moment, "What's going on?"

We laugh, the mirth lifting the heaviness of the moment between us. When we sober up, Maggie takes my hand and holds it while she looks at me with concern. "You have become a good friend to me, Kerri, and I love you loads. I know I'm the one who encouraged you to take a chance with Alex, and I am the reason you are so shattered. And I am so sorry."

"Maggie, you have nothing to apologize for—"

"No, Kerri. I do, because your light is no longer so bright, and I feel that if I hadn't encouraged you to go out with Alex, your heart wouldn't be broken. If I hadn't meddled, you would be the free, joyful Kerri I met. I'm worried about you, KB."

"Oh, Maggie," I smile as I blink away tears. "Maggie. It was my decision at the end of the day. And besides, Alex and I had a good time while things were good, but it wasn't perfect or what I wanted—it had its perfect moments. You have nothing to feel guilty about. Promise me?"

She shakes her head and shrugs. "I just keep seeing your face when you found out. And all I remember is making you go to Illicit that night. And I made you go to the Hamptons with me, and I can't help—"

I shake her hands to get her to look at me. "Maggie, come on. You know me well enough to know that if I didn't want to go anywhere with you, you couldn't make me go. But *I did*! I wanted to get to know my colleagues and make friends. I *wanted* to go away with you and Demi and have a fun weekend, which I *did*—I had so much fun! You've reminded me what it is like to let go from time to time and not to be so serious, and I love you for that. So, please, don't exclude me from any parties you are planning because you're afraid I might get heartbroken?"

She laughs. "Okay."

Sniffing away tears, we hug each other and just hold onto the beauty that our friendship has become.

"Oh, I have to tell you about this guy that's renovating our house. Kerri—he is gorgeously fantastic! You need to meet him! And those low-rider jeans are to die for!" She fans her face, and I am relieved to see the old spark back in her eyes.

"Hey, you're not supposed to be throwing yourself at other guys!"

"That's why I'm throwing you at him!"

"Maggie!" I gasp, and for the first time in a long time, I laugh with sincerity.

~~~

I pin the large white hibiscus behind my ear before stepping back from the mirror to inspect my appearance. Alex is picking me up for dinner and to visit an art gallery that we've both been wanting to see for a while. It's the first date we could settle on all week, and I am looking forward to spending time with him. I run my hands down the sides of the plum wide-legged jumpsuit and smile in anticipation at the look on his face when he discovers the surprises, I have underneath.

I am a few minutes early, and I sit at the counter to drink the tea I made earlier and scroll through my emails as I wait. Still smiling at a silly Instagram post, I answer the video call from Alex. I can see that he is still at his office, and I can feel the disappointment stealing over me.

"Butterfly, I'm sorry, but I'm needed at the office to sort out some paperwork. I won't make it tonight."

I smile, trying not to show how disappointed I am. "I'm sorry, too."

"You look phenomenal. I really wish I could show you
~~~

off tonight." He pulls off his tie and opens the top button on his white shirt. "Believe me, I'd much rather be walking around a gallery with you than doing contracts."

"I understand. Besides, there's always the weekend."

"I love how supportive you're being, Kerri. I will make it up to you, I promise."

"Alex, I want to be supportive, but I need to know it's mutual."

"Butterfly, I'm trying. I promise I've been speaking to someone that can help me figure out a way, but I want something definite to put into action, Kerri, so that we can live the rest of our lives without issues."

I want to believe him, but I know he can't guarantee anything, so I say instead, "I'll miss you, though."

"I'll miss you, too." He looks up and then back at the phone. "I'm sorry, but I have to go."

"Sure." We hang up, and my shoulders sag. The shitty feeling, I have as the call ends is made even worse when a text message comes through, and a photo of Ana and me appears on the screen.

Unknown: I told you, bitch, I will let the world know who you really are.

I shiver as I read the message a few times, the realization

sinking in. They weren't sent to the wrong number. They are meant for me!

Panic overwhelms me, and I struggle to control my breathing. My muscles tense, and my stomach threatens to empty itself. I clutch my head with my hands as it spins, the room blurring around the edges of my vision. The personal photo makes me heave for breath; the idea that someone—*a stranger*—knows my personal number, and has unlimited access to me, makes me feel sick to the depths of my soul. The way this person can use my personal information makes me think it is someone who knows me intimately, almost as though the person has a bird's-eye view of my life. Is it someone from home? Someone from my past?

Taking deep breaths, I eventually gain control of my runaway emotions. Slowly recovering my breathing to a normal level, I make the decision to take control of my life and not let some unknown person spoil my night any further.

With resolve, I dial Maggie's number. "Hey!"

"Kerribel! What's happening?"

"Are you busy?" I am relieved that my voice is not as shaky as I thought it would be.

"Not yet…" she drawls, a hopeful note in her voice.

"How about dinner and an art gallery opening?"

"Will there be wine at the opening?"

"Of course."

"I'll meet you at Le Bon Aperitif in fifteen?"

"Perfect!"

Chapter Twenty-One

A cold wind is blowing over the roof after this morning's rain when I come out at lunchtime, so I have the area to myself. I savor the mouthful of warm chili I brought with me and think about the past week. Alex made it a point to have lunch or dinner with me every day since the night we were supposed to go to the art gallery, and some nights he stayed with me until the early morning hours. I would wake up cold and alone, biting back the tears as I ran my hands over the pillow, trying to find some of the warmth he left behind. I don't quite believe him when he says that he wants to get a few hours of sleep before going to work, but my heart needs to believe that he doesn't go to her.

I remember how my heart filled with hope when he told me that he had moved the last of his stuff out of their house and into the condo earlier in the week. The shadows in his eyes told me that the move hadn't been easy for him. I get the feeling that there is something he isn't telling me, but he just smiles and says everything is fine when I ask. Though I don't believe him, there is nothing more I can do but accept that he is fine.

A soft breeze brushes against my skin and I shiver, pulling my denim jacket tighter around me, the colorful silk patches reflecting like jewels in the dark, dark blue. With a determined shake of my head, I try to forget about the overwhelming challenges between Alex and me and focus on the positives, like visiting the Statue of Liberty and having a picnic on the viewing platform. Or having dinner on his balcony surrounded by colorful Chinese lanterns. I still smile at the memory of the star-studded sky and the glow of the candles as I scroll through my Instagram page, realizing that it's been weeks since I last posted something.

I read through my messages as I finish my tea, but then I put my cup down and quickly scroll through them. There is one person who has sent several messages, both in comments on my posts and as direct messages. The messages are dark and give me goosebumps as another shiver racks my body. Some of them say *"Bitch"* or *"Murderer"* and they were posted more than a month ago.

With my heart beating hard against my ribs and my breath panting at the craziness of the messages, I untangle my fingers from my chain, and my thumb hovers over the delete button, but something tells me to hold onto them.

An email alert beeps through, and I gasp when I look at the clock, jumping to my feet. I quickly gather my things to make it to my desk in time. The messages won't leave my mind, though, and I am distracted.

I look up at the shelf Maggie had surprised me with to put all the tiny gifts that Alex had sent me, thinking about all the excitement he gives me. I didn't have the heart to replace the trinkets when we broke up, and now it is a quiet reminder of what our relationship is at the moment. I squint at the shelf. Something isn't right, and I frown as I get to my feet to look for the helicopter under and around my desk. I find it lying behind my computer screen, the windscreen shattered and one of the propeller blades bent as if someone had stomped on it.

"Oh, no," Maggie coos as she sees the broken toy in my hand. "What happened?"

I shake my head. "I don't know. I found it like this."

"Oh, Kerri, it must have been when they delivered the new furniture to the office. I'm so sorry." She strokes my arm, and I smile at her, glad of her support.

"Yea…maybe. It just sucks." I place the helicopter in its place and turn to her. "Are you here to torment me or to ask something?"

She laughs. "I needed to speak to you about the Jensen account. They love the graphics and want to discuss the second phase when you have a minute?"

"Sure," I agree, and I forget about this afternoon's incidents as we talk about the new phase.

I check my socials regularly over the next couple of days and find the same types of messages and even some comments on photos that I post. A comment on a photo I shared of a colleague of our evening at Illicit has the worst effect on me. *Prowling for your next victim, Kerri? Will this murder be as easy to get away with?*

Elise calls me to find out about the comments. "You need to block this person—in fact, *people*—because it's not the same username."

"I have, Elise," I say, not wanting her to hear my panic. "Hopefully, it should stop them."

"Let's hope so. Anyway, I sent you something for your birthday, so you can expect it any day now."

"Oh yeah! My birthday is coming up!" After Ana died, Elise went out of her way to help me celebrate our birthday. Every year, she decides on a theme and will start a month in advance by sending me little decorations that will give me hints about the madness she has planned. It is this tradition that I look forward to rather than the actual day on which Ana and I were born.

~~~

Two days later, I whoop as I receive the text from the delivery man—my package from Elise has arrived, and the
~~~

photo shows it waiting for me at my door. I am so excited! It is a couple of days before my birthday, but this is how we've always celebrated. I stifle a laugh at last year's theme, which had my mom fluttering around the house, too embarrassed to invite her friends to the party—which was a big relief for Elise and myself. We were tired of smiling over tiny porcelain teacups while containing our boredom. Maggie is as excited as I am, and we make plans to meet up at my place after work.

I'm too impatient to wait for the elevator and race up the five flights of stairs, breathless when I reach my floor but giddy with anticipation. I stand at my door and look down at the empty space, not sure if I'm imagining things. The box is gone. I scroll through my messages and find the photo of the box on my tiny yellow Welcome mat. The text has today's date, and the time is just after 3:00, barely two hours ago.

"Hi, Kerri." I turn to Mr. Granger, our building manager, and smile at him as he passes me with his toolkit.

"Oh, Mr. Granger?"

"Yes?"

"I received a package this afternoon, and it's not here now. Did you maybe see what happened to it?"

"Oh, yeah." He lifts his cap and rubs the bald spot in the middle of the tufts of his black and gray hair. "I saw the box earlier, but when I came through to fix apartment

121 B's sink, it was gone. I assumed you'd come home earlier and taken it in."

"Oh… thank you," I say softly, confused as to what could have happened to it. Maggie arrives as I unlock my door, noticing the concern on my face.

"Kerri, what's wrong?"

I shake my head and shrug. "I don't know. It's just so strange."

"What is?" I tell her about the missing delivery and confess that when I got to my desk yesterday, the balloons on the apology bear were cut off and lying all over my keyboard. She stares at me in horror. "Kerri! You should have said something! I'll have security be stricter with visitors. No one at the office would do that."

"I know, and that is what makes this even more confusing."

"I tell you what. Tonight, we have fun, and tomorrow we speak to people who will know what to do."

"Like the police?" I ask, not sure this issue is serious enough to call them.

"No, silly! I was talking about Demi and Elise!"

"Maggie!" I groan, feeling my mood lift at the idea.

<div align="center">~~~</div>

My day is hectic, filled with meetings and conferences that run through lunch. When I reach my desk, I have several calls and some texts that I try to answer while I drink a cup of tea. I leave the messages from my parents for when I get home, but there are a few from an unknown number that I open, thinking it's for business. When I open them, though, all I hear is someone breathing heavily into the phone. The next few are the same—someone just breathing—and I rub the goosebumps that explode onto my arms. Once again, my thumb hovers over the delete button, but one of my colleagues calls me, and I close my screen as I turn my attention to her. My phone rings as I'm speaking to her, and I kill the call without checking the display, sending the call to voicemail.

I reach my loft tired and drained and sink onto my couch, my purse still slung over my arm. My stomach rumbles, and I groan, dropping my head onto the cushions and closing my eyes. I mentally review the contents of my fridge. Leftover Chinese will be dinner, my mind not willing to cooperate with my stomach to plan anything better. Those creepy messages still tickle the hair at the back of my neck.

~~~

Saturday morning greets me with watery sunshine, and I decide to go for a run, needing to clear my head of the things that have been happening the last week and that had me tossing and turning all night. By the time I finish a circuit of the park and return to my building, I am
~~~

breathing easier, and I feel less stressed. I click the connection on my earbud when my phone rings, at the same time coming to a dead stop at the doors of my building.

"Kerri?" Maggie's voice on the phone is a whisper at the chaos that fills my mind when I eventually break through the crowd of people that are gathered on the sidewalk, staring at the large, angry letters spray-painted across the glass doors. Mr. Granger scratches his head in worry. The letters are in deep red, possibly four feet high, and where the paint has run, it resembles drops of blood flowing down the wall. I feel my head moving from side to side of its own accord at the sight of the jagged heart painted in black, surrounding the condemning words. A line is drawn down the middle, supposedly resembling a broken heart, and my stomach turns as nausea fills my mouth at the smell of the fresh paint. I feel the blood draining from my face as I stare at it, my head spinning like I'm on a broken merry-go-round. The stares of my neighbors bore into me as they turn shocked eyes at me.

When I left for my run this morning, there had been nothing on that door, and in the space of an hour, the entrance is vandalized so traumatically. How batshit-crazy must someone be to do this at eight in the fucking morning?

"Kerri! You need to tell me what is going on?" Maggie sounds just as panicked as I feel.

Maggie's demand pulls me from the scene, and I swallow the nausea closing my throat. "Maggie, I honestly don't know," I manage in a hoarse whisper.

"I came to work to do some admin, and someone spray-painted your name all over the building."

"What?!" I stare in shock at the words painted for the world to see.

"Someone spray-painted '*Kerri Townsend is*—'"

"'—*a murdering bitch*'..." I finish her sentence in a whisper. It is the same words I am staring at.

Chapter Twenty-Two

"Hey, Kerri, call me when you get a chance. A box arrived at my place with your details on it. Not sure how it got to me." The voicemail from Alex has me frowning as I try to think how a package for me landed with him. I dial his number.

"Hey, I'm just about to go into a meeting." His tone is rushed, and there is the sound of papers rustling.

"I'm sorry, I only got your message now. What package? Did you open it?"

"Quite honestly, I didn't need to. It was so badly damaged, and the stuff inside took quite a beating, most of it nothing but trash at this point. I kept it, though, in case you wanted to see what it's all about?"

"Thanks, sure," I respond, trying to contain the shivers racing down my spine.

"Okay. I'll bring it along tonight with dinner?"

"That sounds great, thank you, A—" I stop myself before I say his name as Maggie passes close to my desk.

"Sure." He pauses, and I am about to hang up when he calls my name. "Kerri, are you okay? You sound… distant."

"I'm fine," I reassure him, but my mind is filled with the calls I received from the unknown number as well as my name splattered on the walls of my loft and work over the weekend. At first, the caller sounded like they were just breathing, but then I realized that someone was breathing the word '*bitch*' over and over until I hung up.

"I've got to go, but we'll talk tonight. I want to know what's going on." We hang up, and I turn back to my computer. Mr. Granger had called the police, and after a brief conversation with me, they had shrugged and left, not filling me with much hope. I sigh as I massage the headache from my temples, my elbows resting on my desk. They had told Maggie the same thing when they came to check out our office building.

I look up at the hand that massages my nape, and I smile when I see Maggie standing beside me.

"I just came to check how you're doing, KB." Maggie

has been a great friend and an even better boss. She paid a contractor extra to have the words removed before my colleagues arrived on Monday morning; the only evidence is the photos taken by the police officer lying in a folder on someone's desk. It reminds me of the added cost on my rent bill at the end of this month.

"I've been trying to wrap my brain around this, Mags, but I can't think who'd do something like this." I can feel the tears of frustration—and fear—brimming on my lashes.

"We'll figure it out," she reassures me, her hand on my back a silent comfort in my turmoil. "Have you told your mystery man yet?"

For a moment, I am confused, but then quickly I remember she is referring to the person she believes I am dating. The person who is not Alex. And my headache just intensifies. I shake my head. "He's coming over tonight to drop off a package of mine that was dropped at his place."

"What package? Wait! Your birthday package?" She lets out a loud breath when I nod.

I shrug as I shake my head. "Maggie, I've been trying to think what I could have done to someone that they would do this, but…"

She leans down until we are eye-to-eye. "You listen to me, Kerribel Townsend. You are the sweetest, most caring and compassionate person I know. You don't have a vicious bone in your body. Whatever is going on, it is totally the other person's issue. Okay?"

I give her a small smile and nod, but I am not as confident about that as she is.

~~~

Over the next couple of weeks, Alex is busy with work and Nicole has him attending several social events that he can't get out of, so we don't get to spend as much time together. The night he brought the package over, I recognized Elise's handwriting on the box and knew it was the delivery that had gone missing without opening it. My heart sank. Elise puts so much effort into this celebration every year, and to see it destroyed makes me angry as much as it saddens me. Everything in it had been smashed or cut up, even the beautiful birthday card that she had sent. I cried myself to sleep over the destruction of her beautiful gesture.

The question that's beating like a bad chorus in my brain is: *Who would do this?*

I close my eyes and massage my temples to ease the threatening headache, but instead of going away, images of old newspaper headlines flash into my mind, headlines and social media comments that I wish I can forget but know I never will.

"Twin hampers rescue of sister at Juniors Final: Is jealousy a role
~~~

player?"

"...Ana dying is just Kerri's way of catching the limelight..."

"Sister clutches winning twin at a swim competition, causing her to drown..."

"This is Kerri's opportunity. She's been waiting a long time to be as popular as Ana!"

"Well, well, well, now that she got Ana out of the way, little Kerri can shine!"

I put the back of my hand into my mouth to smother the scream I feel tumbling out of my chest and past my throat to quiet the voices that are filling my head, scenes from my past, snide looks and comments that followed me through the rest of my high school years. Comments that haunt me to this day.

The messages and calls are also quiet except for the occasional voicemail where the person is chanting *bitch*. I don't answer calls from unknown numbers anymore, and even emails from unfamiliar sources are kept in a separate box that I don't open.

Instead, I am focusing on New York showing off her change of season, the colors changing from a deep green to soft ambers, browns, and golds. The days are cooler, and I can't believe how refreshing it is to take a run through the city and see how the buildings seem to prepare for winter. Their sparkling facades seem to glow darker and warmer, making me feel more at home and comfortable than I did during the summer. It is also interesting to see the leaflets advertising upcoming Halloween parties. I close my eyes as I stare at one in particular as I take the elevator up to my office. I need to get a costume for our Halloween party at the office tomorrow.

"Kerri!" Maggie exclaims as I put my purse under my desk and switch on my computer. The office is normally a hub of activity, but this morning everyone is super-excited about the party and spending more time decorating their cubicles than working. It doesn't help that there is a competition for the scariest workspace happening as well. One colleague nearly gives me a heart attack when a cackling skull pops out of his drawer as I ask to borrow his stapler.

It also doesn't help that the office is decorated like the inside of a haunted house, every corner and available space covered in spiderwebs, huge spiders dangling from them and the ceiling. There is a witch flying on a broom in the corner, her pitch-black cat wrapped around her purple hat. Jack-o-lanterns litter the hallways, and a graveyard scene decorates the foyer that our elevator opens to, a bony hand sticking out between the moss-covered tombstones. Michael Jackson's "Thriller" is playing from someone's speakers as I walk past the eerily decorated desks. Apart from a mini jack-o-lantern candle holder and some spiderwebs, my desk is bleak compared to some of my colleagues.

"What can I help you with, Maggie?"

"I need a costume. What are you doing for lunch?"

"Looking for a costume too?"

"Good. Now get to work; I can't wait to see the finished product."

I check my emails and accidentally click on one with an unfamiliar address. Before I can close it, I am frozen in shock at the image on my screen. It is the picture of Ana's accident that accompanied the newspaper article ten years ago. Beneath that picture is one of me and Alex in the park the day he told me about Nicole, leaning over the bridge, but the headline is changed to *"Enticing the Next Victim?"*

I close my eyes and try to do the deep breathing exercises I have been taught in therapy shortly after the accident, but the intrusion into my life—and especially into my past—has me angry, fearful, and anxious. For someone to know about my past and use it in such a way is scary. I remember the rumors that followed me after the accident—that I was jealous of Ana.

None of them hurt more than when Ana's boyfriend accused me of pulling her under the water—

No! It can't be Michael!

I pick up my phone to call Elise, but an email alert pings through, and I check the address before I breathe a sigh of relief when I see it's from a client. With my attention diverted, I forget about the email and concentrate on my work.

~~~

"Amazing!" I breathe in admiration at the many costumes swirling around the office. The conference room is set up as the food center, and everyone is either dishing a plate or dancing in the small area set up for the occasion. Everyone turned off their computers at exactly 11:00 and rushed for the bathrooms to change for the party. I had waited until almost everyone had come back before taking the opportunity to change into my costume.

I put my glass of punch on my desk and reactivate my screen, wanting to finish the last of the design I am working on when I hear someone mention my name. "What the—!"

I am not a fan of clowns, and to see the scariest one of the lot walking toward me has my heart rate tripling. I put my hand to my chest to stop it from breaking through my rib cage, too afraid to confirm my name in case it decides to pull me down some sewer pipe. I back up against my desk, almost sitting on it completely when the messenger holds out a box and an iPad, his hands painted white with bright red blood dripping from his pointed nails. I shudder and hold out a shaky hand to sign for the parcel, not wanting to look up at the grotesque smile he has painted over his full lips, the red lipstick dripping down his chin in
~~~

the form of blood drops.

"This is fantastic!" Maggie admires his costume before sitting on the edge of my desk. She's dressed like Wednesday Addams with a black miniskirt, fishnet stockings, knee-high platform boots, and a black leather jacket over a crimson shirt, her hair smoothed over her shoulders and down her back, the tips sprayed a blood red. "Come on, open it! I want to see what kind of gift someone will send you on this auspicious day for pranks."

I roll my eyes as I take the box, making sure not to touch the clown's freaky hands. It is heavy, and I put it on my desk to remove the lid. There's no card or note, which is unusual for Alex—he always sends a sweet note.

I peer into the box and frown when I see a long pink tail curled around a large brown, furry body nestled in white tissue paper. I glance at Maggie and the Pennywise-look-alike who is suddenly very pale under his makeup.

"That's not right…" he stutters. "We don't transport animals."

We glance at each other again before leaning over the box. My mind is numb at what will be revealed when I pull back the rest of the paper, and it feels as though I am floating above my desk, not part of the things unfolding in front of me. I see my hands shaking so much as I reach for the paper that I clench my fingers together before taking the corners and pulling it open.

I don't know who screamed louder, *Pennywise II* or me at the sight of the headless rat.

~~~

I am vaguely aware of Maggie quickly closing the box, her own face pale and her green eyes wide with shock. She pushes me into my chair and reaches for her phone to call the police.

"What the hell is going on? Who would do something like this? This is so totally against company policy! They're going to fire me! Oh no, I can't get fired from this job! Please tell me if this is some sick joke! Tell me that is not an actual rat! Ah, shit, I'm going to lose my job!" Pennywise wails.

"No one's going to lose anything," Maggie hushes as she hangs up the phone. "The police are on their way. We just need to wait for them. You too... uh, Pennywise."

The wait for the police is a blur as Maggie escorts us to her office for privacy. She makes us each a cup of tea and paces the space until we spot the dark uniform of the police officers making their way between the obscene costumes. We fill them in about the messages and the vandalism, and they take photos of the box only after Maggie insists.

"Miss Townsend, please understand that with this holiday, things go crazy, and we have our hands full with petty crimes. We'll see if we can find anything but—as I said—our labs are backed up. It could be a while." I look
~~~

at the officer who is more interested in the festivities of the office than investigating my package.

"Ok, so what are you saying, Officer?" I ask.

"I'd move on from this, Miss Townsend. We have nothing to work with." Maggie and I gape at him as he answers a call on his radio. He shakes his head and shrugs when Maggie opens her mouth to challenge him. "I'm sorry, Miss Sheffield. I have another call I need to get to."

Chapter Twenty-Three

"Kerri, it can't be Michael," Elise says softly after she listens to my theory.

"Why not, Elise?" I can't understand why she would defend him. He caused us both so much pain after Ana died. "He was the one who told everyone that I pulled her under, that I was jealous of her success. That I killed her to be with him!" I shudder at the memory.

Michael was the all-American boy. His mom was a doctor at the same hospital my parents worked at, and his dad had his own business. Michael had been obsessed with both Ana and me and would often joke about having a threesome with us. At 17, he was over six feet tall with broad shoulders, and extremely athletic, being the star of both the football and basketball teams. I could never understand what Ana saw in him because he was a spoiled ass who used people and had a mean streak, especially when he didn't get his way. And when he tried to kiss me at Ana's funeral, I rejected him. I still remember the laughter that I couldn't suppress as I moved away from him, his vow to *make me regret it* reverberating through the memory.

"Kerri, Michael is locked up for drug dealing. He has been in prison for about a year now. There is no way he can be in New York, or even close to technology to do this."

"Oh." The fight whooshes out of me like a deflated balloon. That takes me back to square one. Someone wants to destroy my life, and I have no clue who it can be. "What do I do now, Elise?"

"You take the weekend to relax and live your life as you are meant to. Whoever it is will reveal themselves eventually."

"Ugh… You're reading Confucius again," I groan.

"That's Oprah actually, but that's not the point." She takes a deep breath and says softly, "I always just want you to be happy, no matter what. I was skeptical that Alex would have done that, but he was a good distraction for you."

I bite back a moan of misery and guilt and feel a sense

of relief when a message alert beeps through as we speak. I suck in a breath as I read the message from Alex. "Elise, I… uh… have to respond to this email from work. I will speak to you tomorrow. I want to grab a shower after I answer it. I need it after this hectic day."

"Okay. Be careful, KB."

"Always, Elise." I hang up, and I'm just pulling the loose-fitting sweater over my yoga pants when Alex knocks on the door 20 minutes later. I adjust the lilac material to casually hang off my shoulder as I open the door. The heat that flashes in his eyes finds a corresponding pulse deep in me, but I push the feeling aside and turn back to the living room.

But he barely closes the door before grabbing hold of my hand and pulling me into his arms. With relief, I sink into his warmth and sigh as he gently massages the muscles in my lower back. I close my eyes and enjoy the feeling of him around me, and I know that somehow everything will be okay.

"Want to tell me about it?" he asks as we settle on the couch.

"It's just been so weird." I lay my head on his shoulder as I curl up at his side. "When my sister died, I was in the water with her. She touched first, and I was so close behind her, but by the time I surfaced, she was struggling to breathe, and I tried to get her out so fast. But we were too late, and her boyfriend was so bad, accusing me of being jealous. That's why all this stuff just reminded me of the worst time of my life. And then today, it was just too much."

"Ah, baby, I'm so sorry." The gentle stroking motion of his fingers on my shoulders has me relaxing.

"The one person I thought it could be is in prison, so he can't be responsible for this." I lick my lips and hesitate to voice my thoughts because they are so new, and I'm not sure how he might react to them. "Alex, some of this shit started escalating after that weekend of your anniversary. Could it maybe be someone from the party? Maybe someone who saw us together? A friend of yours? A friend of Nicole's, maybe?" I sit up to look at him. "Maybe Nicole herself?"

He stares at me intensely as if he is in deep thought and then abruptly pushes to his feet, and I watch him clench his fingers as he paces before pushing them into the pockets of his gray pants. He stops in front of the window and leans against the frame as he looks down at the street for a few seconds before looking at me over his shoulder. "Kerri, Nicole is a lot of things, but I don't think she knows anything. It must be someone else."

"Why are you defending her?" I hiss feeling a slight tinge of anger rumbling inside. I need to understand how much she still means to him.

"I'm not defending her, Kerri. Nicole is vain and won't do anything that could cause wrinkles, never mind damage her reputation or image of perfection. She will do what it takes to ensure that the world sees her as superb and nothing less. She won't risk that image."

He sounds so sure of himself that I'm tempted to believe him. "Can you think of someone who'd do this?"

"I've not told anyone about you, Kerri, other than you're a friend I like to spend time with." He frowns as he stares out the window again. "I wish I could find out who it is so that I can protect you from them. I just feel so damn helpless."

I walk up to him and put my arms around him, resting my cheek against his back. He folds a hand over my own, and I can hear his heartbeat slowing down. I never thought about how much my situation is affecting him too.

He turns around and kisses me so sweetly that I smile, and I feel him smile against my lips in response. He slides his tongue along the seam of my mouth, and when I open it, he pulls back and nibbles my bottom lip so gently. And when he blows on it, I feel my juices flow. He grazes my cheek with his beard, and the sensation is so sexy that I grab hold of his shirt as my knees buckle. "Fuck, Kerri, you smell so good."

I cup his face bringing his mouth back to mine for a kiss that is deep and hungry. His soft lips caressing mine has my body heating up from within. His slightly cold hands slip under my sweater and find my bare breasts. Alex groans as if he is pleased to find me without a bra on. He pulls my sweater over my head and stares at my breasts like he hasn't eaten in days. I watch as he kneels in front of me staring so intensely.

Gently, he places a kiss on the tip of my nipple, licking a path to the other, and sucks it softly. I moan bending my back and my head falls onto my shoulders as he slowly licks and sucks. I gasp when he slides his tongue down the center of my chest until he reaches my belly button, and then spirals around it until he dips into it, making my stomach muscles jump beneath his fingers. His beard grazes my skin as he kisses his way to the waistband of my pants. With everything happening this is exactly what I need to relieve my stress. It's like he can read my mind. He knows exactly what I need.

"Alex…" I gasp, my hands cupping his head. In one quick move, he gets to his feet and lifts me into his arms, then carries me to my bedroom. I reach for his belt to free his hot erection, but he pushes my hands away before kneeling in front of me, giving me a devilish grin. He opens my legs and places them over his shoulder as he breathes in my scent. *Damn.*

"I'm going to tongue fuck you until you cum all over my face, baby" He whispers and very lightly traces his tongue down my center, hooking his fingers into my slick seam. The look in his eyes is so intense, I can't look away, and gasp when he pushes his fingers inside me. He draws a deep sigh when he pulls out, and then I moan when he thrusts into me again. I rock my hips forward for him to go deeper, but he withdraws, slight disappointment comes over me until I see him licking my juices from his fingers.

"Fuck, yes," I say with a laugh when he pushes his fingers deep into my center again, the sound of my wetness almost as loud as my moan. Alex finds the spot that makes me come unglued every time. My breath stops when he opens his hands, my juices pooling in his palm, and he sips it up. My hands fist in the sheets as he grazes my clit with his teeth before licking it with his tongue. And then he licks his way back to my tunnel, withdraws his fingers, and thrusts his tongue deep inside, making me cry out with pleasure. And just when I think that I am about to fall over the edge, he places his thumb on my clit and slowly, ever so lightly, circles it, teasing me in a way that has me sobbing his name as I prepare for an intense explosion.

And just when I feel my muscles tighten, he withdraws, and I am immediately filled with his hard erection stretching me with pleasure that only Alex can give me. "Fuck" he moans. "You feel so fucking good." His compliment comforting and I melt when I feel his seed released inside me.

"Kerri, my beautiful butterfly," he murmurs against my lips, and I suck them, still tasting my essence on his tongue. He kisses me. "Let me remember you like this, please? Just something to carry me through the long days away from you?"

I lick my lips as I consider what he's asking. I know I can trust him to keep this to himself, but I'm still hesitant. "Alex, I don't know…"

"I'll take care of it, and no one has access to my phone. I promise you that."

"Okay," I agree after a moment. "Only you."

"Only me," he says as he smiles. He takes his phone out of his back pocket, and I lean back on my arms, arching my back and thrusting my breasts at him, my feet braced on the edge of the mattress, my legs splayed to give him a good angle of the parts he loves so much. He snaps a couple of photos, and I can see that he is hard again, but an alert comes through on his phone, and he sighs as he reads the message. "I need to get back to the office. I'll call you later?"

"Sure." I am still lying in the same position when the door closes behind him, the touch of his rushed kiss still stinging my lips.

Chapter Twenty-Four

For the next month, I hold my breath for the next thing to happen, but as each day passes, I relax and find myself enjoying the little things again. Between Maggie and Alex, my evenings and weekends become jam-packed.

Maggie was even able to salvage my birthday celebration with a surprise visit from Elise, and the four of us spent the entire weekend in my loft, doing tipsy karaoke while sampling different types of Jell-O shots. When they asked me about my 'mystery man,' I told them about my dates with Alex, but I didn't mention his name. I know that I need to tell them the truth and now that I've kept this secret for so long it just makes it harder and harder to come clean. The timing just doesn't feel right to me. I didn't want to spoil our moments together, especially as it was the first time in months that I'd seen my best friend. I guess I hesitate to tell them because I know they will want me to walk away from him when I selfishly want to continue seeing him, despite his…situation.

As I finish up my latest design on my computer, I look up and see someone walking toward me with a small, rectangular box in their hand. I hold my breath as I watch a delivery man make his way to my desk, and I can feel my hands start to sweat. My heart's rhythm is slowing down so much that I cannot breathe. The office becomes quiet, as everyone is aware of what happened at Halloween and is on extra alert. I watch in slow motion as the man hands me the iPad. I wipe my hands down my skinny-legged jeans and clench them to stop their shaking as I sign for the package with stiff fingers. I reach for the white envelope taped to the box and pull out a card.

> I don't mean to be that guy, but I miss surprising you and this would be the perfect place to escape for the weekend.
>
> -Alex.

I sag against my chair, my body weak with relief as I read Alex's note again. The buzz in the office goes back to its normal volume when they realize that everything is fine. I reach for the pretty white box with the silver butterflies embossed on the surface. Holding my breath, I lift the lid and see two tickets to Usher's concert in Vegas. Oh my god! An overwhelming sense of excitement consumes me because I've been wanting to go see him ever since he announced his residency there. I cannot believe he got these! My stomach flutters at the thought of being away from everything and just spending quality time with Alex. We've never really gone anywhere outside of the city, and I think it would be a nice change of scenery. With my anxiety rising from the crazy things that's been happening this will take my mind off it, at least for a while.

"Kerri!" Maggie calls me from the door of the conference room, and I nod at her to show I'm on my way before sending a smiley emoji to Alex and rushing off to the meeting.

~~~

He picks me up on Friday afternoon and we head to JFK International Airport to catch our flight. Since Vegas is all the way across, on the other side of the country, we stop at their snack store near our terminal to load up on delicious and totally fattening snacks. We have six hours of flight time to get through. I hadn't noticed that Alex bought us first-class seats until the lady scanned our tickets at the gate. I have never flown first class before. I could never afford it. In fact, I haven't really flown too many places at all, just Chicago, New York, and once to see an aunt in Oklahoma.

The flight attendant comes around asking everyone in our cabin if we'd like anything to drink, which is odd because usually, they don't ask that until halfway through
~~~

the flight, pushing a huge cart down the aisle. I think Alex notices I'm taken aback by the question and decides to answer it for me.

"Old Fashion with Makers for me. My girlfriend will have a strawberry mojito."

Girlfriend? That's new. I must admit, I do like the sound of it. Alex has never referred to me as his girlfriend before. I know it may be a small thing to some, but it just makes me feel like all this is real. Like he feels exactly how I feel.

We chug our first cocktail before the flight takes off and Alex squeezes my hand tightly as the plane soars through the air. I form a small grin on my face as I think about our helicopter ride and how he was just as nervous. Only this time he is not trying to hide his fear and is seeking comfort by squeezing my hand. Once we level off the rest of the ride is smooth. Alex and I order two more rounds of cocktails before enjoying the dinner they provided. We land in Las Vegas around midnight and after grabbing our bags from baggage claim, catching a ride share to our hotel, and finally checking in we were both pretty exhausted and decided to crash.

I'm startled out of my sleep around 9 am by Alex's phone alarm blasting at what seems to be the loudest decimal. He doesn't move a muscle, just moans placing the pillow over his head. Slightly frustrated, I decide to bite the bullet and get out of my super comfortable position to turn it off. When I reach to grab his phone, I notice 3 missed calls and 2 text messages from Nicole. Undeniable it's from Nicole because the name he has her saved as is "The Wife." I instantly get annoyed, a reminder that my life has low-key become a soap opera and I'm not quite sure how I got here.

"Hey," I nudge Alex to wake up.

"Mmm," he moans back to me.

"Alex. Wake up." I nudge him again and place the phone in front of his face. "It's The Wife"

Alex pulls the pillow from his face and looks at me confused. His eyes veer down to my hand holding the phone and he rubs his eyes to clear sleep from them. He grabs the phone, unlocks it, and spends a few seconds reading the messages she wrote.

"Well…" Curiosity eating me alive.

"It's nothing. She is just asking where I am." He places his phone back on the nightstand.

It never occurred to me to ask what he told her. Now that I think about it, I'm sure he didn't tell her the truth. So, what did he say? I grimace at the thought of Alex needing to lie to come on this trip with me. The whole thing feels wrong.

"And what did you say?" I swallow nervously.

"I told her I'm here for a work conference all weekend. She won't ask any more questions. Don't worry about it, Kerri." Alex pulls the white linen comforter off his legs and heads to the restroom.

Don't worry about it. That's practically impossible. This just stirs more questions for me. Like what has he been saying all the other times he's managed to hang with me? He's working late? I exhale one big sigh at the cliché of this entire situation. The reality is sinking in deeper that I am his other woman. And now I can't even be mad at anyone but myself because I am fully aware of it. I know he's married and yet here I am, in Vegas, in bed with him. What the fuck is wrong with me? I sulk for another ten minutes before Alex suggests we get dressed and have brunch on the strip.

As the day progresses, we cruise up and down the Vegas strip eating, shopping, and meeting so many people I've lost count. Alex even takes me to a few major casinos to play on the blackjack table and slot machines. I don't know what I am doing but Alex is so freaking good at it. I think after his Rain Man moment he manage to walk away with $7,000 in winnings, which Alex balled up in a wad and placed in my purse for me to keep like I'm the girlfriend of El Chapo or something. Holy crap! I really could use this money because I get paid out commissions through completed projects and I haven't been able to close one in the last few weeks. Things have been really tight. Shout out to my new sugar daddy.

"Butterfly, come here," Alex yells across the casino floor waving his hand towards him.

He points at a huge banner displayed near the entrance to another section of the casino. As I walk up, I notice it's the details for Usher's concert tonight. There is a VIP all-access option, and he was purchasing the add-ons for our passes. My eyes grow big full of excitement when he tells me we are sitting in the front row and will get a 5-minute meet and greet backstage after the concert.

"Alex, stop. Are you serious?" I squeal jumping up and down, wrapping my arms around his neck and squeezing tightly.

A deep rumble comes from him as he bursts into laughter. "OK…OK…relax butterfly. I'll do anything for you. You know that."

I smile and give a slight smirk. I couldn't help but think his statement wasn't 100% accurate. I do know he'd do a lot for me this proves it. But I can't help but think the one thing I really want he is unwilling to give to me. I shake the thoughts out of my head not wanting to risk changing the mood and give Alex a huge kiss on the lips showing my appreciation.

~~~

As I apply the finishing touches of my make-up at the bathroom sink, I notice the time is now nine-thirty and I still need thirty more minutes before I'll be ready to head
~~~

to the concert. Having naturally curly hair is time-consuming and requires so much attention. I usually have to start super early on it. Alex, however, is just now getting out of the shower and will probably beat me getting ready. Men have it so easy.

"Now that I'm clean…wanna get me dirty again?" Alex murmurs in my ear as he steps behind me, wrapping his arms around my waist. Fuck. There goes a perfectly good pair of panties. I feel my juices flowing as I feel his breath tickling the back of my neck. My breaths go shallow.

"Yes, please." I mouthed as I turn around needing to feel his lips on mine. He grabs hold of my hips and grinds his erection on me. His tongue delves deeply as his fingers pull my skirt up to my waist and push down my panties and sheer tights. I shimmy out of them, teasing him as I sway my hips side to side against his hardness. I lift my right leg and place my foot on top of the bathroom sink, exposing everything for him to see.

"Mmm. You waxed." He bends down and softly begins kissing my inner thighs leading up to where I needed him to kiss most. I squirm on the counter and hiss as his sucks and licks inch closer and closer to my middle. And with one gentle and slow movement, he slides his tongue from my slit up to my crown.

"Yes...yes...yes…" I hiss softly, taking in every supple kiss leading me to euphoria.

Both Alex and I freeze in motion when we hear three loud knocks at the door. Slowly coming down from my euphoric high, I quickly put my leg down, pull my panties to an upright position, and adjust my skirt.

"Did you order room service?" I ask confused remembering how late it was.

"No. I didn't." Alex wraps his towel around his waist and walks to the door peeking through the hole to see who it is. He pulls back, rests his forehead on the door for a split second, and peeks through the hole again.

"Damnit!" Alex whispers.

"What's wrong? Who is it, Alex?"

A serious look washes over his face "It's Nicole."

For a second, I must've zoned out because I see Alex's lips moving as if he is telling me something, but I cannot hear anything. His body is moving in slow motion as panic rises from within. Fuck. She's here? Why?... How? I'm looking at Alex and see him approaching me.

"Kerri!" He grabs my shoulders and shakes me. The jolt snaps me back into reality and I furrow my eyebrows.

"What is she…" I stumble finding my words.

"I have to answer the door, Kerri, or she will never go away. But you cannot be here when I do."

"So, what the hell do you expect me to do, Alex? I can't just jump off the 42nd-floor window."

He sighs. "I know butterfly. I'm so sorry to ask you this but I need you to hide. Please, Kerri."

"Are you kidding me? I am not hiding, Alex."

"Baby. Listen to me. I am being honest with you about everything. I promised you I would never hurt you like that again by lying. But I told her I was at a work conference to keep the peace. If she knew I was with you she would cause a big scene. I promise you I'm working on a way for us to be together out in the open. But we aren't there yet. I need you to trust me. Ok, baby? Please." He points at the wardrobe closet that holds our luxurious robes and iron. "Go there. It won't take long. I'll get her to leave. I promise."

Against my better judgment, I comply with his request, step inside the wardrobe, and close the door. I feel the softness of the terrycloth robe brushing against my arm as I'm standing inside the small wardrobe closet. Luckily, I am still able to see the entire room completely due to the 1-inch faux wood blind inserts that are built in. The blinds face slightly downward so I can see out, but no one can see in. I watch as Alex scans the room, tidying up and hiding any evidence of me before opening the door.

"Honey! Finally. I was just about to go back downstairs and convince the front desk to get me a key." I hear

Nicole's voice as she enters, immediately smelling her expensive perfume permeate the room. Baccarat Rouge 540. I can recognize that perfume anywhere.

"What are you doing here?"

Nicole walks further into the room, and I get a full view of her. She's tall. Possibly 5'9" in height and undeniably very beautiful. Her light caramel skin is smooth like a porcelain doll. She's thinner than I remember, wearing dark, denim jeans and a pink blouse with black high-heeled boots. Her long, honey-blonde hair has soft curls shaping her face.

"Is that any way to greet your wife?" I watch as she studies the room, looking at the bed and his suitcase on the floor.

"I wasn't expecting you, that's all." He sighs and puts his hands on his hips.

"I thought I'd surprise you and come hang out while you're on your work trip. Remember… like old times." She walks towards him and runs her hands down his arms stopping when she reaches his hands and grips them tightly.

"You really should have called first, Nicole." Alex hitches, repositioning his stance and releasing the grip of her hands.

"Well, I did sweetie. And you never answered my calls. So, what's a girl to do? You left me no choice but to come. If it's the only way I can speak to you." She reaches for his hands again.

"This isn't a good time for you to be here. I'm very busy." Alex walks past her avoiding her grip.

"So what? I know how to occupy my time when you're working. But you're not right now. Now seems like the perfect time for me to be with you." Nicole walks to Alex and yanks the towel from his waist, exposing his full birthday suit.

I swallow the bile that's rising in my throat suddenly feeling nauseous. She is trying to be with him. She is trying to connect with him. Like any normal, loving wife would do, not like a wife who is living separately from her husband. I think I'm actually going to be sick. I'm suddenly aware of how small the wardrobe closet is. Even one slightest movement from me and this iron and ironing board will come tumbling down. And maybe it should. Maybe I should intentionally move to blow this whole thing up, exposing all the secrets Alex has been keeping.

"Nicole, please stop. I've got a big day tomorrow and really need to get some rest." He bends down to reach for his towel.

"Baby, c'mon. It's been so long. I miss you inside me. I need to feel you again." Nicole blocks him from getting the towel with her foot and lifts him back upright. I watch as her hands begin stroking his cock.

"Nicole, stop. I'm not in the mood." Alex spats.

"That's why I'm doing this baby. Just relax. I'm going to make you feel good." Nicole continues stroking him increasing her speed and gazes into his eyes.

Alex presses his lips together and I see the muscles in his jawline pulsing. I can tell his frustration is rising. "No! Nicole. Stop it. Now."

Nicole suddenly stops and releases a loud sigh of frustration.

"Ok, fine Alex. If this is how you want to play it." Nicole takes a step back and immediately starts screaming at the top of her lungs.

"Help! No, stop! Please don't hit me. Stop it!"

"What do you think you're doing?" Alex yells and rushes to Nicole, placing his hand over her mouth.

I manage to hear a laugh escape her mouth from behind his hands. When she stops yelling, he releases her.

"Fuck me right now, Alex, or I will say you hit me."

Holy crap! She cannot be serious. I can hardly believe my eyes and what I just witnessed. How could she just lie like that? A profound ache creeps inside of me for Alex and I feel bad for not believing him. I know he lied to me. And that lie almost tore my heart into two but watching her manipulate and threaten him like this makes me feel sorry for him.

"Well, what's it going to be?" Nicole continues.

There's a long pause and Alex doesn't say a word. Nicole walks over to him, places her lips on his, and begins kissing him. I watch as Alex stands there motionless. His eyes are staring straight at me. He's not kissing her back or touching her, just looking directly at me. She begins rubbing on him again, but this time twisting her grip when she slides to his tip. I avert my gaze feeling uneasy about watching him get a hand job from his wife. But I quickly look back at them when I hear a familiar sound.

"Mmmm" Alex moans. Nicole is now on her knees giving him a blow job. Oh…My… God! This cannot be happening. Alex is still looking directly at me. He hasn't moved his stare, which makes me think it's intentional. What the fuck? Is he seriously looking at me while his wife sucks him up? I frown in disbelief but quickly open my eyes wide as I notice Alex take his right hand and place it behind his wife's head guiding her.

"Yea. Like that." He says biting his bottom lip.

Alex now has both hands placed on the back of her head swaying his body towards her, forcing his erection deeper into the back of her throat. I hear choking sounds coming from Nicole and my heart begins pounding so hard the thuds echo in my ears. Please make this end. Please make this end. I chant over and over in my head wishing for me to be anywhere else than here watching the man I love get off from another woman's mouth.

Thinking my prayers have been answered, Alex pulls her off him and stands her up. Relieved I close my eyes and let out a loud exhale.

"Turn over," Alex commands.

My eyes open back. No freaking way is he going to fuck her while I'm watching. All the air escapes my lungs and I suddenly find myself realizing just how tight this space is. I've never been claustrophobic before and now is definitely not the time to become it but if I have to watch any more of this I will literally die. As much as I try to look away, I cannot help but watch. Alex has not stopped looking in my direction. I know he wants me to watch him. It's why he is staring at me, enticing me to watch him fuck his wife. How twisted is that?

"Ok baby," Nicole whispers and turns around bending over on the bed.

Alex yanks her pants down dropping them to her ankles and rips her panties off at the seams. Nicole whimpers anticipating Alex's entry. He pushes her head into the bed muffling her sound and places his cock at the entrance of her. With great force, he slams inside of her, and a loud whale comes from Nicole. Alex turns his gaze back at me and continues giving long, hard, strokes to her. One after another. Bam. Bam. Bam. And Nicole whimpers and whales each time he does it. Alex's muscles are contracted showing every definition under the dim lighting. I run my eyes down his body, gazing at the same way it flexes and contracts when he strokes me. And I can't understand why but my nipples get harder the longer I continue to watch. All the anger I felt inside is now turning into sexual frustration. It's like my body knows his body is near and is yearning for him.

"Slow…down" Nicole says releasing each word in unison with each thrust.

"No. You want it. This is how you're getting it." Alex slams into Nicole three more times and pulls out just before exploding, letting all his juices flow into his hand. Nicole's body goes limp and deflates onto the bed.

The air around me feels thin and my lungs throb from the lack of breath I haven't taken. Did he enjoy it? I honestly couldn't tell. He came so hard, so he must have. My body is yearning for that same explosion inside of me, but I grimace at the thought of being totally aroused and disgusted at the same time. I don't understand it. I hate that he can affect me like this. Fire burns inside of me. How could he do this to me? How could he allow it? A part of me understands she twisted his arm but surely, he can control the situation better than just succumbing to her demands. The man I know is not fearful. The man I know commands attention and respect. Alex steps back from the bed and walks over to the wardrobe, placing his hand on the door to support his stance. Standing right in front of me, only a wooden door separating our bodies, I look into his grayish-brown eyes searching for answers, watching his chest rise and fall in heavy breaths.

"You've got what you've wanted, Nicole. Now leave."

Chapter Twenty-Five

Monday morning rolls around quickly but my mind is racing even faster thinking about the events of this past weekend. I hadn't spoken to Alex since we arrived back at JFK International Airport. I took a ride-share home instead of allowing him to drive me in his Audi. I just needed some space to clear my head and having him near me just made things worse. I think pure shock has been my feeling for the most part, perhaps a little bit of disbelief. After he kicked Nicole out of the hotel. I burst from the closet, falling to my knees grasping for every ounce of air my lungs would take in. I shake my head, freeing myself from my own thoughts, and pick up my stylus pen to finish this final sketch.

My phone starts beeping several alerts, and I freeze at the sight of the Unknown Number flashing across my phone. I open the message to see a picture of Alex and I kissing in the lobby of the Casino in Vegas. Another of us holding hands walking down the strip. The last image is of us groping each other underneath the table at the Peppermill Restaurant.

As I close out from the third picture sent to me, I notice multiple chimes and dings reverberate around the office. Everyone begins looking at their computers to check their email notifications and a small rumble begins. As more minutes pass, a few people whisper to one another, and I begin to receive odd stares and looks. Confused, I grab my keyboard to log onto my desktop to see what is going on and my phone begins ringing. This time the Unknown Number is calling me.

"Kerri!" Maggie yells my name and I see her running down the hallway in her Louboutins, which is really odd because I've never seen her move this quickly in them before. As she reaches my desk, we both look down at my phone as it is still ringing. "Don't answer it" she commands but I swallow my fear and swipe right to answer the call.

"I thought I warned you about fucking my husband, but it seems the last message wasn't strong enough. Stay away from him, or I will kill you." There was no denying the voice on the other side of this phone. And in this moment, everything came crashing down into reality.

"Kerri…" Maggie whispers as she wraps her arms around me. "Come on, let's get you some tea."

I nod absently, unable to believe that it's been Nicole this entire time. And her voice…she sounded…furious. The anger and betrayal I can understand, but to threaten my life? A shiver runs down my spine thinking of the intensity in her voice. I remember Alex saying that she would do anything to maintain the image of perfection, but would that include *murdering* someone? Murdering… *me?* An immense amount of guilt floods me. All of my selfish choices have caused real pain and I've been so stupid thinking things could actually work out with us.

I'm not sure if Maggie heard Nicole's words, but her face is pale and her eyes wide with panic and concern. Her natural exuberance is subdued as she takes my hand and leads me to my desk. Then I realize that Maggie had met me at the elevator as if she was looking for me and had tried to stop me from answering the call… Who did Maggie think the caller was going to be? And why did she have that panicked look on her face when she met me at the elevator?

I break out in a cold sweat as another shiver races down my spine. My knees are starting to shake as I make my way to my desk, and I am glad that I have Maggie supporting me. I am vaguely aware of tension filling the office space. It's only when all sound goes quiet that I realize everyone is looking at me. Some of my colleagues are staring at me in shock, some in embarrassment, and one of them turns away from me in contempt. I swallow the knot of apprehension, and I sink into my chair because my legs can't support my weight.

My hands are shaking so badly that it takes me a couple of attempts to reactivate my screen and log in to my email account. I stare wide-eyed at the unknown email address at the top of my inbox. My cursor hovers over the item, and I *know* I shouldn't open it, but I need to see what is being said about me that has my colleagues in such a state. I *know* this email is going to tear my life apart. And with a resolute click, I open the email.

"What... the... fuck..." I gasp as I stare at the pictures—*my* pictures! All of them exposed me to the people I have worked so hard to accept me, to respect me. And everything is shattered with the click of a mouse. I am horrified as I stare at my screen. Somewhere, deep inside, I hear a little voice telling me that I am about to lose the job I love so much.

The photos that were taken in the privacy of my bedroom have me posing on the table in our conference room, a man kneeling between my legs, my eyes half-closed in pleasure. Another photo has me on my desk, pleasuring myself. I am hyperventilating as I stare at my screen. Fear, anger, humiliation, and shame all fill me, and I can barely lift my head. I am frozen and can barely move to close the images.

My head is heavy as I drop it into my hands, tears flowing freely over my cheeks. I am too despondent to wipe them away. Maggie's sweet perfume makes me gag as she folds me into her arms after hurriedly placing a cup on my desk.

"Kerri, I'm so sorry." I glance up at her. "It seems everyone received the same email. The people in the IT department are already trying to get it removed."

I don't respond. Instead, I pick up my purse and get to my feet. "I need to go home… I, um… I'm not feeling well."

"Yes, of course." She watches me with a concerned frown. "Kerri, it will be okay."

I shake my head as I look at her, a sob wracking my body from deep within me, and I put a hand to my mouth to stop it from escaping. "No, Maggie. This is not going to be okay."

I stumble blindly to the elevator and push the button impatiently as the car takes its sweet time to reach our floor. The doors open soundlessly, and I come out on the street as the reflection of the sun on the glass doors hurt my tear-sensitive eyes. I start walking in the direction of my loft, but the faces of the people I pass are looking at me in judgment, each of them sneering at me and my naïveté. I shake the tears from my eyes, and my pace quickens. I round a corner and bump into a big man in a white suit.

"Watch where you're going!" he growls.

I gasp, and the first sob breaks free. I'm too upset to apologize as I start running. It feels as though my building is miles away, but I can see it the next block over. People are now shouting at me as I knock into them while trying to get to the haven of my home as fast as I can. I need to get away from the accusations that everyone is shouting at me. Logically, I know that these strangers don't know what Nicole has done, but I am too blinded by my emotions to acknowledge the logic.

The door slams behind me, and I race up the stairs to my floor, shaking my keys out of my purse and hurriedly opening my front door. As soon as it closes behind me, I sink to the floor, my purse dropping open and spilling its contents. I don't try to stop the sobs that are now tearing through my body. My phone rings, and I reach for it, not hiding my anguish when I click accept when I see Alex's name, anger mixing with the other emotions swirling in my head.

"Hey, butterfly—"

"What the fuck, Alex?!" I gasp through the sobs. "You promised me! You said no one else had access to your phone! How could you do this to me?!"

"Wait! Kerri?" I can hear the shock in his voice at my attack, but I can't shake the feeling of betrayal. "What are you talking about?"

"What do you mean *what am I talking about*?!" I can't seem to stop shouting at him, taking my anger out on him because there is no way I can direct it to the person responsible. "Ask your crazy fucking wife what I'm talking about!"

"Kerri…about Vegas. I've been meaning to call so we can talk about what happened."

"No! Not Vegas." I hiss in anger. "But now it all makes sense why she just popped up. I should have known it was Nicole all along." I begin rambling under my breath as I pace the floor back and forth.

Wait. What are you talking about? What do you mean all along?" His voice is raspy with the shock of my accusations.

"She fucked up my career! Sending me crazy texts of *us*! In Vegas! She called me, Alex." My sobs subside into crying, taking some of the edge off my emotions. "She called me and told me that she was going to kill me. Actually… kill me, Alex…"

"Kerri, please, I'm coming over." His voice softens.

"No, Alex, please don't…" I know that it isn't a good idea for him to be with me, instinctively knowing that it will make things even worse if he comes over.

"Kerri, you shouldn't be alone," he protests.

"No, Alex. Just stay away from me, please." I need to call the police, but it'd be bad to get him involved. It would hurt his reputation and especially his chances of becoming a judge if this should ever become public. And besides Alex, going to the police means that my life will be open to scrutiny and judgment, but it will mean involving my parents, their concerns brought to life in the most dramatic way possible. What would my friends say, considering that I wasn't supposed to be seeing him after the event in the Hamptons? That I had been lying to them about the person I am dating for nearly a month?

"Kerri, what did you mean about the access? Access to what?" he asks softly as if he already knows what I am going to tell him.

"Our photos, Alex. She posted *our* photos to my entire office, as though they were taken in our conference room." The humiliation rolls over me again, the condemning looks of my colleagues filling my mind as the images from the email play like an old movie on a reel. I close my eyes, but they burst open again at the sight of the condemning eyes of the strangers I had knocked into on my way home. I bite down hard on my lip to stop the sob threatening to break me again.

"Shit, Kerri," he groans. I drop my phone on the floor after I hang up on him, then wrap my arms around my knees, lean my head against the door, and cry.

Chapter Twenty-Six

My knees, thighs, and butt scream in protest when I eventually kick off my shoes and push myself upright with the help of my front door. Leaving everything where I dropped them, I walk into the bathroom and run a hot bath overflowing with bubbles. I sink into the soothing cocoon and lay my head back as I close my eyes. My head is pounding, my eyes feel scratchy, and my throat is raw from all the crying. I stay there until the water turns cold and my skin is shriveled and wrinkled. Slipping into my favorite flannel pajamas, I crawl into my bed and wish the world would disappear. I wish that when I wake up, I will be back to the time before all this hell started.

I'm not sure how much time has passed, but I do know that I hadn't fallen asleep. I'm not totally conscious either, though, my thoughts and emotions seem to be fusing together. Everything that has been happening over the last few weeks blurs in my mind until I can't remember what came first. I keep seeing Nicole as she was at their anniversary celebrations, clinging to Alex while she looks at me and repeats her threat over and over. It's worse when I close my eyes, so I keep them open, too afraid of actually sleeping.

My stomach rumbles, and I peer out of my comforter, hoping that it is mistaken. But then I realize that the sun is hanging low, and my room is covered in a dusky shadow that makes it seem gloomy. To escape it, I make my way to the kitchen and put on some water for tea.

My phone beeps an alert, and I glare at it, not wanting to interact with anyone, but I also need to see if they can sort things out at work. I drop my head onto the counter and groan aloud when I think about facing my colleagues again. I need to start looking for other work. Maybe I should start thinking about going back to Chicago. The kettle whistles, and I lift my head, reluctantly getting to my feet and making my tea.

With my cup in my hand, I pick up my phone and curl into the corner of the sofa, pulling the blanket over my legs before I look at the item that had become the menace of my existence. I ignore the messages and check my missed calls. Three from Maggie. With a deep breath to brace myself for the next thing, I call her back.

"Kerri, hey," she greets me, her voice breathy with

relief. "How are you doing?"

"I've been better, obviously" I sass, but then bite my lip in regret immediately. Maggie doesn't deserve to be the brunt of my bad mood. "I'm sorry, I just needed to tune out for a while."

She's quiet for a few seconds. "I can understand that." Her voice apprehensive as if she has something else, she wants to say.

"Look, Maggie, I'm so sorry about the whole mess at work. I don't normally have my personal life interfere with my work life and this… This is just…."

"Hey, I know. Anyway, you know me, always looking at the bright side of things."

"Yeah? What could possibly be bright at this moment?" I barely contain the sarcasm.

"Well, two things, actually." I can hear the smile in Maggie's voice, and that makes me give a reluctant smile. "One, not everyone opened their email yet, so IT was able to scrub it from their systems unopened. And IT was able to fix it… ninety percent of it, at least."

"Oh, great, so not everyone is judging me at the office."

Maggie laughs. "No one is judging you, Kerri. Shit happens to everyone."

"Sure, it does, but it doesn't get emailed to everyone at the office." I look down at my phone when an alert comes through, and then gasp when I see from whom the email is.

"Kerri, what's wrong?" Maggie asks.

"I'm not sure. Give me a moment." I open the email and start reading it aloud to Maggie.

Dear Miss Townsend.

Please know that we regret the event that occurred this morning, but due to the nature of the photos seeming to take place in the workplace, an investigation is required. For this process to take place, you will be on leave pending the outcome of the investigation. Please know that this is done in your best interest. We will send you further correspondence when the investigation is concluded.

Yours sincerely,

Tanya Houghton, HR Manager.

Placing the phone back to my ear. "HR just emailed me. Did you know about this?"

"It's just procedure, Kerri. We know that you wouldn't do anything like that, but we need to get it on record." I don't realize that she hears me sniffing away the tears. "Oh, fuck this! Demi and I were going to have dinner, but we're going to bring dinner to you. You shouldn't be alone."

She hangs up before I say anything. And I am honestly relieved, because I am going crazy with the things that happened this morning. I must have fallen asleep after our conversation, because I wake up to the smell of fried shrimp dumplings, Chicken Chow Mein, and other titbits that make my mouth water. Maggie is kneeling on the floor beside me, gently stroking my hair out of my face, her eyes wide with worry.

"Our poor KB," she croons softly. She helps me to sit up, and Demi hands me a box of warm comfort food before sitting beside me. "The office was so quiet after you left today. Everyone is so worried about you."

"Sure," I drawl as I push my chopsticks through my noodles. My appetite disappears, and I can feel the misery forming a cloud over my head.

"Hey." Demi takes my hand and squeezes it. "We're going to find out what psycho-is messing with you, and we're going to cut off their *cazingas*."

I have to laugh as she uses Elise's favorite words. I'm sure that Nicole wouldn't stand a chance between Demi and Maggie. The smile dies from my lips as Nicole's voice reverberates through my mind. I am still trying to marry the images I saw of her in the hotel room with the voice and words of the phone call, never mind the emails, texts, and creepy photos.

I can feel Maggie's eyes piercing my face. "You know

who it is!" Maggie accuses, and I can feel the guilt turning my cheeks pink. I don't have a choice but to nod my admission. "Who the hell is it, Kerri?"

"Nicole." I mumble under my breath.

"Who?" Maggie snaps back.

"Alex's wife," I mumble around a large mouthful of food.

"Say what?" Maggie demands. She narrows her eyes and purses her lips as she waits for me to finish chewing and grabs my chopsticks before I can fill my mouth again.

I sigh deeply. "It's Alex's wife."

They gape at me, neither saying a word as they absorb the information. "I thought you broke up with him."

I can see the confusion on both their faces, as well as the hint of accusation in Demi's voice, and I bite my lip as I realize that I will have to tell them everything. "I did break up with him after what happened in the Hamptons. For a month."

"Kerri!" Maggie cries and buries her face into her palms.

"I feel good when I'm with him, Maggie. He makes me feel things no one else has ever made me feel, and for the first time since I lost my sister, I feel alive." I try to defend that relationship, but every word I speak sounds flat and doesn't justify my decision.

"Kerri, in theory…that's truly amazing, but you must realize that you can get hurt, and not just emotionally." Demi nods her head in agreement as Maggie wipes a tear from my cheeks.

"I'm so torn, guys. I'm not sure how I'm supposed to handle this." I start talking, unable to stop the thoughts that fill my mind. "I don't know what to do at this point. I can't just let him go. I've tried! How do I step back and let it all go? What we have feels real to me! And then, should I call the police? This could really affect him, and he promised me she wouldn't actually carry out her threats. But after today…" I sigh then take a deep breath. "I don't know if I believe that anymore."

"First," Demi says as she holds a finger up. "You need to go to the police. Second, you need to fight *for yourself*, not for Alex or a relationship that's hurting you, but for your well-being. Third, you *need* to walk away from him until he has sorted out his shit, Kerri. That bitch is crazy!"

"Kerri…" For the first time, I see the shadows in Maggie's eyes as she takes my hands. "I understand being in the position of having a partner who is committed and being offered something you don't find anywhere else. And I get the question of whether or not you should take the plunge. But, Kerri, I am pleading with you to walk away. I don't want anything to happen to you."

"I can't go to the police, guys. It might set her off to become totally unhinged, but it will also affect Alex, and I can't put him in that position." I hold up my hand as I see Demi getting worked up. "And going to the police is going to make it a public spectacle that will reach my parents. And as it is, I'm trying my damnedest to convince them that I am doing okay."

"Well, unfortunately for you, I will need to inform the police, especially after the vandalism incident. And the fact that she hacked company computers." Maggie rubs my arm as she tries to comfort me while letting me know that her job is at risk as well.

"And she was obviously on the premises to take the photos," Demi adds.

"And that." She shrugs sadly. "But the major factor is you, Kerri. You are the one that this is directed at."

I sit back against the cushions, wrapping my arms around my knees, trying to hold the tears inside. But when Maggie sits back and pulls me down so that my head is in her lap and Demi curls up behind me, the tears accept this as a license to fall freely. A brief surge of anger fills me with sobs, but when Maggie strokes my hair out of my face, I give in to them, wondering when the relief will come. I cry for what Alex and I could have been, but also for every beautiful memory that Nicole has tainted.

"We're so sorry, Kerribel."

Chapter Twenty-Seven

"Kerri?"

I wake up with my legs curled up under me, my head pounding, my muscles screaming, and my eyes raw from crying. I am still on the couch, the comforter from my bed tucked around me and a pillow under my head. The loft is tidy; all the take-out boxes are thrown away, the kitchen is clean, and even my purse is put on the armchair now once again holding everything that had been lying all over the floor.

The girls have shown me their love by doing these things that steal my heart. I moan and put a hand to my head as the pounding on the door reverberates through it. My throat is scratchy when I croak, "I'm coming."

"Kerri!" Alex… he can't hear my throaty response. I sit

up and something pokes my ass. I reach beneath me and find my phone; the battery having died in the night. I put it on the coffee table and stumble to the door. I open it just as he is about to knock again. "Kerri, thank God."

I allow him to pull me into his arms, savoring the warmth that he offers. His smell surrounds me and makes me feel so secure. But he is not supposed to be here, and I push away from him in anger. "What are you doing here?"

It irritates me that my voice is raspy as I turn on him. I fold my arms over my chest and make myself look at his face rather than at how tempting his body is. What irritates me more is that he is standing there, looking at me as if *I'm* crazy, and this makes me want to lash out.

"Where else would I be, Kerri?" I tilt my head as I look at him. "You need me, and you wouldn't let me be here."

"So, you just pop up here, anyway?" I raise my eyebrow at him, the sarcasm sharp in my tone.

"Yes." He narrows his eyes as he looks at me. "Kerri, what is going on? Why are you being like this?"

He tries to reach for me, but I pull away. I turn away from him to put water on for tea, but he follows me. I spin around and lift my hands in the air so that he can't touch me when I find him close behind me. "How can you ask me that?"

"Kerri, make me understand what made you so angry?"

I gape at him. Can he seriously not see what is happening?

"Let's recap, Alex. Your wife just might have gotten me fired."

"Come on, Kerri, that's not fair—"

"*Fair*?!" The rasp in my voice breaks into a squeak as I turn to him. *Is he fucking serious?* I clear my throat and hold up my hand, lifting a finger as I recount each event. "She has been tormenting me for months with emails and text messages. She has been digging into my past and is spreading twisted versions of the most tragic time of my life. She is following us whether it's you or me, she has photos of us and popped up in Vegas! She threatened to kill me if I didn't stop seeing you. And she sent… she sent an email… to my *colleagues*, Alex…Need I say more!"

My voice, and my defiance, cracks, and fades, and I wipe angrily at the tears that fall. Deflated, I fall against the counter and stare at him with fear in my eyes.

"Kerri, I don't know what to say. I never thought any of this would happen. And I'm so terribly sorry it has. Nicole is not a bad person. If I could just figure out…" I feel my mouth drop as he defends her. "She is one of those insecure people who need constant validation. She is very possessive, but she won't hurt anyone."

"She hurt me! She emailed photos of me—photos *you*

promised me would be safe—to my colleagues! She vandalized my home!" I shake my head. "She vandalized my *office!*"

He closes his eyes as he leans on the counter before looking at me. "Kerri, Nicole will say many things in anger, but she would never act on it—"

"Alex, where was she in August? You were free to spend so much time with me. Where was she then?"

"She was supposed to be on a trip with her friends,'" he answers softly.

"Yet I got photos of the two of us walking in the park during that time." He closes his eyes and breathes loudly. "Alex, she has you so tightly bound to her, almost blinded to her insanity."

"I'm not blind to her, Kerri!" He slams his hand on the counter, making us both jump. He scrubs his hands over his face and blows out a rough breath. "I'm sorry."

"You are, Alex. You are so schooled, so manipulated, that you don't even realize that you're defending her." I can't believe he is one of the smartest people I know and yet he can't even recognize when he is being manipulated. It's beginning to really piss me off. My frustration is stirring. "Alex, we can't do this anymore."

"Kerri, please." He reaches across the counter for my hand, but I fold it against my waist. "Nicole has been a large part of my life, but I don't want to lose you or hurt you. I need you."

"I need to report her to the police, Alex. She has gone way too far."

"I think trying to get her committed is a better solution than calling the police, Kerri? I can call her psychiatrist and have him speak to her. Kerri, we don't have to be extreme—" I feel my jaw drop for a second time since he walked through my door. "Kerri, please! You're the best thing that has happened to me. Don't make any decisions while you are this emotional."

I go breathless as my heart expands, and I feel my bones start to melt. And then the rest of his words filter through the haze that had settled on my mind. "*I shouldn't make any decisions when I'm this emotional.* How did that work out when you said it to Nicole? Is what she did to me a calmed-down version of what she would have done before you spoke to her—"

"*Kerri!*" He explodes, making me jump at his tone. He paces to the window, and I watch his shoulders rise as he takes a few deep breaths. Then he turns back to me, and I feel the anger leave me at the lost look in his eyes. "I'm sorry. There's just so much more about her you don't understand. And I can't really explain it. I just don't know how to protect you."

"Alex," I whisper as I find myself in his arms, seeking

comfort from him as much as I comfort him. We stand like that for a long while, just holding each other. Then he tilts my chin up and kisses my forehead, the gesture so sweet and endearing that I smile. I am so angry at him but when I feel his lips on my forehead all my anger resolves. I realize I'm sad this has become my life. I desperately want Alex to stand up for me and stop her, but he tells me it's more complicated. I have no choice but to take his word for it. Despite everything, I want to trust him. I want to believe what he is telling me is the truth because I love him. And I believe he loves me. I reach up and cup his cheeks, absorbing the feel of his beard in the palms of my hands. I cling to the shape of his square jaw and sharp cheekbones, and I realize that this is possibly the last time I will have him this close.

I pull him closer and kiss him, brushing my lips against his—softly, gently, teasingly. I tickle the corner of his mouth with my tongue, and he opens with a groan. Slowly I insert the tip of my tongue between his lips before I withdraw. The next thrust, I brush against his tongue, enticing him to react, but he stands still. The only signs that he is affected are his hands grasping my hips tightly and his hardening erection against me. I place a soft kiss on his cheek, a light trail to his ear where I suck his earlobe softly, grazing it with my teeth. The muscle in his jaw jumps, and I can't help the smile as I kiss the column of his throat.

I unbutton his shirt and place a kiss on each bit of skin I expose, his heart beating beneath my lips. I pull it off his shoulders, capturing his hands behind his back in the cuffs. His sculpted stomach muscles are jumping slightly, and I lightly lick first one, then his other nipple before softly blowing on it. I watch the gooseflesh pop around the tiny buds with satisfaction. I glance up at him as I sink to my knees.

His lids are lowered as he watches me, his cheeks sunken and his nose flared as he tries to control himself. I lower my own lashes to hide the satisfaction glowing in my eyes as I trace his abs with the tip of my tongue, and they clench tightly beneath my teasing. Loosening his belt, I undo the clip and zipper of his pants and watch as they slide down his strong thighs. With a sense of mischievousness, I circle his belly button with my tongue and follow the spear of his hair until it disappears into his boxers. He is so hard, the tip is lifting the waistband, and I blow on it softly and smile as Alex sucks in a sharp breath, his cock twitching. His shoulders jerk as he struggles to free his hands from the shirt, but I pull away, leaning back on my hands, the action thrusting my breasts upward and pulling the gaping neckline of my flannel shirt open and exposing my cleavage to him.

"If you touch me, I will stop." The struggle is clear; the need to touch me is as great as for me to touch him. I see the muscle in his jaw jump fervently as he stops struggling, and I smile, feeling myself flush at the power I have at this moment. With slow movements, I pull his briefs down his legs and stare up at his impressive, long-hanging erection as it juts from his hips, so thick. The vein throbbing along its length has an echoing throb inside of me. I give in to the temptation and place a kiss where his shaft meets his balls, and he grunts softly, but I want more from him.

I lick the spot before grazing it gently with my teeth, and then I suck it hard and moan when he growls out my name as his hips jerk forward. A drop of his essence runs down to meet my lips, and I follow its path with my tongue to its source, wanting to taste more of his salty sweetness. Slowly encircling his girth with my hand, I lean forward and take his sensitive tip into my mouth, gently making love to it with my tongue before sucking it into my mouth as deep as it can go. Alex's hoarse cry has me tightening in anticipation, and I can feel that my panties are soaking wet. He thrusts forward, and I brace myself with a hand on his thigh as my other folds around his balls and clenches softly. I can taste more of his cum in my throat, and I feel disappointed when he steps back, pulling out of my mouth and sucking in deep breaths to gain some control over his body.

"You have too many clothes on, butterfly," he groans, and before I realize it, he is reaching for my shirt and pulling it open even as he tugs me to my feet. I gasp as I hear the buttons pinging off the hardwood floor. I was so engrossed in giving him pleasure that I didn't see him free himself from his shirt. He tosses my shirt on the floor, and his hands burn my skin as he unclips the hooks of my bra nestled between my heated breasts. He buries his face between them and groans as his hands slide along the ridges of my ribs, down my hips, and under the waistband of my panties, pushing them and my pants down in one move. "I never thought flannel could be sexy, but fuck, Kerri, I'll never see flannel the same way."

I laugh, the husky sound ending in a gasp as he lifts me to his waist, his engorged tip separating my wet folds to give him access to my throbbing pussy. I cry out as he drops me onto his length, the sudden invasion causing me to clench around him with pleasure. Cupping my ass, he walks to my bedroom, each step jostling me from side to side, the friction driving me crazy, and I grind on him, chasing my orgasm.

"Oh no you don't," he groans as he withdraws from me, placing me on the bed and crawling over me. "You're not the only one that can tease."

"Alex!" I wail as he places his hardness against my slit, our juices lubricating my folds and allowing him to thrust hard against me, the base of his shaft gloriously stimulating my clit. I run my nails down his spine, and a shudder shakes his body.

"Fuck," he growls, adjusting his hips, and he fills me once again, both of us gasping. I hook my knees high around his hips, taking him deeper into me. I hold onto his shoulders as he thrusts into me, and I inhale deeply, trying to hold onto his scent—the freshness of his cologne, the smell of his skin, and the smell that is exclusively Alex when he is deep inside me. Closing my eyes, I memorize the way his hardness feels as it fills me, the way the strong, throbbing vein massages my inner walls as it moves against them, the way his tip finds that spot deep inside as he thrusts in and out of me. Angling my hips upwards, my clit finds the base of his shaft, and the sensations are almost too much for me. And then I explode when he cups my butt and changes the angle so seamlessly.

His movements become frenzied, and I feel the fire reigniting even as he pounds into me, my breasts bouncing against his chest. The hair tantalizes my nipples and adds another line of fire that leads to another explosive orgasm, his hips furiously pumping his seed deep inside me.

He collapses on top of me, and I wrap my arms and legs tighter around him, placing soft kisses along his neck and shoulder, not wanting to break contact with him yet. His hands tighten momentarily on my hips, and he turns us so that we are lying on our sides, his fingers lazily stroking from my hip to my shoulder and back again. I savor this moment we share. I will miss it a great deal, but I survived without Alex Carter before, and I will have to do so again after this.

"Hey, why the tears?" he asks huskily, brushing them from my lashes. "Everything will be okay."

I fold my fingers around his hand and kiss the palm, trying to gather the courage to look at him—to do what I know needs to be done. I cup his face as I look at him, my heart breaking as the realization darkens his eyes. I swallow back the tears and take a deep breath, hardening my resolve.

"I'm sorry, Alex, but things will never be okay as long as she is in our lives." I place my fingers over his lips to stop his protests, knowing that I will never be able to follow through if he speaks. "You say you love me and don't want to hurt me, but your excuses for her *are* hurting me. I can't be with you anymore, not while she is a part of your life."

He clears his throat as he pulls my fingers away from his mouth. His voice is a raspy whisper when he asks, "What are you saying, Kerri?"

"You need to make a choice. You need to let her go if you want to be with me." I bite my lip to hold back the emotions I can feel clawing at my heart. "You need to go now, Alex. This is goodbye."

He shakes his head, but I nod, the tears burning a path down my cheeks. With a shaky hand, he wipes his own tears from his eyes, and then silently leaves my bed, immediately leaving a cold space I know won't be filled anytime soon. I hear him putting on his clothes in the living room and the door opening. I hold my breath as I sense his hesitation, his need to try to convince me otherwise. The sound of the door closing is the catalyst that releases the heartbreak within me. He's gone.

Chapter Twenty-Eight

"Kerri, Tanya Houghton from HR," the friendly voice says. I never thought two weeks could be such torture, and yet my nerves are stretched to their breaking point, and I hold my breath every time my phone rings as it did just now. The disappointment that fills me is so painful, it feels like I'm being cut by a thousand tiny knives.

"Hi, Tanya." I sip my tea as I watch the snow fall past my window. The weather has been dreary since Alex left, and the snow that has been threatening for the last few days eventually fell, and it is still falling.

"Kerri, I'm not sure how to say this." Her tone is compassionate, but I know the news is not good. "We're still working through the video footage, but as it's a week before Christmas, we're working with a skeleton staff, so things are going very slow at the moment. I'm so sorry about this."

"Surely it will be easy to show that I never did those things in the office?" My frustration gives my words a bit of a sting, and I hear Tanya draw a sharp breath. I close my eyes, breathing slowly to stay calm. "I'm sorry, Tanya. I'm just going out of my mind about this. I wouldn't do something so stupid to put my job in jeopardy, and to have someone intrude into my life like this…" I sigh.

"I can't imagine how that must feel, Kerri, but I can't speed things up from my side."

"From your side? So, you're saying there's something I can do?" I feel hope blossoming.

She is quiet for a heartbeat before she answers. "You could go to the police. They can subpoena the footage, and it could be reviewed much quicker. They'll be able to back your claims of innocence."

The hope dwindles into a tiny dark hole, her insinuation clear. But I still can't bring myself to hurt Alex by involving the police. I did some research, and Nicole's family is New York elite. Having her arrested will be a publicity shitshow, and it will include lawyers and court cases that will bankrupt me, never mind the public humiliation and judgment that it will bring into my life. And how it will affect Alex's future also makes me hesitate.

"What do you suggest I do?" I ask Tanya softly.

She sighs softly. "If that is not a route you want to take, I'd suggest you trust the process. Go visit your family for the holidays, come back in the New Year, and things could look so much clearer."

I nod slowly. "Thank you, Tanya. That sounds like a good idea."

"I'll let you know if anything comes up."

"Great." *Great.* My career, and ultimately my life, depends on a committee of people who doubt my innocence. *Wonderful.*

I check for flights to Chicago as I sip my tea after I hang up, and I book a ticket for later this afternoon. This is really not the mood to which I want to return to my parents. I had hoped I could show them that everything was perfect, maybe even introduce them to Al—*someone*—and show them how well my job is going. I had not planned to return with my tail tucked between my legs, and to give my mom the opportunity to say, "*I told you so.*"

With a groan, I finish my tea, tidy up, and pack my bags for a trip that I am not looking forward to. I glance over my shoulder at my loft—my home—and hope that the next time I return, it's not to pack it up completely. With a soft click, I close the door and roll my suitcase behind me. I don't leave much time between checking in at the airport and my flight because I know that I will change my mind if I wait too long.

~~~

Two and a half hours later, I exit O'Hare airport, the cold Chicago wind flapping the edges of my caramel coat against my legs. I make my way to the line of cabs standing at the curb, and all too quickly, the driver has my suitcase loaded and we are on our way to my childhood home. I stare up at the imposing red brick façade with the poinsettias lining the walkway, each pot decorated with white fairy lights. Even the wreath on the white door holds perfect tiny poinsettias among the holly leaves.

I try the door and am relieved when it is locked, meaning that both my parents are still at the hospital. The red ceramic heart sitting on the wooden bench beside the door smiles up at me as it always has, its eyes not quite aligned. It had been a Christmas gift to our parents when Ana and I were eight and in our DIY phase. The top half of the heart is open to reveal the brain inside, an homage to our parents' professions—my mom is a heart surgeon, and my dad is a brain surgeon. I am always surprised to see it still on the porch, considering that my parents had packed up all of Ana's stuff almost immediately after she died.

I lift the brain and pull out the spare key, quickly opening the door as the snow starts falling into the collar of my jacket.

"Mom? Dad?" I call into the large entrance hall, my voice echoing through the empty house. Good, at least the
~~~

hellos won't take place immediately, and I can get some rest before they get home.

The way to my bedroom is slow, and I stop at the door that hasn't been opened in 10 years. I put my hand against it and bite my lip at the coldness I feel through it now. Before Ana died, I believed that I could feel her warmth through the wood, and she could do the same. The house had become so empty without her—soulless, a huge mausoleum that began to feel like a gilded cage. It was beautifully and artfully decorated by my mom, but life had left it. It is a gorgeous showpiece.

My fingers tangle with my charms as I feel the loss of my sister with a pain that still cuts deep. Furiously blinking away tears, I rush the last few steps to my room and stare at the soft purple and lavender accents that always bring me peace. Mom never allowed us to have *tasteless* boy band posters on our walls, only elegant frames of art that neither of us understood, but today, as I look at the endless fields of tulips in my picture, I wish I could be there, away from the world as it is for me now.

I unpack slowly and reluctantly make my way to the kitchen, my fingers gently brushing the tiny gold bells that hang from the green garlands decorating the grand staircase. The house is, once again, professionally decorated, with every accessory to make the perfect Christmas setting, up to the dainty angel that sits on top of the perfect Douglas Fir. The kitchen cabinets are decorated with miniature replicas of the wreath on the front door.

Mom always sets the things she's going to use for dinner in the fridge, and I take out the bowl to get started.

With the chicken slowly roasting in the oven and the peach cobbler just about ready to bake, I am peeling the vegetables when I hear Mom's footsteps coming into the kitchen.

"Kerri?"

I give her a small, uncertain smile. "Hi, Mom."

"Oh, baby, this is such a wonderful surprise!" Her familiar perfume surrounds me as I enjoy the feeling of my mom's arms around me. "You should have said that you were coming. I could have taken the day off."

"It was a last-minute decision," I prevaricate, knowing she would see through anything else I tell her.

"Don't you eat in New York? You're too thin." She pinches my cheek as she studies me.

"Mom," I drawl, turning back to the vegetables as she continues to look at me.

"If it's not the food, then it's man trouble." She holds up her hand to stop my protests. "I'm not going to ask. You're a grown-ass woman and can mind your own business. I just hope he's worth it."

"Thanks, Mom," I say softly.

"I'm going to get changed and do the carrots. You always burn them."

"I do not!" I argue as she leaves the kitchen. I suppose being at home is not so bad after all.

My reception from Dad is so different. He pulls me into a one-armed hug, not looking at me or meeting my eyes, and I wonder when I've become okay with this. Since Ana died, he barely looks at me, and I am convinced that it's because he blames me for her death. Anabelle had been daddy's girl, and they had a special connection that I could never understand. I was never jealous of it because Dad spent as much time with me as he did with her, but they had a language all their own. Mom always said it was because he was the first one to hold her when she was born. I just wish that his connection with me was strong enough for him to look at me like he used to and tell me that he loves me. He hadn't said it since I was 15.

After convincing Mom that she should go to work and not change her plans for me, I call Elise, and we make plans to spend the next few days shopping for Christmas presents and catching up. We visit the Christmas market and spend too much money on Christmas trinkets, candy canes, and heavily whiskeyed, hot chocolate loaded with marshmallows.

We find a bench next to a small fire, and Elise looks at me. "Okay, so for two days, you've pulled me from store to store, nostalgic lunches, and laced hot chocolate, but not once have you mentioned Alex. So, spill."

I chuckle at my best friend. She knows me so well, and I tell her everything that has happened since the Hamptons, including the last time he was at my apartment. "You were so right about everything, Elise."

"Oh, Kerri. I'm sorry you went through this alone. I can't believe you didn't tell me."

"You warned me, Elise, and I didn't listen. I was such a fool."

"Girl," she drawls as she waves her hand at the people walking past us. "Show me one of these women who is *not* a fool for love. And since when did either of us listen to the other when it comes to boys? You warned me that big teeth Tony was not the right boy to give my V-card to."

"Damn, I forgot about him!" I laugh, brushing away tears as I remember Elise's teenage crush. The poor boy had been so excited that he wasn't able to perform when the time arrived. Elise had been so pissed she spent the night in my room and told him she had been with a college boy.

"He's married now with five kids."

I choke on my drink. "*Five?*"

"Yup." She laughs. "That will teach me."

We laugh a bit, and then the silence falls between us. "Kerri, you need to go to the police about that crazy bitch. Alex can take care of his own career, but your sanity is more important than him sitting on some judicial bench."

"Her family is huge in New York. They have the means to make my life hell."

"Isn't she already making your life hell?"

I bite my lip as I consider her questions. Yes, Nicole is already making my life hell, but I just want this issue to blow over so that I can pick up the pieces and go on with the rest of my life. "I can't argue with you, Elise."

"No, you can't." She gets to her feet and collects the mountain of packages together. "Come on, my ass is frozen. Let's go see how much bourbon your dad put in his eggnog this year."

I laugh fully for the first time in a very long time. "The older he gets, the heavier the bottle."

"I'm just glad we're old enough to drink it now." Elise giggles as she hooks her arm through mine, and we walk home.

"Oh, Kerri, you're home." Mom greets us as we close the door behind us, stamping the snow from our boots. "A package came for you while you were out."

Elise and I glance at each other, and I drop my bags on the floor as I lift the box my mom put on the hall table. My heart starts beating so fast I can hardly breathe. Alex has not contacted me since he left and seeing this fills me with excitement… and fear. *What if it isn't from him?*

My hands are shaking too much, and I hand the envelope to Elise, who frowns at me. "Open it, please?"

"Okay." She shrugs and reads the note aloud.

> "Dear Kerri. Something special for you to open on Christmas morning. Don't spoil the surprise."

We stare at the flat, red box, no larger than the envelope that is attached to it.

"Open it," Elise urges, and I shake my head, my stomach churning in trepidation. "It's two days until Christmas, and how will they know that you opened it early?"

I rub my hands and pick up the box. It weighs nothing, and I frown at her. "I don't have a good feeling about this."

"Neither do I."

I slowly lift the lid, and the nausea rises to my throat as I remember the last gift that was shrouded in tissue paper. Looking at Elise again, we simultaneously reach for the white wrapping and pull back the corners. Inside is a black and white sonogram, the image of a fetus clear in the blurred background.

"What the fuck?" Elise gasps.

I lift the glossy picture and flip it over.

He's mine forever. Merry Christmas, bitch.

Chapter Twenty-Nine

For the rest of my time at home, all I can think is there is no way Alex is leaving her now that she is pregnant, and I am relieved I let him go—so I can't understand why my heart won't agree. Though I join the rest of the festivities and try to laugh when I need to, my heart is not in it, and Mom keeps glancing at me with a worried frown.

I look down at our backyard from my window, finding a quiet moment to pack before I leave in the morning. The snow falling to the ground in the colorful lights of our neighbor's house catches my eye, and I unconsciously tuck the light sweater I am folding under my arm as I watch it drift past the window. I remember Dad walking into the entrance hall just after Elise and I read the message from Nicole.

"Everything all right, girls?" he had asked, his deep

voice filling the air.

"Yes," we chorused as we spun around. He nodded, looking at Elise but barely glancing at me as he walked to the kitchen.

The yard is dark, but I can still see the swing under the oak tree that we had fallen off so many times as little girls, the tiny rock pond where we tried to raise frogs, and the back porch steps where we had shared our secrets. This house had not been my home since I was 15. Both my parents had immersed themselves in their careers after Ana died, and I was left to navigate the grief on my own. And now I am packing to return to a place I am trying to make my own, but my sense of belonging is once again jeopardized.

The anger at this is deep and slow-burning, a steady heat that won't go away with the unfairness of the situation. The pattern is clear and painful. Not only do I lose someone I love, but I also lose the place that is supposed to be my haven. The sadness of these tears at me, and the wetness rolling down my cheeks surprises me at the thought. The relationship between my parents and myself is so fragile that I didn't tell them what is happening in New York, or that I might be returning to Chicago.

I turn back to my open suitcase and drop the sweater on the other clothes, my fingers tangled in my charms as I look up at the knock on my door. Neither of my parents had sought me out in 10 years, so it is a shock to have one of them approaching me. Even Mom will do the courtesy call, but our conversations will often revolve around general things and never cross the line of how Ana's death affected us.

"Yes?" I am able to squeeze out of my constricted throat. My breath whooshes out of me when my father opens my door and hesitantly steps over the threshold. "Dad?"

He looks at my packed suitcase, then glances around the room before he turns his gaze on me, and I can see the many emotions in his hazel eyes as they eventually meet mine. He moves toward me, and it seems that time is standing still. I gasp softly when he cups my cheek, and I hold onto his wrist, not wanting the contact to be broken too soon.

He clears his throat and then smiles at me. "You know that you can always come home."

I choke and nod slowly. "I know."

"Good." He pats my cheek gently before he turns away from me.

"Dad?" I call as he reaches the door, and he turns back to me. "Do you blame me?" He arches an eyebrow in question. "For Ana's death?"

He looks at me for a long time before looking at the floor. My heart constricts, and I berate myself for asking the question, knowing that it would just bring more pain to us and our torn relationship. There are tears in his eyes when he looks up again. With slow steps, he comes to sit on the edge of my bed. "The night before the meet, Ana told me she wasn't going to swim. She couldn't explain why, but she didn't feel right about swimming. I talked her into swimming, anyway, asking her how fair it was to you if she didn't swim."

He wipes away the tears, and I rush to sit by his side. "Dad…"

"It's my fault, Kerri. I made her swim even when she didn't want to. And every time I look at you, I see your pain, and I keep thinking if I had only listened to her." He shakes his head. "I failed you both in the worst possible way."

"Oh, Dad!" I throw my arms around him as we sit and sob in my childhood bedroom.

~~~

My steps falter as I walk toward the door of my loft, my suitcase knocking into my legs as I stop. The door is standing slightly open, but that is not possible, I know I locked it before I left. Could I have accidentally left it open? I was pretty upset when I took off, and could have left it open, thinking that I had locked it. I slowly push the door open and call, "Hello?"

There's no answer or noise, and I walk in. This is
~~~

strange because nothing seems out of place, and there is no damage except for the door jamb. I close my eyes and take a deep breath to stop the panic from setting in, and through my racing thoughts I know I need to call the police, so I take my phone out of my pocket and dial 9-1-1.

I am put through to the local precinct. The policeman asks me some questions, and when I tell him that I wasn't in the loft and that it doesn't seem like anything was stolen, he patiently explains that under the circumstances, it doesn't constitute an emergency and advises me to get my locks changed. I thank him politely, biting back my frustration and holding back the urge to scream at him. Before I realize it, I've dialed Alex's number, but before I can disconnect, he answers.

"Kerri? What's wrong?" I can hear the worry in his voice as well as a door that is being closed, and I realize that he is with… someone… I push the jealousy aside and prepare to apologize and hang up, but my mouth doesn't obey, and I stifle the sob that erupts.

"I think someone broke into my apartment," I sniff.

"Hold on, I'll be right there." The sound of keys jingles faintly, and the muffled sound of another door closing comes through the line before he hangs up.

I sink onto the armchair and squeeze my hands between my knees as I wait. With a deep frown, I groan in frustration. What am I waiting for? For Alex to come in and rescue me? I grow angry at myself for even calling him.

I scroll through the neighborhood's handyman list until I get the number for a locksmith. After making the call, I put my suitcase in the room and put water on for tea, making sure that everything is in order around the loft. I can't seem to put my finger on it, but the feeling of someone invading my space makes me shudder with fear and anxiety. I can feel myself hyperventilating, so I try to focus on the breathing exercises I was taught so long ago.

Alex and the locksmith arrive at the same time, and he checks the lock as I pay the man, neither of us saying a word to the other until the man leaves. At the click of the door, I realize how much the last few days have affected me when my tea sloshes over my shaking hand.

"Careful," Alex mumbles and takes the cup from my hand as he pulls me onto the sofa. "Kerri, are you okay?"

I shake my head, tears spilling from my eyes, and he pulls me into his arms, his hands stroking my back in large circles. I sigh as my emotions calm down, and my hand fists in his shirt as I listen to his steady heartbeat… except it's not as steady. It actually stops. He has gone so still, his body tense against my own.

"Alex?" I look up at him.

He is distracted as he gets to his feet and walks to the shelf that holds my picture frames. He takes a frame and turns it to me. I gasp at the picture of Nicole and Alex taken the afternoon of their anniversary celebrations. There are others filling all the frames in my loft, even the one of Ana that I keep on my bedside table. Each picture is of Nicole and Alex throughout their marriage. The wedding photo shifts as I lift the frame, and remove it from under the glass. *He'll never be yours* is scrawled on the back of it. I drop the photo as though it's burning my fingers, the glass shattering in the frame.

Alex meets me in the kitchen and fans the other photos on the counter, face down, each with their own message on the back.

You'll never have him.

He's mine, bitch.

Find your own fucking man.

Shameless whore!

"Enough!" Alex barks as he scoops them up and walks over to the trash can. He is about to throw them away when I spot the photo lying at the top of the bucket.

"No, no, no, no," I moan as I take the torn picture out of the bin and piece it together like a puzzle, my tears falling again at the large tear scarring my sister's beautiful face.

"Fuck. Kerri, I'm sorry," Alex whispers as he pulls me

into his arms again. I shiver at the thought that this woman has invaded my space and once again destroyed something so beautiful. How much more is she going to intrude into my life? How much more power is she going to take from me? And why am I tolerating her abuse?

I reach for my phone and begin to dial the number for the local precinct.

"What are you doing?" Alex asks.

"Calling the cops like I should have done weeks ago," I retort, but he grabs the phone and disconnects the call.

"Kerri, you can't do that." Even though his tone is calm, his expressive eyes can't hide his panic.

"Why not?" I demand, anger burning through my body like molten lava.

"What else are they going to do besides have her arrested? Her father's a high-powered judge—how well do you think that will work?" He grabs hold of my arms to make me look at him.

"Alex, at this point she *needs* to be stopped! She is scaring me so much." I reach for his hand and hope he can read how fearful I am of her. "What if I'd been here? What if she came in and found me sitting there?" I wave at the couch. "Or asleep in my room? Or what if you'd been with me?"

"Kerri." He turns his hand and captures my fingers with

his, kissing my knuckles. "I know the situation is fucked up, but for both our sakes, please don't report this?"

"What do you suggest I do, Alex?" I break free from him and pace to the window. "I can't go on like this. It has to stop."

He circles his arms around me, and I lean against his chest. He takes a deep breath and exhales slowly. "Let's go away for a few days. After everything, it'd be good to just get away. Maybe until after New Year's, and figure out a plan of action then? My family has a place up on a lake; we can take a few days and just... breathe."

I shake my head against his shoulder. "I don't think it's a good idea, Alex. I can't even think about relaxing at a time like this."

"Kerri." He sighs my name, his breath tickling the hair at my temple. "Just for a few days. It will do us both good to get away from the situation. Maybe it will help us find another perspective on this."

"Sure," I laugh. "Finding other ways of dealing with Nicole other than calling the police, you mean."

"There has to be another way, Kerri." He tightens his arms around me when I move to turn toward him. "I know that what she's doing scares you but going away for a few days will help us talk it out."

I look out the window and stare at the view in front of

us. It is so tempting to run away from everything that has been happening, to escape the mental hammering I've endured over the last few weeks. To have a few stolen days with Alex. But I can't shake the feeling that it is the worst thing I can do.

"A large cottage. Enchanting interior. Warm shaggy rug. Wide fireplace with wood …" His voice is low in my ear as he sells the idea of going away. "It will be fun…"

I groan when he rotates his hips against me, his meaning clear. "Alex…"

"Just a few days… We'll be back after the new year."

"Until after the new year," I agree reluctantly. "But if she does one more crazy stunt Alex I swear to God."

I feel the rumble of his soft laughter against my spine. "Noted."

I take a deep breath and go to my room to get my suitcase and head to my closet to get my denim jacket. But it's not there, and I check the bathroom to see if I left it there. But it isn't. Nothing is where I put it… No, that isn't quite right. I check the counter in my bathroom, my reflection in the mirror showing the deep frown on my face. The shampoo is where it should be, but the bottle isn't familiar. Neither is my body lotion or my perfume.

"Alex!" He immediately appears in the doorway to the bathroom. I hand him the perfume. "This is not mine."

He looks at the bottle and I notice his face goes slightly pale. He places the perfume down on the counter, quickly strides to my room, and opens my closet doors. I don't recognize anything that's hanging. Even my shoes are gone. All I have are the clothes I packed to go home with. His eyes are wide and his face paler when he looks up at me. "It's Nicole's."

I close my eyes and feel my knees buckle and I grab hold of the doorjamb for support. *What the entire fuck.* Fear grows increasingly as I stare into my unfamiliar closet. The thought of her accessing my home has me terrified she could come back and really harm me. The gravity of this situation is undeniable. "Alex…I…" The log in my throat prevents me from speaking. I clear my throat and try again. "She has gone too far."

He looks at me, his eyes dark with disbelief, fear, and something I don't recognize. "Come on. Let's get out of here."

Chapter Thirty

Alex carefully negotiates the city traffic as he makes his way north, the roads sleek with fresh snow. I stare out of the window, watching the scenery change as we drive further away from the city, but I'm not seeing any of it as my mind is filled with images of Ana's ruined photos. What kind of person would do this to someone? A slight guilt fills me. I mean I know this relationship with Alex is the root of all my problems, but I never imagined the stakes would be this high. I guess I never really thought about the consequences of our actions…my actions. Taking this trip away feels reckless considering what Nicole has already done but there is no way in hell I would stay in my loft right now. If we weren't going away, I'd probably ask Maggie to crash on her sofa.

The sound of my phone ringing draws me from my

reverie, and I frown at my father's number on the caller ID before quickly answering the call. "Dad?"

"Hi, Kerribel." He only calls me on my birthday, and this is definitely not my birthday.

"Is everything okay? Is Mom all right—"

"Yes, everything is fine, baby," he assures me, and I release the breath I didn't realize I was holding.

"Okay." The conversation is awkward between us, and I am unsure of what to say to him.

"Honey, I just… is everything okay? There's nothing you want to tell us, maybe?" I can hear the hesitation in his voice. I haven't told my parents anything about Alex and me, so I am not sure what my father is asking me.

"What are you asking me, Dad?"

"It's just that I was cleaning out the grate in the living room." I close my eyes as I remember Elise and I burn the photo of the sonogram before my parents enter the room. I didn't have enough time to see if it was gone.

"Uh, no, Dad." I am aware of Alex glancing at me as he drives, curious about my hesitant answer. As spacious as his Audi SUV is, it doesn't offer much in terms of privacy. I am chewing my lip, hoping my father doesn't ask me more because Alex can hear every word. "It was just a picture."

"Kerri, I know things haven't been great between us, but if you—or Elise—need to talk, you know you can come to me or your mom."

"Thanks, Dad."

"Having a baby is a big thing, and I wouldn't want you to feel that you're on your own." I want this conversation to end before more is said. Alex glances over at me, and I can see the happiness brightening his eyes. But it flickers out when I shake my head.

"Dad, there is no baby. It was something sent to me."

"Oh, okay. But I meant what I said, Kerri."

I try to speak past the lump in my throat. "Thanks, Dad. I have to go. I'll speak to you soon."

"Tomorrow. I'll call you tomorrow, Bel." The old nickname warms me from deep within. My dad and Ana are the only ones who ever called me that. I hang up, and the car is immediately filled with a tense silence.

"Well…" there's a brief pause before Alex continues, "Are you going to tell me about it?"

I can hear the confusion and anger simmering in his tone, but I don't look at him as the anger of Nicole's *gift* blazes through my mind. My dad's call just made all my emotions resurface causing my temperature to rise. Why are we going to his family cabin when his wife is about to have their baby? Why did I agree to come? My anger rises as I chastise myself for being a fool all over again. Always a fool for Alex Carter!

"When were you going to tell me about the baby, Alex?" I try to keep my tone calm, but it is difficult for me to contain my temper.

"Wait! What?" He turns to look at me as my words sink in. "What baby? What are you talking about?"

"Oh, come on, Alex!" I scoff. "Are you seriously going to play the 'dumb' game?"

With a curse, he pulls into the parking lot outside a diner.

"I can't tell you about something I know nothing about!" He returns, turning in his seat to look at me.

"Seriously?" The question is drenched in sarcasm as I look out the window, my arms crossed over my heaving chest. I gasp when he pinches my chin and makes me look at him.

"What the fuck is going on, Kerri?"

"You want to tell me you don't know that Nicole is pregnant?"

"Nicole?!" He rears back against the driver's side door.

"Please, Alex! You cannot make me believe that you didn't know."

"Kerri." He shakes his head as he gives a wry chuckle. "If Nicole is pregnant, it sure as hell isn't from me."

I arch my eyebrow at him, my disbelief clear as I look at him. "Sure. Please explain the sonogram I received, with a note saying you'll never leave her."

He closes his eyes and releases a loud sigh. "Vegas was the first time I've touched her in over a year." He cups my cheek. "Kerri, I know it's hard to believe, but I promise you, Nicole and I are only married by name. And since I've been with you, the thought of her or any other woman is sickening. I need you to understand I didn't have a choice that night. I would have been taken away in handcuffs if I hadn't given her what she wanted. Baby…I need you to believe me. And Vegas wasn't that long ago, it's not possible for her to test positive and have a sonogram this early. She would have ruined me with blackmail. You're my forever butterfly. Not her. I just need to figure out how to end it."

I stare into his eyes, and I want to believe him, but how can I when he is still defending her and making excuses for her? "What are you going to do about her, Alex? She is not stable."

A muscle in his jaw tenses as he looks out of the windshield. With a heavy sigh, he starts the car and pulls onto the highway again. "When we met, she was the life of the party. Everyone wanted to be near her. I had a close friend—not a girlfriend—just someone I had a lot in common with. When we saw Nicole on campus, others would always say there was something off about her. We never socialized in the same circles until we attended the same party, and she decided she wanted me."

He shakes his head again and stares through the windshield, but I know his mind is not in the car. "She was charming and friendly, and she could always make me laugh. At that stage, I thought she was teaching me how to find a balance in my life. Things changed after the first miscarriage. The only time she laughed was when she drank, and she started texting me several times a day to check where I was and who I was with.

"When we went to counseling, she explained that she had become insecure and was afraid I'd find someone else. Things went well for a while, but..." He shakes his head again. "I kept trying. I kept going back. I never had the motivation to break things off with her. I never thought I'd find a reason for me to walk away."

He takes my hand and strokes his thumb across the back before kissing it. "For the first time, I've found something that I'm afraid of losing more than I am of losing my career, Kerri."

Hearing those words sends a warm wave throughout my body and I suddenly feel sorry for him. Listening to him open up about his marriage looking into his eyes and seeing how vulnerable he has become in this moment makes me want to throw caution to the wind. But I know

Ana would not approve of it, so I gently remind myself and straighten my posture. "But if you keep holding on to her, then you will lose me, Alex."

His hand tightens around mine before he nods and concentrates on the road again.

As we pull over to grab some snacks, Alex absentmindedly plays with an app on his phone. My mind is still spinning from our conversation, and the emotional roller coaster I've been on for the past few days has left me utterly drained, both physically and emotionally. I can't wrap my head around what he's telling me. The one thing that baffles me is why Nicole is so unhinged, considering they don't live together or sleep together. If it's all just for show, then why would she go to such lengths?

Approaching the cabin, I am struck by its majestic presence. It's not your ordinary cabin; it's a two-story mansion made of wood and stone. Bathed in a sort of warm glow, its large windows reflect the golden light onto the snow-covered landscape. Behind the house, a picturesque lake stretches out, and as we drive up, Alex mentions that there's a jetty and a couple of boats available if I want to venture out onto the water.

"We should have the place warmed up by now," he assures me, leading the way up the stone steps to the porch adorned with inviting Adirondack chairs and a table that beckons me to sit and savor a cup of chamomile tea. As he opens the hefty, double-wide door, I find myself mesmerized by the beauty of its grand presence. Stepping into the expansive room, I'm greeted by a high ceiling adorned with skylights, allowing the sun's rays to illuminate the open balcony leading to the second-floor bedrooms. A magnificent stone fireplace occupies almost an entire wall, while a plush sectional couch and armchairs create a cozy seating area opposite it. A luxurious, thick shaggy rug ties everything together, and I can already envision his family gathered around the crackling fire, basking in the warmth of the setting sun filtering through the large picture window.

"Dad always keeps tetrazzini pasta in the freezer. We can put that in the oven and make a salad. It shouldn't take too long."

I nod. "The advantages of having a chef for a father?"

"There has to be some benefits." He smiles unapologetically. While the pasta is in the oven, he collects some wood and starts a fire, and I look at the photos that are hanging on the walls all around the room. I laugh at the cheeky smile a young Alex gives the camera as he shows off his catch on the dock. So many of his memories are tied to this place, and as I watch him, I realize that he is free here. Even his smile comes easier.

We sit on the rug in front of the fire as we eat, and the setting makes the last few months seem like a horror movie that missed the box office hit list. We quickly clean the dishes and settle on the sofa, my head on his shoulder, after he puts another log on the fire.

"Tell me about Ana," he says softly, his voice warm and inviting me to confide in him.

I lift my head to meet Alex's eyes and my heart instantly starts pounding. I knew this moment would come. Of course, he would only naturally want to know more about Ana. Every fiber in my body is telling me to fake food poisoning so I can escape. But I know Alex just opened up to me and shared his situation with Nicole. It would be relationship suicide to shut down now. I inhale one deep, long breath hoping to keep my heart from jumping out of my chest. I close my eyes as I prepare to share the most painful story of my life.

"Ana and I were inseparable from the moment we took our first breaths. Growing up as identical twins, we were constantly mistaken for one another, but we never minded. In fact, we loved it when we were mixed up because we loved to play tricks on our friends. Only Mom, Dad and Elise could tell us apart. Our childhood was filled with countless adventures and mischievous escapades. We were each other's partners-in-crime, always finding ourselves at the center of some thrilling escapade. Whether it was climbing trees in their backyard or exploring hidden caves in the nearby forest, we were unstoppable, and our bond was unbreakable. We both started swimming at 5 years old and quickly fell in love with it. We always wanted to be in water, whether it was lakes or swimming pools."

My mind begins to drift back to that day when everything changed.

~ ~ ~

Her voice echoes in my mind as I'm sitting in the front pew of the church, her white coffin covered in a huge wreath of lilies, roses, and baby's breath with a huge photo of my sister's beautiful smile. Everyone is dressed in somber black except me. I am dressed in a dove gray suit a color I've never worn again. Everyone else is crying but I'm numb, unable to cry since the day the EMTs couldn't get her heart to beat again. Even Pastor Davids can't get more than a few words out before he needs to clear his throat.

My mind is stuck on the image of my sister on the side of the pool, her body jerking as the coach administers CPR, the spectators so quiet I can hear her shoulders slapping on the floor. My mom is kneeling next to the coach, calling Ana to breathe. My father is standing behind her, his arms wrapped around his chest, his body so tense that I'm not sure if he is breathing. My eyes are drawn to the scene from where I am sitting at the edge of the pool, my knees pulled up to my chest, my chin tucked between them. I am rocking back and forth as I try to process what is happening in front of me. One second Ana was a half-length ahead of me, her wake carrying me to a close second after her finish; the next, her body was convulsing and shaking, the movements causing small tidal waves across the surface of the pool. Our eyes met briefly in her struggle, the pain and terror in them drawing a soul-wrenching panic from me. I couldn't get to her fast enough, the lane-dividers hampering my movements as they bounced on the unsteady water. By the time I could dive under the bulky red buoy to get to her, Ana's eyes had rolled up in her head and she had disappeared under the water.

My muscles burned as I wrapped my arms around her and pulled her to the edge of the pool where the coach took hold of her and laid her out to do CPR. But I knew, deep down, it was too late. I had felt her give her last breath in my arms. Ana was dead.

~~~

"After the accident, Mom insisted on an autopsy report. It was an undiagnosed traumatic brain injury she had received earlier in the summer at a previous competition. One of the other swimmers had stumbled off her diving block as Ana passed her, and in the fall, Ana had knocked her head against the edge of the block. She said she was fine, and Dad gave her a thorough exam and said that it was a mild concussion. Nobody saw the bleeding from a torn blood vessel."

I look up at him as he strokes my shoulder, his eyes dark with compassion. "Kerri, I'm so sorry."

I nod and stare at the fire. I feel him grab my hand to stop the trembling and I take another deep breath summoning the strength to speak "I haven't been in the water since. It feels like a betrayal to enjoy something we both loved when she's not here to share the joy. As much as I told myself that her injury was an accident, I can't shake the fear. And I keep asking myself if she would still be alive if she didn't compete or if I had gotten to her
~~~

sooner."

I curl up against the couch as I feel the tiredness sweep over me after my emotional purge and feel myself doze off against his shoulder. I wake up when I feel him shifting me to a more comfortable position on the rug. He lies down next to me, and I hook my arms around his neck and pull him down to kiss him softly.

His taste is of the coffee he had after dinner both warm and delicious. He slants his mouth across mine and takes control of the kiss, seeking entrance, and I gladly open for him. We spend the next hour talking and staring into the fire while he holds me tightly. My body perfectly nestled with his, wrapping my arms around his strong shoulders, I hold onto him, absorbing some of his strength. And I know I'm exactly where I am supposed to be.

After a while, the room cools down as the fire dies. Noticing the draft, Alex gets up to add more logs to it. When he's done, I settle into his arms when he comes to lie behind me, his hands stroking the skin beneath my sweater. We watch the fire for a while, and I wonder if we'll always have to sneak away to get more of these memorable moments together.

My thoughts are suddenly interrupted at the loud bang and the immediate sound of glass shattering. I scream as Alex covers my head when a million shards fly toward us, their tiny cuts stinging as they make contact with any exposed skin. I lift my head past his shoulder in time to see the brick bounce off the large mantel and ricochet onto my ankle, and I gasp at the pain.

Chapter Thirty-One

Alex immediately jumps to his feet and turns off the lights, plunging us into near darkness except for the fire. He peers out into the night, trying to see what is going on, his body tense. Scrambling to get onto the sofa and trying to find my shoes in the gloom, I notice the brick at my side and squint at the wording etched into it, the darkened room making it difficult to read. Picking it up, I lean toward the fire as I trace the letters that are carved into the beautiful orange stone that I recognize as one of those lining the footpath to the door, the markings ugly and angry in the firelight. *Bitch!*

I can't believe that just minutes ago, Alex and I were entangled in the most intimate moment we could have, just to be plunged into another nightmare of Nicole's making. My emotions see-saw between fear and anger, confusion and sadness, regret, and hate, everything directed at Nicole as I think back over the last few weeks and what my life has become.

A shiver races down my spine at the word, the familiar writing making my breath hitch, and I look over at Alex, who is suddenly silhouetted against the shattered picture window as bright lights are directed into the room. The sound of the howling wind is loud through the gaping hole but not loud enough to drown out the sound of the car being revved. I turn my eyes away from the sudden glare and wonder how she is always able to spoil our beautiful times together. "Alex, I think—"

My sentence dies on a scream as Alex dives at me, folding me against his body and rolling me toward the stone wall of the fireplace, the heated bricks warm against my back. I pull my head up to look past his shoulder, frustrated at not being able to see what is going on, but he pushes my head tightly against his chest just as a loud crash shakes the cabin.

More glass splatters around us, but they are joined by splinters of wood. The foundation is still shaking at the impact, and it is only then when I hear the high-pitched revving of a car engine that I realize that Nicole has driven her car into our oasis. Above the sound of the creaking supports, falling glass, and whining engine, I am able to hear her maniacal laughing. I lift my head, fighting the stronghold that Alex has on me, and gasp in shock at the sight. I push away from him and get to my feet, using his shoulder to help me stand.

Shaking my head, I look at the destruction. The picture window and its supporting wall are gone, exposing the debris to the light layer of snow that is now drifting into the cabin. And in the middle of the chaos, a badly crushed BMW is idling, filling the cabin with the sweet toxicity of engine fumes, its front tires chewing up the white oak wood floors as they spin uncontrollably. The airbags have deployed, and beyond them, I see the silhouette of Nicole, her head thrown back as she laughs, the sound sending shivers down my spine. I'm so focused on the sight that I'm barely aware of Alex standing behind me.

"What the fuck?" he whispers, and I glance over my shoulder at him. His eyes are wide as he stares at the scene, shaking his head as if he can't believe it. "What the hell is she doing?"

"Do you think she's still harmless, Alex? All talk?" I can't help the sarcasm as we watch her punch the airbag flat before she steps out of the car. She is a beautiful woman, I can't help but notice, as she steps around the car door. Unlike the special event I had seen her at or the hotel in Vegas, where she was poised and elegantly coiffed and dressed, this Nicole is wild and uncontrolled, and I don't think that reasoning with her is going to work tonight.

Her black high-heeled pumps kick the wood and

broken furniture aside as she walks to the front of the car. The black pants encasing her long legs like a second skin are now lightly coated with dust and snow, and the short black leather jacket hugs her body. The fuchsia pink blouse beneath it is dotted with blood from the gashes on her forehead and cheeks, and that brings my focus to her face. Though beautifully made up, there is mascara smeared beneath her eyes, giving her face a gaunt appearance, but at the same time, making her gold eyes large. There is no way either of us can miss the demented look in them, especially with her hair wild and standing on end in the gust of wind that is blowing through the missing wall. Nicole has lost her shit.

And then I notice the hand she is waving around is holding a gun, and I freeze in fear. My heart thuds painfully in my chest as I realize that she is going to make good on her threat, and that I am going to die tonight. A small amount of joy fills me at the thought that at least my last minutes on earth are spent with the man I love. But that joy is quickly overtaken by terror as she points the gun at me.

"You really are unbelievable," she spits, her voice raw and mechanical as she walks toward me, her breasts heaving with each ragged breath she takes. "I cannot believe that someone can be so stupid. Did you not believe me?"

I start as she screams at me. "Alex…" I whimper.

"You are probably the stupidest bitch I have ever come across." She shakes the gun at me, her mane of hair shimmering around her head. "I kept warning you, telling you to keep your smutty hands to yourself! I even sent you a picture of our baby, you stupid-assed whore!"

There is a sharp hiss from Alex as she screams the last part. I glance over at him and see the confusion and shock on his face. His brows are drawn together, and I can see the worry in his eyes. His hands tighten around my waist as Nicole steps closer. "Nicole, what are you doing?"

But she doesn't hear him, as her hate-filled gaze is stuck on me. "But I can understand why, his dick is addictive… But, honey, as I kept trying to tell you, it belongs *to me*! I don't know what voodoo shit you doin', but it won't be enough to keep him inside of you, because he'll *always* come home to me!"

The gun goes off as she screams the last words at me. The report is so loud, I barely hear myself scream as Alex turns us. The impact of the bullet hitting his body knocks us both to the ground, and a loud *whoosh* leaves me as his weight covers me with a grunt of pain.

"ALEX!" Nicole shrieks. The gun drops from her hand, and another shot is fired as it hits the floor, the bullet ricocheting off the edge of the fireplace and lodging into the high ceiling. Nicole carefully struts over the debris as she lunges toward us.

"Alex," I mumble as I pull out from under him, his blood seeping into my sweater. He is breathing hard, and his face is pale with shock. I scan his body and find the bullet hole in his shoulder, blood flowing from it in a steady stream. The white rug that we had just eaten on is now soaked in red. I sob as I see his lifeblood seeping away. "Alex."

He pushes my hands away from him as I try to staunch the blood. "Go! She's going to kill you…"

"No." I shake my head at him, tears flowing down my face and onto his.

"Kerri… you need to go *now*…" His words are beginning to slur with pain. The sound of Nicole stumbling over a piece of wood brings my head up to see her a few feet away from us. "I love you…"

"Alex, I can't leave—"

"Look what you've made me do, you bitch!" Nicole screeches as she stumbles over the broken coffee table.

"Kerri, RUN!" he shouts. The last thing I remember is the smell of Chanel No.5 cloying my throat as Nicole drops to her knees at Alex's head. I scramble to my feet and escape through the space that Nicole created with her car.

Chapter Thirty-Two

Passing the glaring headlights of the car, I fall under the blinding darkness, stumbling over the debris. I drop as my injured ankle twists in a portion of the window frame. I land hard on my ass and use the tail end of the car to pull myself to my feet. Through the shattered windshield, I see Nicole bending over Alex as he lies on the ground. I see his lips moving, but I can't hear what he is saying over the beating of my heart, the revving car, and the howling wind.

Nicole rears back from Alex, falling to her backside as she stares at him, her mouth open in shock. Her eyes stretch even wider than they were before. And then she looks up, and my heart stops at the hatred radiating from her gaze as she looks at me. She turns onto her knees and searches for the gun behind her, and I have a renewed sense of urgency to get away from her. Whatever Alex told her has just inflamed her madness.

I turn and stumble off the porch, dropping to my knees as my ankle refuses to take my weight. With a frustrated groan, I push to my feet and stumble toward Alex's car. I know he left the keys under his seat, and though I'm not sure which direction to go, I'll be getting away from Nicole. I duck behind the fender as a shot reverberates in the nighttime quiet, and a bullet whizzes past my head. Using the tire to get to my feet, I frown when the usually sturdy rubber gives me no resistance and instead sags against the pressure of my hands.

"No, no, no, no, no," I beg as I feel around the tire wall and find the deep slash in it. My stomach flutters in fear as I move to the back wheel and discover that it has also been slashed. Though my instincts tell me that she has slashed all the tires, I still feel the need to confirm it. As I move around the back of the car, I catch a glimpse of Nicole stepping out of the hole and standing on the porch.

The image is terrifying! The headlights rebound off the inner wall surrounding Nicole. Her flying hair seems to be lit up with tiny flames while her black suit keeps her body in shadow, making her seem like a specter from a haunted house. My heart is bouncing hard in my chest as my lungs squeeze out the little air I am able to drag into them, only to expel it with a gasp.

She throws back her head and laughs, the sound sending shivers down my spine and making me break out in a sweat. "Kerribel *fucking* Townsend, you can't escape me! I will find you!"

I wonder if she hurt Alex after what he said to her. I grimace at the thought. Did she shoot him again? How could she just leave him to die like that? My fear for his life has me choking up, and I stifle a sob with my hand.

"You think you can come into our life, dangle your young, new piece of ass in *my* husband's face, fuck him and get away with it?" She screams so hard, her voice now becoming raspy. "You bottom bitch!" Another shot fires grazing the dirt ground near my position. "I've known about you since the beginning. Watching your smug face turn pale white when you saw Alex standing next to me at our anniversary party was the best fucking anniversary gift, he could ever get me." Nicole laughs echoing through the night sky.

Another shot rings out against the car, and I hear her step off the porch and onto the gravel. I peer around the car and see her heading toward the driver's side, so I ease around to the other side. Gingerly testing my weight on my injured ankle, I move to the front of the car. I need to get away from Nicole, but hiding behind the car is not going to help me achieve that. Closing my eyes, I think about Alex, trying to remember what he told me about the cabin and its surroundings.

"... There are two boats, and in the summer, Dad and I would take one across the lake to the local bait shop and then spend hours on the lake catching our dinner..."

The lake! My heart slams hard against my ribs at the realization that I'll have to go onto the lake. For a moment, my muscles tense, and I feel my body shrinking into a tight ball as fear immobilizes me. I unclench my tight fists and stretch my fingers, psyching myself to loosen my body in preparation to flee.

"Little Kerri!" Nicole sings out. "What are you going to do, sweetie?"

I shudder again as she laughs, a sound I will be hearing in my dreams for a long time to come. Looking around, I don't see another way to escape, leaving me with no choice. I need to go to the water. That is the only way I will be safe—that I will save Alex.

"I know about your poor sister. She was so desperate to get away from you, she was even prepared to die!" I gasp at the pain of that remark. How dare she use Ana to hurt me? With a spurt of anger and adrenaline rushing through my veins, I sprint across the open ground to the side of the house, ducking my head as a bullet fly past me.

There is a hundred feet of open space between the cabin and the lake, the area dark and menacing, making me hesitate. I see the black surface of the cold lake ahead of me, the two boats bobbing on the side of the dock, their chromework like a beacon under the weak moon that peers between the clouds. Could she catch me if I take the chance?

"Apparently, Kerri, you were so jealous of your sister that you held her under the water instead of helping her!" She giggles, the girlish sound contrary to the bitterness of her words. "You're one bad bitch! Bet you didn't count on me, though!"

And then I hear the unmistakable sound of a high heel breaking as Nicole steps off the gravel path. With a deep breath, I push away from the wall and sprint across the yard, my feet flying over the coarse grass. My mind tells my body to zigzag, feeling ridiculous as I imitate the action stars from the movies, and as I dodge to the left, a bullet kicks up dirt to my right.

"Stand still, you scrawny cunt, so that I can shoot you!" Nicole screams in frustration. I glance over my shoulder as I reach the dock and see that she is limping across the lawn. Her pace is not as quick as mine, as her heels are catching in the soggy ground, slowing her down. The sound of the wood slapping under my feet has me sobbing in relief, and I head for the first boat at the end of the pier. I quickly untie the ropes, my hands fumbling in the weak light of the moon. With a hard grunt, I push the boat off and jump on board.

I have never driven a boat before, and I stare down at the controls before me. My hands are so sweaty that they slip off the steering wheel as I inspect the dashboard. I turn the key, but the engine doesn't take as the key twists back in my slick hand. I take a deep breath, rub my hands down the thighs of my jeans, and try again. This time, the powerful engine immediately vibrates to life beneath me, and I gasp in relief. I push a button, and light streams out over the lake, illuminating enough of the dashboard for me to see what looks like a gear stick with the word "Throttle" embossed on the woodwork.

I push it forward tentatively, and the boat moves forward. I allow a moment of exhilaration to fill me as I push it forward completely, and I hold onto the steering as the boat surges across the black waters. I am so intent on piloting the vessel that I don't realize Nicole has stepped onto the dock.

"KERRI!" My name echoes across the lake in a bloodcurdling scream, and I glance over my shoulder as I make my escape. Nicole is standing at the end of the dock, waving her arms wildly. She stamps her foot and directs the gun in my direction. I see two flashes from the gun in her hand and the distant pop of the two shots she fired. I push the throttle forward, hoping to get as far away from Nicole as I can.

As I get deeper into the lake and the inky water surrounds me, I feel my heartbeat increase as my fear and anxiety invade my mind. My hands are so sweaty that they slip on the controls, and I have to wipe them on my jeans again. I struggle to control my breathing, feeling the darkness on the edges of my mind as my body is becoming deprived of oxygen. *Come on, Kerri, think about Alex.*

I glance back at the cabin and then gasp when I see Nicole climb into the other boat. Air whooshes out of me, shallow and uncontrollable, and I feel the tears of fear and frustration roll down my cheeks, freezing in the cold wind blowing against my face as I speed across the water. The sound of the other boat's engine starting has me clutching the steering wheel, my knuckles shining white in the moonlight. I have never been as desperate in my life. *Help me, Ana—please help me!*

As I look over my shoulder to see how far Nicole has progressed, I gasp as I shake my head, my body frozen in anguish and terror. Water is seeping into the boat! The crazy bitch had shot a hole in my escape vehicle!

"Please, no! Please don't do that!" I plead with the water that is filling the boat, making it heavier by the second, and as its icy tentacles curl around my feet, I start to sob, tears blinding my route and effectively shutting down my ability to think logically. I instinctively take hold of my charms and twist them around my finger as I try to fight the panic that is engulfing me completely.

Nicole's crazy laughter echoes over the quiet waters. She must've realized that my boat is sinking and that she is gaining on me. The engine in my boat stalls as water fills it, and it doesn't take as I try to start it again. I am in the middle of the lake, so far from the shore, but I know the only chance I have to survive is to swim. Panic brings me to my knees, and I hang onto the steering wheel, my ribs hurting with the effort to breathe. *No, Ana, I can't do this!*

Of course, you can. You are Kerri fucking *Townsend!*

Taking quick, shallow breaths, I regulate my breathing, drowning out all other sounds and thoughts, just like we did on the starting blocks. Ana always stood to my left, partly as support, partly as my competition. We would encourage each other, timing our strokes with the others as we kept pace. And the calmness I felt during those times comes over me. With a resolute nod, I get ready to do what I need to do.

As the water reaches my knees, I look over at Nicole, take a deep breath, step onto the side of the boat, then launch myself into the water. I barely get the chance to register that I am three feet underwater, totally enclosed in the inky depths as my body fights the surge of cold. I surface several feet from the boat, gasping for breath, the air forming white puffs in front of me. My nose instantly burns as I take in more air. I kick off, not sure if I am swimming in the right direction, but I just know I need to get to shore as quickly as possible. My survival depends on it.

"Come on, Kerri! Keep up!" Ana's voice carries over the water. I look over to the left, and I can swear I see a splash of water just ahead of me. That is all the motivation I need to move through the water and swim for my life.

Chapter Thirty-Three

With my muscles screaming in protest against the cold, and the obvious fact that I haven't used the group of muscles needed for swimming in 10 years, I continue heading toward the shore—any shore would be great, for all I care. I am spurred on by the sound of Nicole's boat so close behind me I can feel the stern wave pushing me away from her, and I gasp at the small reprieve. As I take in another breath to continue my escape, I resign myself to the knowledge that she is going to catch up to me.

It is exactly 10 strokes later when I hear Nicole pull back on the throttle, and the engine goes into a slow rumble as it idles, stirring the water around me and impeding my way. I cry out when she grabs a handful of my hair, my head banging lightly as she pulls me up so that she can look at me. I reach up to hold on to her wrist to lessen the harsh tug on my skull. She laughs hysterically, spittle splashing down on my face, her face almost demonic in the moonlight, freezing me even more than the water ever can. I quickly gulp in a lungful of air as she pushes me under, her madness giving her more strength than I thought she was capable of. I scrabble against the side of the boat, trying to get a handhold, but it is so smooth and slippery that I am sliding even further under the water than I expect.

Just when I feel my air supply diminishing, she pulls me up. "*You* made me kill him!"

I gasp for air as she pushes me under, and I realize that fighting will only use up the air and energy I need to survive. She pulls me up again. "If you had stayed away from him, I wouldn't have shot him." She slaps me hard before plunging me beneath the surface again. "But you had to be fucking greedy!"

This time, she holds me down longer, and panic seizes me again as I feel my strength leaving me. The icy water, lack of swimming exercises, and fear sap me of the strength I need to stay afloat. The coldness of the water eats away the feeling in my fingers and toes. And the knowledge that Alex is dead makes me feel heavy, and I allow the last of my breath to bubble to the surface. But I am suddenly pulled back out of the water, and I stare up at Nicole.

I'm not sure if it's the coldness of the water penetrating

my brain cells, the trauma of the last few weeks, the idea that Alex could be dead, the painful memories of Ana revisiting me, or just the thought of this crazy-assed bitch taking my last breath, but something burns inside of me from the pit of my stomach. It flares hotly and zaps along my nerve endings, and I recognize it as the rage that is taking over my soul.

The bitch had invaded my life, going into my past and using the most painful part of it to torment me. She had humiliated me in front of my colleagues. She had made the sweetest memories I'd made over the last few months with Alex so bitter. She had broken into my apartment and put her stamp over what was mine. She had killed the man I love. She's even made me dive into a fucking icy lake when I had vowed that I would never enter the water again. *And she is now trying to drown me in the very essence I had loved as a child?* Oh, hell no!

I'm not sure where the last burst of strength comes from or what makes me use her power and momentum to pull myself up the side of the boat. With my other hand, I grab hold of her ankle and use it as an anchor as I scramble on board.

"What the fuck are you doing, you crazy bitch?!" She tries to stomp on my arm, but I'm already using it to sit up. She lifts her leg to kick me, but I catch it and push it away from me. She tries to catch herself, but the deck is slippery from the water running from my body, and her shoe slips.

I see her falling. She knocks her head against the dashboard, but she blinks the darkness away and launches herself at me, grabbing hold of my throat.

She's taller than me, and this allows her to be just out of my reach. I can feel the blackness enter my vision as she cuts off my breath. My eyes start to close, and I am fading. A memory of Ana and me flashes into my mind. Though we were close, we were also competitive, and tussling was a regular occurrence between us. With a last effort, I clasp my hands together, pull my arms up between us and knock her locked elbows as hard as I can with mine. When her arms buckle, I hit upward with my fists, hitting her on the chin, knocking her from me.

I struggle to my knees, gasping for breath, but she grabs my hair again, yanking my head back sharply. I feel her nails digging into my windpipe. I stare at her in horror as I realize that she is prepared to tear out my throat. I blindly reach behind me for a weapon—anything that can stun her enough for me to get to my feet. She pulls me up and slams my head on the deck hard enough for me to see stars. My hand falls limp, but it brushes against a rope, and I blink away the dizziness as I look at the toolbox that is open above my head.

I try to grab hold of the rope, but it slithers from my nerveless fingers. I use my other hand to find something, and my fingers curl around an item that fits perfectly into my hand. I pull it out, and I gasp as I realize that I have found the flare gun. For a second, I feel myself letting it go, not able to use it on someone else. But then her nails tear through my skin, drawing blood that I can feel trickle down my throat to drip to the deck. With as much strength as I can, I swing the gun down and knock the butt hard against her temple, the impact shifting my finger on the trigger. With a long whistle, a flash of red speeds to the sky, covering us in a red haze.

"You stupid bitch!" Nicole screams as she tries to grab my wrist. She has been mumbling and screaming at me the entire time we fought, but my need to survive has been blocking out her voice. She straddles my waist and bashes my wrist against the edge of the box, and the flare gun spins out of my fingers as my bones break. I buck her off and push back to the front part of the boat, cradling my broken hand. Nicole laughs when she realizes that she has me cornered. My eyes drop to her feet, and I see that she is still wearing her pumps, her one foot flat where the heel had broken off. I find this hilarious and start laughing, the sound mingling with hers, both tinged with hysteria.

"Do you know what's crazy, Nicole?" I ask as soon as I can sober up.

She stops laughing long enough to look at me as though I have lost my mind, which I probably have. "What?"

"That when you kill me, I'll be spending eternity with Alex and away from your crazy ass!" I taunt her, the jab making her eyes widen even more. I don't know what the intention of my taunting is but watching her lose even more control of her sanity is satisfying enough.

"And do you know what's *crazy,* Kerri?" a twinge of evil seeping through her pores as she directs her gaze at me. I give in to curiosity.

"What?" I sass.

"Everyone will look at you like the pathetic, insecure little bottom feeder you are. Everyone will say you had it coming. I didn't think my honey would fall in love *oh so easily* with a stupid tramp like you. Alex is not a good man. But he's *mine.* I own him! He tried to leave before, but I showed him he can't leave me just because I've made a few little mistakes. Who gives a shit if he doesn't love me anymore. Love doesn't matter! What about all the years I gave him, supporting him in his career, grooming him and for what…for him to run off with a younger model?" Veins are beginning to bulge from her neck and her laughter growing louder "he tried so hard to keep you a little secret—his little emotional support animal. But even pets die too." Nicole screams as she lunges for me again, but the intact heel of her shoe hooks into the trigger guard of the flare gun. The smooth soles of her shoes give her no grip on the slippery deck, and her foot slides out from under her. She falls backward, and I watch in horror as she drops. I'm not sure what is more sickening: the sound of her head as it bounds off the engine or the sight of it as it strikes the red and white cover, her honey-blond hair tangling in the mechanics. The sound of her neck breaking as her body falls over the side and splashes into the water has me rushing for the side, and I empty my stomach, no longer able to hold back the nausea.

I sink to my knees, and my uninjured hand tangles in my charms as I thank God that helped me stay alive. I crawl to the dashboard and slump into the chair as I push the throttle forward gently. The engine makes a strange sound as it shifts into motion, but the need for excess is passed, and the speed is not as fast as when I entered the lake.

A house has its lights on as I get near the shore, and I see people standing on the dock. I head in that direction, and a tall man pulls the boat closer to the dock and ties it with a rope. He quickly helps me out and steadies me when my knees buckle.

"We saw the flare and called the police," he explains as his wife drapes a blanket around my shoulders. They lead me to their house and sit me in front of the fireplace. The wife magically puts a cup of hot cocoa in my hand and folds it around the mug, the heat stinging my fingers.

"Please, we need to call the police again. My boyfriend was shot…" I sob. "He needs an ambulance…"

"Who's your boyfriend, dear?" the wife asks as the husband dials 9-1-1 again.

"Alex… Alex Carter," I stutter.

"Oh, the sweet boy," she murmurs as she rubs her hands over my arms to warm me up.

A few minutes later, I am sitting in the back of the police cruiser as it speeds towards Alex's home. The car screeches to a halt, the flashing red and blue lights glowing against the destruction of the beautiful home. The tail of Nicole's navy-blue BMW is sticking through the wall, and a portion of the porch is dropping as the support column is cracked and leaning to one side. There is wood and glass lying everywhere, and a light dusting of snow covers everything.

"What the fuck happened here?" one of the officers asks in shock as he stares at the spectacle.

I hardly hear him as I pull at the lever to open the door and cry out when it won't budge. Panic fills my mind and body as I struggle to be free. I need to get to Alex—I need to see if Nicole had really killed him. One of the officers realizes what is happening and quickly gets out of the car to open my door from the outside. I rush out of the car, falling to my knees as my ankle gives way under my weight, my body no longer running on pure adrenaline. I vaguely feel my knees burning where I skimmed them as I push onto the officer who offers me his arm to help me to my feet. I hobble to the hole in the wall and lean against the car as I move forward.

"Alex!" I cry out his name, but he doesn't move, and my heart sinks at the thought that I am too late. The house fills with red lights as the ambulance pulls up, and I use this to guide me over the debris and toward Alex. I fall to my knees at his side and cup his face. The blood has spread even further, but there is a small flutter in his throat when I search for his pulse. I kiss his mouth, willing him to open his eyes, whispering his name over and over.

Chapter Thirty-Four

It's been six months since the nightmare at the cabin happened. All my physical battle wounds have healed for the most part but the wounds that cut the deepest fortunately aren't known to anyone but me. Starting therapy was the best decision I've made in a long time. Dr. Fisher is blessed with my presence every first and third Tuesday of the month. As a matter of fact, if I don't hurry up and leave now, I will be late…again.

"Shit" I whisper as I check the time on my phone.

"It's a little early for lunch don't you think? Plus, I wanted us to go together today to celebrate your promotion! I need to catch up with my girl. I miss her!" Maggie pouts standing at the entrance doorway to my brand new, rather large office. She's got her arms folded tightly almost wrinkling her plum colored, pin stripe suit jacket. Her bottom lip is poking out trying to sell me on how sad she is to see me leaving.

I return a devilish smile "And I thought by having my own office would mean you would stop popping up unannounced. But we all don't get what we want. Do we?" I tease as I stand up to grab my purse and we both burst into laughter. It has been some time since I've hung out with Maggie or Demi. After everything that happened, I haven't felt like being around anyone.

"How about we meet for drinks later this evening and catch up?" I offer instead.

"Deal." Maggie's smile drops almost instantly. "I just want to make sure you're really doing OK after everything that happened. Hearing about everything on the news almost gave me a heart attack, especially when you weren't answering my calls."

Wanting to change the subject as fast as possible I interject "Listen, Maggie, I know we have a lot to talk about, but I've really got to go now. I promise I am fine. Tonight. 8pm! You pick the place." I walk past her to exit my office and head for the elevators.

~~~

My palms are starting to turn sweaty, and my heart is pounding so hard I swear the gentleman next to me can
~~~

hear it. I've been waiting in the lobby for Dr. Fisher for fifteen minutes now. It's unusual for him to have me waiting so long but I can hear the tempestuous couple screaming at each other on the other side of his door. From what I gather the woman is upset she and her husband didn't go skiing like she wanted over the holidays but had to stay home because his mom was sick.

"Sir." The receptionist calls to the man sitting next to me. He is on his phone typing an email or text message to someone and doesn't budge. "Sir." The lady calls out again. He finally looks up to see who is speaking and locks eyes with the receptionist. "Dr. Williams is ready for you." He stands to his feet and walks down the hallway, opens the door, and disappears into the office.

I check my phone to see it is now twenty minutes past ten o'clock. I notice a few alerts from my dating app and one missed call. Seeing his name on my phone makes everything around me go still. I haven't spoken to Alex in several months. After the paramedics rushed him to the hospital, I spent so many nights praying he made it. I miss everything about him, especially his smell. It was a combination of his shower gel and cologne that made me go wild so many times before. I close my eyes to drift deeper into memories of him.

"You look like you've just seen a ghost." I open my eyes to see Dr. Fisher standing over me. I look around and realize the office is empty and his door is open. I guess I didn't notice the theatrical couple had left and he was waiting on me. "Sorry I ran over a tad bit, Kerri. Thank you for waiting."

"Of course, it's no problem." I follow him into his office and take a seat in my favorite spot on his blue, leather chesterfield sofa. This spot has the best view in his office. You can see the entire city skyline. We are on the 47th floor so I can pretty much see everything for a hundred miles. His office is cozy, not too big and he has a collection of Banksy artwork on all his walls which I've grown to love looking at while talking to him.

"So" Dr. Fisher gets my attention tapping a pen against his infamous brown leather portfolio. What I would give to read the notes he keeps on me. I clear my throat and cross my legs.

"He texted me, again." I blurt out.

"I see." He responds, not taking his eyes off mine. His facial expression staying the same making it hard for me to read his thoughts.

"A penny for your thoughts," I say nervously.

"I'm more interested in your thoughts."

I take a deep breath and close my eyes, "well I haven't spoken to him yet and he keeps calling. I…don't know what to say."

"So, the reason you haven't answered is because you

don't know what to say? Or is it perhaps you know exactly what you want to say but are not ready to do so?" Dr. Fisher says very matter of fact.

I pause for a minute unsure what to say. *God. I hate it when he shrinks me.* "I don't know. I'm afraid if I see him, I will not have the courage to tell him." I finally admit. Every time I get around Alex my whole world turns to mush and it's like I can't think straight. Well, that's at least what I've gathered over the past few months of therapy.

"Sometimes, the band aid method is most effective" he replies. "Just do it. Rip it off."

I spend the next thirty minutes talking through my feelings around Alex, my sister's death, and my relationship with my parents before he ends the session. Remembering his last session ran long mine felt a tad quicker than usual but still rejuvenating. It has been the one thing I look forward to each month. Something I've grown to depend on to put me in better spirits. Dr. Fisher has a way of making me feel like my world is not so bad after all.

As I walk down West 32nd street, I notice I am only a couple blocks away from Harriet's, so I take a quick detour to get a few macarons to settle my sweet tooth. Another chime comes from my phone, and I see it's my dating app again. I only activated it a week ago and so far, haven't really had much success. I decide to open the app and see who has messaged me. It's Kevin, a thirty-year-old man from Tribeca who is six feet tall, loves hiking with his dog, and does a lot of DIY projects from ideas he gets from the HGTV channel.

"Ma'am! You ready?" I hear a familiar voice call out.

"Yes, sorry. I'm ready." I walk up to the cashier I've grown to know over the past year and order my usual macarons with a coffee to go. I have no choice but to stuff my phone in my purse to carry both the coffee and macarons back to my office. But every five steps I take a new chime sound comes from my purse.

"Oh, what the hell" I exclaim and move my macarons underneath my armpit freeing my right hand and reach for my phone.

> Kevin: I'm not very good at this.
>
> Kevin: I think you're absolutely stunning.
>
> Kevin: Ugh. Was that cheesy?
>
> Kevin: Anyways, I'm Kevin.
>
> Kevin: If you look at my photos, don't judge me.
>
> Kevin: I don't take selfies.
>
> Kevin: But I guess that's the only way to judge if you like me, huh?
>
> Kevin: Did I mention I'm not very good at

this?

A slight grin surfaces and I feel inclined to respond. The poor guy is trying. It's like he literally writes what he thinks before actually thinking about what to write. The feeling is nice actually. It feels... *honest*.

Me: Lucky for you I am not a fan of male selfies

Me: I'm Kerri :)

Still carrying a slight grin on my face, I walk the remaining blocks to the office taking in the warm air and allowing the sun to shine directly on me. After the year I've had I still find myself in love with New York City. The busy streets and loud honks from cabs and people in a hurry gives me a thrill and sense of adventure. There's still so much to explore. I spend the remaining 4 hours sifting through emails and sipping on my lukewarm coffee before calling it a day and heading home to change for tonight.

~~~

"Well, well, well. If it isn't Kerribel fucking Townsend." Maggie shouts across the bar commanding everyone to turn and look at me. I roll my eyes and suddenly get nervous with the entire bar staring.

"Boy, have I missed you!" I giggle as Maggie hands me my first drink. She looks like a rich supermodel as usual. Her hair is wavy and slightly messy, rocking Coco Chanel earrings and red lipstick. Tonight, she has on a rather tight,
~~~

form fitting navy blue cocktail dress with a Chanel purse to compliment.

"Well, I feel like I should have chosen a different outfit tonight." Looking down slightly regretting my blue jeans and white crop top shirt from Fashion Nova I decided to wear.

"Oh please. You look fabulous! Demi is on her way, and I have a *big* surprise for you. In the meantime, I've ordered another round of drinks while we wait so come sit down!" Maggie points at the chair next to her.

A few moments pass and the bartender brings us two cocktails. He hands me my strawberry mojito and then turns to Maggie handing her a martini glass that's smoking. Slightly intrigued, I watch as she tastes it to gauge her reaction.

"I thought you were more of a strawberry margarita type of girl, KB" a voice from behind me says. Pure excitement fills me because I can recognize that voice from anywhere. I turn to confirm it is in fact my best friend in the flesh.

"Elise!" I scream out and immediately jump to my feet to give her a hug. "Oh my god, I didn't know you were in town."

"Well shit! I had to fly out here to check on my girl because someone was hardly picking up my calls." She smirks and hugs me back. She's right. I hadn't really spoken to anyone since the night at the cabin. I guess I just wasn't sure how to explain everything and if I'm being honest, I guess I didn't want to hear the *I told you so's* I knew would come but having Elise here made tonight complete. I look over at Maggie knowing she was behind orchestrating it all. I take it she knew I needed a little bit of home here with me after everything and Elise was the perfect remedy. She locks eyes with me sending me a warm smile and a *I got your back* look.

Elise and Demi barely give their order to the server before Elise takes my hand in hers. "Are you doing okay, Kerri?"

"Uh, yeah?" I answer hesitantly, her tone telling me that her question is not just out of concern.

"Good." She nods as she sips the water that the server put in front of her. And then she turns her blazing glare on me. "What the entire fuck, Kerri?! How could you betray us like this? How could you tell us—"

Her angry words are cut off when Demi puts a tender hand on her arm and squeezes it. I swallow the lump of guilt burning in my throat as I see the hurt in her eyes. Glancing at Demi and Maggie, I see the same emotions reflected in their eyes. With the lump growing by the second a tear rolls down my cheek, and I wipe it away.

"What she means, Kerri, is that you kept us from a large

part of your life the last few months," Demi says quietly. "You went through so much, and you chose to do it alone, without us. Without us being aware of what was happening in your life. Going through all this shit and keeping us clueless."

"I'm sorry…" I manage to whisper.

"*Sorry?*" Elise wheezes, a sure sign that her frustration with me is high. But she sputters when Demi squeezes her arm again.

Maggie takes hold of my hand. "Kerribel, what we're trying to say is that we're sorry you felt that you couldn't trust us to share the good and bad of your time with Alex. You've listened to us moan and gripe about our stories, and you've had the juiciest stories to tell but didn't." All my emotions are coming to the surface, sadness, embarrassment but mostly my guilt of lying to my best friends for so long. I feel my eyes watering.

Demi gets up from her chair and comes to crouch in front of me, taking my hands in both of hers. "Kerr bear, we've all done stupid shit. We're sorry that our actions made you feel that you couldn't speak to us about things… *anything…*"

"Demi…" I stutter, and before I can say anything more, she pulls me into her arms, and I can't hold back anymore, tears fall down my face uncontrollably. I feel Maggie and

Elise surround me and both place their hands on my back rubbing it to sooth me.

"We love you, Kerribel," Elise says, grabbing hold of my hand when she returns to her seat. "We don't want to see you getting hurt."

"Or watch one of us go to jail because we drop-kicked Alex in the throat," Maggie adds, making us all laugh again. She reaches for my other hand. "Don't keep anything from us again, okay?"

I look at Demi and Elise, who are both nodding. They forgive me with only one condition. A condition that is easy to stick to. "Okay."

After talking through the biggest elephant in the room it takes us no time to catch up and it also feels like no time has passed at all. They are literally the easiest people to talk to and I'm slightly upset at myself because I've been avoiding them for so long. After our third round of drinks, I grab my phone to look at the time.

> Kevin: I have about another hour before I close up shop.
>
> Kevin: Can I call you?

"Oh shit!" I whisper. With all the intense and much needed girl talk I almost forgot about him.

"Oh shit, what?" Demi asks with a concerned look.

I give a blank stare at her and then at Maggie and Elise, not quite sure if I want to mention I reactivated my dating app again and may have a new guy calling me soon. It will only put me back in the hot seat.

"Spit it out, Townsend." Maggie barks.

Dr. Fisher enters my thoughts again...*Rip it off.*

"I may have met someone new...I decided to get back on the app." I casually utter as I unlock my phone to reply to Kevin.

"Oh my god, what?" Maggie squeals. "Let me see!" She grabs my phone and opens the app to Kevin and I's conversation. I suddenly got déjà vu, taking me back to the first night we met for drinks.

"Oh, and he is an entrepreneur too. I love it." Maggie says scrolling through my phone.

"Wait, how do you know that? His profile said nothing about being an entrepreneur." I quickly grab my phone back to take a look for myself.

> Kevin: Or if you're up for it we can meet for coffee?

> Kevin: I own a small bakery shop in West Village called Harriet's.

> Kevin: Ever heard of it?

Immediately my insides start to feel warm. Maybe it's the three strawberry mojitos I drank that's causing it but a part of me feels like it's the sizzling start to a new chance at love.

For the next hour I remained in the hot seat answering questions about Kevin but after about 5 minutes of saying *I don't know* to the majority of their questions they took it upon themselves to find the answers on Google. I left Illicit knowing way more about him than I'd probably get on a first date and that my friends are definitely qualified to apply for the CIA.

Feeling slightly tipsy but with enough liquid courage I decide to reply to Kevin's message as I approach the door to my loft. I type out a response then decide against it and erase the message. I do this combination for a few minutes before giving up. With a big sigh and an undelivered message, I throw my phone into my purse and reach for my keys to unlock the door.

As I open the door, I notice the lights are on and I hear the tv low in the background which is weird because I distinctly remember turning everything off before leaving.

"Kerri." A deep, raspy, and too-familiar voice carries across the room. I know this voice. My body knows this voice because every time I hear it the air around me gets thin and I can no longer breathe. I take a swallow of saliva and a quick inhale before turning my head to face the very person I've been trying to avoid ever since the night at the cabin.

Chapter Thirty-Five

"Alex? What are you…"

"I've tried calling. You won't answer." He says taking a step closer towards me.

I'm standing still, my body frozen in front of him with my mind racing on what to say. I wasn't expecting to see him. I hadn't figured out what I wanted to say to him. I keep staring into his grayish brown eyes and all I see is…*pain*. Dr. Fisher's voice pops into my head and I hear *sometimes, the band aid method is most effective…rip it off.*

"Yea, I know. I wasn't ready to talk." I reply feeling my anxiety rise.

"You look... beautiful." I watch as he stares me up and down tracing every inch of my body with his eyes. "Listen, I have been trying to call you because I just want to say how sorry I am for everything that happened." Alex begins his speech. I'm sure he's worked on saying it a million times in the mirror. As much as I probably really wanted to hear this apology months ago. Now, so much time has passed I don't know that it means as much to me anymore.

"Alex, stop. I don't need an apology." My anxiety now bubbling over I walk to the kitchen counter to sit my purse and keys down and a rush of emotions come over me. Fragments of the night at the cabin flash in my head. All the memories flood my mind about that night I've tried so hard to forget.

"No, it's important you know..." he continues talking but his voice softly fades low, and I'm suddenly taken back to the night when Nicole lost her shit...

~~~

The house quickly fills with emergency personnel. Someone switches on the overhead lights, and the wreckage of the room becomes visible. Another police officer turns off the car's engine and cuts the headlights. More police cars arrive, and the house is soon filled with people walking in and out.
~~~

A paramedic pulls me off Alex and sees to his wounds, hooking him up to an IV bag before turning to me. He pinches my fingers and then curses as he puts an oxygen mask on me. "Miss, you're bleeding. I need to check you for injuries."

I nod vaguely as his partners load Alex on a gurney, and I get to my feet to follow. "Whoa, missy, not 'til I've checked you for a concussion. You have some nasty bumps there."

When he is satisfied, he straps my broken hand and allows me to go with them to the hospital. I hold Alex's unresponsive hand on the drive and only let it go when they rush him into the emergency department. I am escorted to another room, where my hand is x-rayed and then bandaged.

"Miss Townsend, your hand is not only broken, but some of the tendons are damaged and will need surgery to repair," the doctor tells me while he shines a flashlight in my eyes. "Your throat is severely bruised with minor scratches. Your ankle is badly sprained. You are excessively hypothermic, and your body is suffering from exhaustion. I'd like to hold you overnight."

"Is Alex still in surgery?" I rasp.

"Your friend was transferred to New York-Presbyterian Brooklyn Methodist Hospital before it could be done. It was a request from his family." His family. Who knows nothing about me. As his mistress, I'm not included in those decisions. As his mistress, I'm nothing in his life.

A hollow feeling enters my heart at that brutal truth, and I find that I can't even cry about it. My tears are all dried up. I nod my thanks at the doctor, who pats my hand and leaves the room. The rush and rustle of the emergency department flows around me, but I can't seem to straighten from the fetal position I have curled into after the doctor left. I don't sleep, because the nurses keep checking my blood pressure every hour, but I am too numb to respond.

"Kerri!" I frown at the familiar voice, but I'm too tired to move. "Oh my god! What did that bitch do to you?"

I blink as Maggie comes into my line of vision. She brushes my hair off my face and gently cups my cheek, her eyes the saddest I've ever seen them. The tears shimmering on her lashes break the bubble I had withdrawn into. She crawls onto the bed beside me when I choke out a sob. I turn in surprise when a pair of arms wrap around me from the other side, and I find Demi holding me as I cry.

They stay with me during my surgery, and after my release, we drive home together. After telling them what happened, the rest of the drive is made in relative silence, mostly because I'm using painkillers to numb the emotional pain rather than the physical pain, causing me to sleep for long periods during the trip. I can now understand what the allure is to use them to escape the shit that is happening around you. They don't only numb my physical pain, but they enfold me in a blurry cloud that helps me to forget about the events that took Alex from me. When we get to my apartment, Maggie tucks me in as Demi brings me a cup of tea. I snuggle into the comforter and wonder how I am so lucky to have such good friends.

"Are you awake enough to hear me?" Maggie asks as she makes herself comfortable next to me, and I smile as I nod slowly. "Good. You need to get better because you need to report to work after the new year. HR cleared you of all wrongdoing. They found camera footage of Nicole entering the offices and taking photos as well as damaging your stuff."

I breathe a sigh of relief, but then my gaze flies back up to hers. "What about my hand? I can't work like this!"

Maggie sighs as she looks at me. "You will be the supervisor on a new project that will—for the time being— be more admin-oriented so you can dictate notes, and someone will type them for you while you inspire your team to greatness. And I'll even put you in your own office. How's that sound?"

"Okay…" I can't stop smiling.

"Rest up. A detective will be here soon to go over your apartment to gather evidence." Demi pats my leg before getting up. "We'll be here the whole time. You get into too much trouble on your own."

"Wait!" I call as they are about to leave my room. "Did they… find… Nicole?"

Maggie and Demi glance at each other. Maggie sits on the bed again as she bites her lip, and I frown at her. Maggie isn't a nervous person, but she is hesitant about something. "Kerri, Nicole's hair was tangled in the motor of the boat, so when you docked, you actually dragged her with you."

I swallow the bile that rises and shudder, taking a deep breath as I feel a ton of guilt settle on my shoulders. I lie down again and wait for the medication to kick in. It is a blissful sensation. I'm not sure how long I sleep, but I wake up to Demi softly calling me. I get up to meet with the detective, who is very apologetic about the police not showing up earlier. He asks me a ton of questions before looking through my loft. He takes the photos from the trash can and says he'll contact me soon. About 2 weeks later, the detective stopped by to give me a report that shows evidence Nicole had private investigators following Alex for months and that's how she knew about me and where I worked.

"What about the baby?" I asked the detective.

"Baby?" The detective repeats confused.

"She sent me a sonogram at Christmas," I explained to the detective, who was shaking his head emphatically.

"There's no baby. There' couldn't be, according to the

coroner. Mrs. Carter had a hysterectomy at the age of twenty-one." I look at him stunned in silence. *She was lying?* He waits for a few minutes and after no response from me, he leaves me with a copy of the report and quietly exits my apartment giving me privacy.

~~~

As I come back to reality, I can hear Alex still rambling. "Alex!" I yell out with every fiber in my soul. I see his eyes get big and he stops speaking instantly. "I hadn't answered for a reason. I've had a lot of time to think about things while you were in the hospital. In fact, that's all I could do because your family and Nicole's family prohibited me from visiting you in the hospital. And with all that time I had to think I realized something." I take a second to catch my breath and continue "You never chose me."

"Butterfly…I'" Alex attempts to cut me off but I now feel empowered and courageous enough to say my truth and don't allow him to.

"Not one time did you actually choose me. But I chose you repeatedly when I shouldn't have. I lied to my friends, to my family and to myself for you. And I'm pretty sure that's not how it's supposed to be. Love is supposed to feel good and safe. Love is supposed to protect you from pain. All I ever felt with you was doubt and shame. I've come to terms with the truth now, Alex. You *do not* love me! And you never have!"
~~~

"Butterfly…baby…I—" he stops mid-sentence and looks down at his left finger where his wedding band use to be. He furrows his brows and presses his lips together. I can tell he is in deep thought. For what I'd give to know what he's thinking. After what felt like an eternity, he looks up at me and takes a step closer.

"Kerri, you have no idea how much I truly love you. Every night I lay in that hospital bed, I hated myself more and more for not being able to come to you immediately. I failed to protect you. I wasn't honest about my situation from the beginning, and I should have been. I know that but you have to know what we had…what we have…is real. You must know that if it weren't for—" he stops mid-sentence again. This time seeming to contemplate his next words.

"If it weren't for what, Alex?" I nudge him to continue. I watch as he takes in a large breath and sighs.

"Kerri, I found my wife… I found Nicole… face down unconscious in our bathtub the night before the 4th of July. She had apparently taken a full bottle of prescription drugs and the only reason I found her was because I saw water spilling onto our wood floors in the hallway when I stopped over to pick up the mail. I had to break down the door after a few seconds of her not answering. I rushed her to the hospital and barely got there in time." He pauses and closes his eyes "When she returned home, she accused me of having an affair and threatened to harm herself again if we didn't renew our wedding vows for a fresh start. I didn't agree with it at first because I knew I was falling in love with you and my feelings for her had changed years ago. Only, every day that passed by I did not agree, she would do different things to remind me of her promise of self-harm. I fucking found her napping on the sofa holding a kitchen knife on her chest. Who the fuck does that? I had no idea she knew who you were. I only thought she had suspicions. And I also thought I was super careful. I would have never knowingly put you in danger, Kerri. Things just got more complicated as I tried to stay at my penthouse more, she began harming herself more. I hated bailing on you as much as I did but at the time, I felt I didn't have a choice."

Holy shit! I stand frozen in place, my mind racing over the information Alex just shared unsure of what to say. I have been grieving the loss of this relationship for the past few months thinking I wouldn't have closure. I was not expecting any of this, him showing up unannounced, the apology, the extra information that explains…so much. Everything is just happening so fast. The walls start to spin slightly.

"Butterfly…you are my world." Alex walks up to me placing both hands on my shoulders and slowly begins running them down the small of my back. *God, I miss his touch. I miss him. He knows exactly what to say.*

"Maybe if I had met you under different circumstances, we could go the distance. But I think it's best our journey stops here. I deserve…better. So much has happened. I don't think we get to come back from this?" I utter using my last breath in exhaustion with my anxiety now fully activated.

Awkward silence fills the growing space between us having realized Alex took a step back from my last comment. Still breathing hard, I push back my curls that have fallen slightly onto my face. My phone chimes and I absentmindedly look at my purse on the counter.

"Alex, you have to go." I look down at the floor unable to look him in the eyes.

"Why Kerri? We aren't done here." Another chime comes from my phone. And another. And another. I'm not certain who could be messaging me at this time but I'm gaining a sneaking suspicion it's Kevin. Multiple texts seem to be his M.O.

Alex looks at me and then at the purse again. In one quick motion Alex grabs my purse, pulls my phone out and looks at the screen. *Fuck*. Immediately, his jawline tightens, and I can see the muscles causing it to jump. His lips are pressed together, and he squints his eyes showing his displeasure.

"Who the fuck…is Kevin" he looks up at me. His eyes are now extremely dark brown, they're almost black.

"I—" stuttering unsure what to say I watch as Alex throws my purse and phone on the kitchen counter and walks towards me again. Feeling freakishly nervous I begin walking backwards until I hit the exposed brick wall of my hallway, my heart beating with anticipation.

"I've been laying in the hospital healing, and you have a new boyfriend?" Alex hisses. He grabs my waist with both hands and in one swoop lifts me up and tosses me over his shoulder and walks towards my bedroom.

Fuck. Fuck. Fuck. My entire body is ignited with anticipation for what I know is about to come. Alex is mad…at…me. In fact, I don't think I've ever seen this side of him before. He seemed angry yet sexually charged. He drops me onto my queen plush bed, my body bouncing to the impact of the fall. I look up and see Alex take his right hand and reach behind his back pulling his shirt over his shoulders and head, tossing the shirt aside, leaving nothing to my sight except exposing his chiseled 6-pack. I had forgotten how defined his body was. I continue to watch as he unhooks his belt and button allowing his pants and briefs to fall simultaneously. I stare at his naked body, his hard erection curving slightly just the way I've grown to love.

"Alex…we can't—" I mumble under my breath.

"Shh…" He grabs both my ankles and yanks them dragging my body to the edge of the bed. "Close that beautiful little mouth of yours or I will fill it with my cock and close it for you." Obediently, I lay in silence.

With one thrust he is inside me picking up speed and strength with each pump. My body is getting lost in the depths of his touch, his heat radiating. I've missed him so much. Much more than I want to admit. I've needed this for too long, to feel him inside me again. My eyes catch as his abs contract and release with every thrust he gives me and the way his veins are bulging from his arms running all the way up to his neck. I try to look into his eyes, but they are glossed over. He is not looking at me, but it seems he is looking through me, a sort of hunger to them. This is new. And I'm not sure what to make of it.

"You're mine, Kerri." He grunts as his thrusts grow harder. "No one else can have you but me." I feel him growing inside me filling my hole deeper pushing to new limits I didn't know I had.

I hiss as I feel his erection touch the deepest parts of me. My walls close in on his shaft as it glides in and out causing more wetness to spill over. A spark of orgasm slowly creeps forward deep from within as he pulls it from me more and more. And when I can't take it anymore, I explode into tiny little pieces relaxing every muscle, letting every juice drip out of me.

Alex lifts his hips and pulls out of me turning me over to my stomach. He places his hands on both of my ass cheeks spreading them apart and rests his erection right in the middle. I feel him hover over me. "Do you trust me?" he whispers.

"Yes!" I answer without hesitation.

"Good girl." He lifts up and I feel a cool wetness drip into my folds and with a small force Alex enters my ass for the first time. The pain is sharp. I can feel every inch of him ripping me open. I squeeze the sheets into a knot hoping it will help ease the pain.

"Deep breaths, baby," Alex says while slowly moving in and out.

I follow his instruction and inhales as he enters deeper and exhales as he pulls out. In and out I breathe for several minutes. After forcing myself to relax more and concentrate on my breathing it wasn't long before the pain subsided. *Damn.* Either it's been so long I've forgotten how good he is in bed, or he is giving me everything he's got tonight. Alex lays his chest on my back and buries his face in my neck.

"Tell me." He says. "Tell me you love me, Kerri. Tell me you're mine."

His voice sounds breathy and raspy with a slight sadness that I couldn't shake. I've been resisting all night and holding back to protect myself because he hurt me so bad before. But I can't fight these feelings I have for him. I love him. I've loved him for a while now and I cannot keep lying to myself. I want him. I *need* him. I needed this. He has never made love to me like this before. I know this is dangerous…I know loving him comes with a risk, but I can't help it. I cave in and give him exactly what he wants. I give him me.

"I love you, Alex. I'm yours. And I will always be yours." And with one more thrust, I feel Alex exalt the loudest grunt and his erection pulsates rapidly inside me. His body deflates and lays motionless for a few seconds, and I take immediate comfort in him lying on top of me. I'm nestled inside like a little cocoon in total physical bliss not wanting this moment to end. In fact, I'm so comfortable my eyelids begin to grow heavy, and total exhaustion takes over. Just before I drift into nothingness, I vaguely hear Alex whisper into my ear.

"Move in with me, Kerri. Let's start over."

TO BE CONTINUED...

ABOUT THE AUTHOR

L.A White is a writer, actress, and entrepreneur from Oklahoma City, Oklahoma currently residing in Dallas, Texas. She spent her early years in school studying business and performing arts. After graduating from Texas Woman's University with a business degree, she quickly realized her biggest impact would be in the arts. She developed a passion for storytelling through acting and writing. Her focus is on stories through the female perspective, bringing awareness to important issues such as mental health, domestic violence, and women's rights.

www.LaurenAshleyWhite.com
Instagram: @LAWhiteBooks | @LaurenAshleyWhite
Facebook: @LAWhiteBooks

What's next?

CITY OF LIES
INTERCONNECTED COMPANION SERIRES

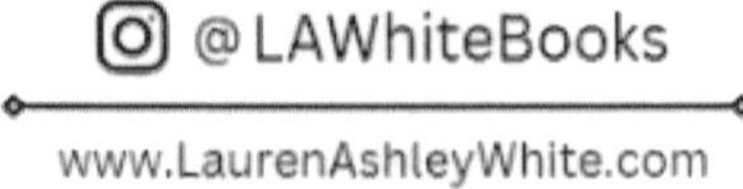

www.LaurenAshleyWhite.com